GIRL, LOST

VIKKI PATIS

For Evie.
And for Isabelle Stevens, who will never read this.

PROLOGUE

We all get what we deserve. A favourite phrase of my mother's, whenever something bad would happen. When we fell out of a tree and grazed our knee, when the neighbour's dog bit us, when we curled up with a bellyache after eating too many sweets. When the violence started. *We all get what we deserve.* I stare down at the girl on the bed, blood covering her legs. So much blood. I can feel it drying on my fingers, see it coating my nails. Will my hands ever be clean after this?

The room is hot and stuffy, the windows shut tight against the lashing of the rain. Her breath comes in short gasps, her hair plastered to her forehead. Pain grips her and she cries out, her eyes screwed shut. I close my eyes too, wishing I could shut my ears to her terror.

'Come on,' a voice says, and my eyes fly open. It's a voice I know, a voice burned into my soul. A part of me. 'You can do this. You have to.'

She tries to call out, but she can't catch her breath. Her eyes meet mine and they widen, pulling me in, desperation written across her face. But I can't help her. It's gone too far. We've gone too far. There's no coming back from this.

I watch her face change as pain washes over her again. Her cheeks are flushed red. A shadow paces in the hall outside, footsteps echoing in the silence between her cries. What have we done? What have *I* done?

'Please,' she says, and her eyes are on me again. 'Please, help me.' My throat constricts, shutting off my reply. And what would I say? What *could* I say? *I told you so. You brought this on yourself.*

No. She didn't do this. She couldn't have known this would happen. But I did. I've known for a long time. I've watched him change from boy to man, watched the darkness devour him piece by piece. The darkness I tried and failed to shield him from; I tried and failed to stop it from destroying him. From destroying us.

And now this. And now, as I have done countless times before, I have chosen the wrong path. But how could I have done anything else? It's my fault, all of it. I did this to him, to all of us.

I watch as darkness takes her, as the nightmare finally ends. For her, at least. For us, a new nightmare is just beginning. We all get what we deserve, after all.

1

IMOGEN

It's been 1,765 days since my sister disappeared. Almost five years. Half a decade. I try to remember what life was like back then, the year she disappeared. That year, 2013, is split in two; before Freya disappeared, and after. Before, a date was set for the Scottish referendum; a blizzard hit the north of England; a terrorist incident resulted in the death of a British soldier. After, same-sex marriage was legalised; the Duchess of Cambridge gave birth to a son after changing the law to allow girls to inherit the throne if they are born first; the hottest temperatures were recorded for a decade. And all the years since, the EU referendum; Trump becoming President of the United States; the terrorist attack at an Ariana Grande concert; the Blue Planet effect. The years I've spent travelling the globe, searching for my sister, never finding her, never giving up.

Before 18 July 2013, I had a sister, a twin, the other half of me. After, I was alone, less than whole.

Where are you, Freya? I send my thoughts into the abyss, imagine I can see them stretching across the ocean, to wherever you are. I left six months after you disappeared. I couldn't stand to sit with Mum in that house, at the kitchen table, tea cooling on the surface between us, waiting for you to come home. But you didn't. You haven't.

I close my eyes against the bright Melbourne sun. It isn't always warm here, you know. Do you know? Are you here somewhere, on this huge expanse of an island? Did you follow our route, the route we carefully planned out, the map Blu-Tacked to your bedroom wall? I followed it, hoping to find you along the way. But I didn't. I haven't.

It was bucketing down when I got here, almost ten months ago now. You wouldn't believe it, would you? It doesn't rain in Australia. But it does. And it's beautiful. It reminds me of home. It reminds me of you.

Do you remember that day at Polperro, when Emily drove across the Tamar for the first time? You were convinced she was going to plunge us into the rushing river below, but she didn't. She was a confident driver, laughing at your anxieties. The windows were down and we drove fast – but within the speed limit – down the A38, all the way to the little fishing village we all loved. The sun was shining the whole way, but as soon as we set foot on the beach, the heavens opened. And you laughed, the loudest, most incredulous, infectious laughter pouring from your mouth. Oh, that laughter. I can almost hear it now, standing on the edge of the Royal Botanic Gardens, ten thousand miles from home.

Is Emily with you, Freya? Where did you go?

I glance back at the building I've just come from, with its shiny glass doors and smiling receptionist. They're not like back home, these receptionists. These women are blonde and tanned and what Mum would call *bubbly*. I smile and rest a hand on my stomach. It's almost time to go home, Freya. But will you be there when I get back?

Max isn't home when I finally let myself into the flat. I drop my bag on a dining chair and sink into one opposite, resting my chin in my hands. Am I really ready to go home? I think of the test hidden in the kitchen bin, the two lines that made my decision for me. I have to be ready. I have to go home, to finally lay Freya to rest. And I need my mum, I realise with a jolt. I need her right now.

Mum's face flashes up on my phone screen and I frown. Freya and I used to joke about the 'Twin Thing', how we could almost read one another's minds, and the coincidence hits me like a wave of cold water. She never rings. It must be important.

I swipe across to answer the call. 'Mum? What's up?' There's a heavy feeling in my stomach as I listen to the silence on the other end of the phone.

'Oh, Imogen. You sound like an Australian!' Mum's words are light, but her voice is thick. I can tell she's been crying.

I force a laugh. 'You say that every time, Mum. I'm still firmly British, don't worry.' Another pause, rustling on her end. She blows her nose and dread settles over me like a shroud. 'What's the matter?'

It takes a few seconds for her to answer, but when she does, the bottom of my world falls out. 'It's Emily. She's back.'

2

EMILY

'Stop fussing, Mum.' Too late, I realise I'm snapping, and I flinch at the pain in her eyes. But she shouldn't be looking at me like that. She doesn't have the right to look at me like that, like I've caused her nothing but grief. But, of course, that's exactly what I've done.

Mum sits down beside me, reaching out to grasp my hand. I fight the urge to pull away.

'I'm sorry, love,' she whispers, her eyes glistening with tears. 'It's just... It's been five years, Emily. Five years.'

I know how long it's been. I've been counting the days, the weeks, since I left. Since I escaped. I never intended to come back.

'Oh, look at you!' Mum gushes, clasping her hands to her chest, as she stares past me. I turn to find Ella standing in the doorway, her favourite blanket slung around her shoulders, her curls standing on end, and I feel the ice in my heart melt a fraction.

'Hey, sleepyhead,' I say, holding out my arms to the little girl. My girl. She steps into my embrace and I lift her easily onto my knee. 'Did you sleep well?' Ella fell asleep as soon as I laid her on the couch a few hours earlier, despite the unfamiliar surroundings.

Ella nods, burying her face into my neck. She's such a quiet child, always has been. Except at the beginning, when we didn't know each other very well. When I was scared she would reject me, reaching her tiny fingers past me, searching for someone else. But I was all she had.

I look around the kitchen, taking in the counters covered in junk, the fingerprints visible on the cupboard doors. Mum was always a neat freak – *a place for everything and everything in its place*, she used to say. Now the house is covered in rubbish, piles of newspapers, cardboard boxes, pizza delivery leaflets. I catch a glimpse of the date on one newspaper – 2013 – and wonder if I'll see my face inside it. *Local Girls Missing.*

Except I was never missing. I just didn't want to be found.

Mum reaches out and gently tugs on a lock of Ella's bright hair. Ella, my shining star. My saviour. I bend my face close to her blonde curls and breathe in her scent. She smells of sleep and sea and the alcohol gel she rubbed on her hands after she ate a chocolate bar on the train. She doesn't like having sticky fingers, never has. She takes after Mum in that way, I suppose. Or the way Mum used to be. I wrinkle my nose at the grime on the table in front of me. It looks as if it hasn't been cleaned in years.

Mum herself has changed too, almost beyond recognition. Her once thick, bouncy hair is all but gone, a few wisps of greyish curls the only thing left covering her scalp. There are deep lines around her eyes, and her jawline is sagging. Her wrists are bony; all her curves are now thin and sharp. *Cancer. Terminal.* The breath catches in my throat and I look away.

I should be asking questions. I should know what treatment she's having, whether she's in pain. How long she has left. But I can't. All I can think about is the past, the first twenty-two years of my life in this house. The pain, the violence. And the girls next door – Imogen and Freya, the twin sisters who knew me better than I knew myself. Both gone now, their lives torn apart by us. By this family.

'I'm so glad I found you,' Mum whispers, dragging me back to the present. 'I'm so glad you came back.' I want to ask how she found me, how she tracked us down to our cabin in the middle of nowhere, but I can feel her gaze on me, hot and searing, and I close my eyes and bury my face in Ella's hair again. The memories are flooding back and I can't look at her. Not after what they did. Not after what they made me do.

There are some things you just can't forget.

3

IMOGEN

I almost trip over my own feet as I hurry towards the taxi rank. My rucksack bounces on my back, my suitcase rolling along behind me. I didn't really need to book a taxi – there are usually black cabs waiting outside Heathrow, despite the early hour – but I had to make sure I could get home as quickly as possible. I have to get home, to Emily. I have to find out where she's been. Where *you've* been, Freya. Why you're not with her.

I throw myself at the passenger window of what I suspect is my taxi, making the driver jump. 'Imogen? Imogen Rivers?' I splutter, already climbing into the back as he nods.

'In a hurry, love?' he asks, eyeing me in the rear-view mirror. I frown. Why do middle-aged men always feel the need to call you something? Love, dear, sweetheart. I think of the old Cornish men who propped up our favourite bar on a Friday night. 'All right, maid?' they'd say, grinning toothless grins, and we'd laugh, young and confident and tipsy. Untouchable together.

'Yes,' I say shortly, pulling out my phone and sending a quick text to Mum.

In the taxi. Train is in an hour. Be with you by eleven xxx

The past forty-eight hours have been a whirlwind. As soon as I got off the phone to Mum, I booked myself on the next available flight – after 2pm the next day – out of Melbourne, and, after a quick stop in Hong Kong, here I am in Heathrow. I snatched a few hours' sleep on the flight, but my mind hasn't been able to switch off for any decent period of time, the same mantra flying through my head. *Home. Emily. Freya.*

'It would've been quicker to hop on the tube, love,' the driver says, breaking into my reverie. I open my eyes to see cars slowing in front of us and suppress a groan. He's right, but it's too late now. I'll still make my train. And then I'll be home, and Emily can tell me where she's been for the past five years. And why my sister isn't with her.

I spot Mum's car as I exit Plymouth train station, idling in a spot meant for taxis. But Mum always dropped us off here when we were younger, Freya in the front, me and Emily in the back. The three of us spilling out of the car, waving goodbye before linking arms and heading into the train station, on our way to a gig or a party. Always the three of us, together. And now I'm alone.

Mum gets out as I approach, her smile wide, her eyes brimming with tears, and I throw myself into her arms. 'Mum.' It's been so long since I last saw her in the flesh, last held her tiny frame, my chin resting on top of her head. I breathe in her scent – tea-tree shampoo and her bubblegum car freshener – and close my eyes.

'Imogen. Oh, Imogen.' Her words are muffled, her voice thick with emotion, and I pull away to look at her. I notice lines at the corner of her eyes that weren't there before, purple bags poorly hidden beneath concealer. She looks older, I realise with a pang, worn down. Have I done this to her? Have we, Freya? She tugs on a curl that's escaped from my bun and smiles. 'Come on, you. Home.'

In the car, the overpowering air freshener hanging between us, Mum drives in silence, lifting a hand to wipe her eyes every few seconds.

'No more tears, Mum,' I say, nudging her shoulder with mine. It's something we've said since we were little, when Freya read the bottle of Johnson's shampoo as *tears*, not tears.

She smiles and glances at me as we approach a roundabout. 'Oh, Imogen, just look at you. You're so tanned! And so skinny. Too skinny. I've got a stew on.' I roll my eyes and she laughs. Only Mum cooks a stew in June.

'How long has this heatwave been going on?' I ask, rolling down the window. The car is stuffy, the sun beating down from a cloudless sky.

'Oh, we haven't seen rain in a few weeks now. My garden is crying out for it. We'll be seeing a hosepipe ban soon, I reckon.'

I smile as I stare out of the window. The city rushes past; the university buildings, the shopping centre. I glimpse our favourite pub, sitting on the corner of Mutley, as Mum waits at the traffic lights. I breathe in. Plymouth. The only home I've ever known. The place we were supposed to come back to, to start our lives, to settle back down after we *got it out of our system*, as Mum used to say about our travelling plans. Two years. We had planned to be away for two years. How did it become five?

We pull up outside the house, the house Mum and Dad bought when they were newly-weds. We arrived here almost twenty-eight years ago, after the cord was wrapped around my neck and Mum had to have an emergency caesarean. There's a photograph somewhere of us all, Mum holding me, Dad holding you, standing at the top of the steps by the front door.

Mum's hair is short and wild, bouncing around her head, her eyes tired, and Dad is clean-shaven with a wide, toothy grin. I wonder suddenly who took that photo, whether it was one of the neighbours.

I try to peer up at the house next door, the house we knew almost as well as our own. Emily's bedroom mirroring mine, Jamie's the same as Freya's – except for the dirty socks and the irrefutable boy smell. Was it Agnes who took that photo? Three-year-old Jamie holding her hand, his dirty blond hair ruffling in the wind, his knees scuffed as usual.

I shake my head and follow Mum up the stone steps. She's carrying my suitcase, and I stifle a laugh as I realise it's almost half the size of her. She sets it down to fumble with her house keys, then opens the front door, throwing it wide. She turns to me, a sad smile on her face. 'Welcome home, love.'

I feel a rush of emotion, and I can't help wondering if she's practised this ritual. But was it me she was welcoming home, or you, Freya? I push the thought away and follow her inside, glancing once again at the house next door, fancying I see the curtain twitch before I close the door behind me.

Mum deposits my suitcase at the bottom of the stairs, and I throw my rucksack on top of it before following her into the kitchen. The stew is bubbling away on the hob, and I wonder what time she got up to start cooking.

'Smells good,' I say, sliding onto a stool at the island. Mum lifts the lid and breathes in.

'Almost ready,' she says confidently. She never needs to taste food to know that it's ready. I wonder if all mums develop a sixth sense for things like cooking and sewing. Or is that sexist? Dad had been a pretty good cook too. A memory flashes through my mind – Mum sitting in the living room, her work trousers slung over her knees. She always had to turn up her trousers, as she stands barely five foot tall. We took after Dad, growing to a respectably average five feet five inches by the time we were fifteen.

'You'll be wanting to keep your strength up,' she says, breaking into my thoughts. She nods at my stomach, and I realise with a lurch that she knows. Sixth sense, indeed.

'How...?' I trail off as her smile widens.

'A mother always knows. As you'll soon find out.' She reaches into the cupboard for bowls. 'When are you due?'

'Not until January.'

'Ah, a New Year baby.'

I stifle a grimace. 'Not intentionally.' Nothing about this was intentional.

'And the father?' Mum's voice is hesitant now. 'Is he... Is he in the picture?'

I shake my head. I can tell she wants to ask more by the way she purses her lips, as if she's forcing the words to stay in her mouth, but she mirrors my silence, and I'm grateful. I don't want to talk about this, not right now. Not when my head is full of you, Freya.

Mum busies herself with dishing up, flapping a hand at me when I get up to help. I sit at the island, drumming my fingers on the pristine counter, staring up at the wall of photographs beside me. I spent six months in this kitchen, watching Mum try not to call me Freya. And she did try, but it isn't easy when your remaining daughter reminds you so much of the one you lost. I should know. My reflection reminds me every time I look in the mirror. I catch a glimpse of myself in a shop window and there you are. Except you're not. You're gone, and I'm left behind.

Mum puts a bowl in front of me, then reaches into a cupboard to grab a loaf of bread.

'Is this the one you like, Immy?'

Immy. Your name for me. Im-my and Fre-ya. Two syllables in your mouth, sing-song. I hear your voice in my head, watch your face as you mouth the words. Sis-ter. Were we the same in every way? I remember the freckles scattered across your nose, the scar in your left eyebrow from the time I pushed you into the side of a large fish tank, our laughter turning into frantic tears as blood dripped down your face. Would this be another difference between us, slashing through the reflection of our features?

'Im?'

I snap out of my daydream. Mum is looking at me expectantly, holding the loaf of bread. I smile. 'You remembered.'

She tuts. 'Of course I did.' She cuts a few slices of bread, placing them on a plate between us, and we tuck in, blowing gently on our spoonfuls of stew to cool it. The stew is delicious. I can see the gravy Mum used sitting on the side and smile at her thoughtfulness. I remember Max getting annoyed when we had to throw out our toaster.

I try to imagine Max opening the front door to our flat, seeing the note I left on the kitchen table. The new one I'd bought last month from a Facebook selling group, after I smashed up the old one and burned it in the garden, embers flying around me as I tried to burn away the memory of that night.

I shake myself, pushing the memories firmly to the back of my mind. I left all of that in Australia, thousands of miles away, and it's not what's important right now.

Right now, I have to speak to Emily.

4

EMILY

'Higher! Higher!'

I laugh as I push Ella on the swing, her little legs kicking in the air as she whooshes back down towards me.

'You'll fly into the sky!' I exclaim, and she giggles.

'To the moon! I want to go to the moon!'

'Can I come?'

I turn to see Mum slipping in through the gate. She slides onto the bench beside the swing, and I feel a tightening in my gut. I can't seem to get away from her now that I'm back. *But you're back for her*, a voice says inside my head, and guilt floods through me. I knew this wouldn't be easy, but I hadn't realised quite how hard seeing her again would be. How hard the memories would hit me.

She's wearing a hat despite the heat, covering her almost bald head. Her face is bare, her eyebrows and lashes so pale they're almost invisible. I try to return her watery smile, then turn back to Ella.

'Yay! We'll all go! We'll all go to the moon!' Ella is giggling, twisting around to look at Mum.

'Face forwards, sweetie,' I say quietly, 'you don't want to fall out.'

Ella does as I ask, her hair flying in the breeze. She's such a happy child, always has been. My sunshine child.

'I've been thinking about schools, Emily,' Mum says, taking out a bottle of water and sipping from it. 'Come September, she'll be old enough to enrol.'

I scowl. School, really? 'I think it's a bit early to be thinking about that,' I say, choosing my words carefully. *We might not stay that long*, I finish in my head.

'But she's old enough for nursery, or whatever it's called these days. Ella deserves the best start in life. I was thinking–'

'She's already had the best start in life,' I snap, whirling round to face her. Ella groans as the swing starts to slow. Mum looks taken aback, and I close my eyes, trying to breathe deeply. 'Sorry. I just... Not yet, all right?'

I open my eyes and Mum nods, sadness written across her face. Guilt flows through me again and I sigh. Guilt seems to be the only thing I'm feeling at the moment, being back here. Guilt, and fear.

'Come on, you,' I say, grabbing Ella under her arms and pulling her out of the swing. 'Time for lunch. What do you fancy?'

'Ice cream!' Ella shouts, pointing at the van that's just pulled up. I suppress another sigh.

'You know you can't, sweetie. It's not gluten-free.'

Ella frowns.

'You remember, don't you? About gluten?' She nods, but I can tell she's disappointed.

'I have some ice cream in the freezer at home,' Mum says, getting to her feet and joining us. She bends down to Ella's level, and judging by the pain that flashes across her face, I can tell it costs her. 'Special ice cream for special girls.'

'Am I a special girl?' Ella asks, peering up at me. I laugh.

'The specialest!'

'That's not a word, silly!' Ella grins, and I pick her up, swinging her round before settling her on my hip. She's too smart for her age.

'Ooh, my apologies, Your Majesty.' I grab my bag and turn to Mum. 'Do you really have ice cream? You know, stuff she can have?'

Mum looks surprised. 'Of course I do. I downloaded that app, scanned it in the shop. It's definitely okay.'

I feel a tingle at her words. 'Thanks, Mum,' I say, trying to infuse my voice with warmth. 'That was nice of you.'

'Only the best for my little Ella,' she says, tucking a strand of hair behind Ella's ear. 'Who wants a race?'

Ella immediately struggles to get down from my hip. I look at Mum. 'Mum, you don't have to, you'll...' What? Wear herself out? Hurt herself? But her eyes are alive with such happiness that I trail off, setting Ella down at my feet. 'Go on then. Just to the end of the field, all right? Ready, steady... go!'

Mum pretends to lag behind as Ella sprints across the grass. She's fast for someone with such tiny legs, but not so fast that Mum couldn't easily catch up with her. At least, that's what I'm hoping. I'm hoping it's all an act, and that Mum isn't so ill she can't move faster than a slow jog. How long has she been like this, wasting away, trapped in a body that is deteriorating far too early? I run a hand through my hair, pushing it away from my face. It's too hot, airless. Suffocating.

'Winner!' Ella cries as she reaches the end of the field, jumping up and down, her T-shirt riding up. Mum grabs her around the waist and tries to lift her, but I can tell she's too heavy for her. I jog towards them, mouth open in laughter, when I catch sight of something and stop dead.

For a second, Mum and Ella and the park dissolve, and it's

just me and her standing a few feet apart, her blonde hair blowing in the breeze, her sea-blue eyes locking me into place. Freya. No, no, no. *Freya.*

'Emily,' she says, and I feel my legs give way beneath me.

5

FREYA

THEN

'No, no, no!' Freya shook her head, pulling the pin out of the map with more force than necessary. 'We're going to Belgium *before* Germany. It makes logistical sense.' She pushed the pin into the word Brussels, obscuring the s's. 'And I want to eat waffles.'

Imogen laughed. 'I want to eat waffles!' she mimicked, putting her hands on her hips and sticking out her chest. Freya threw a cushion at her sister, who ducked just in time. It bounced harmlessly off the door frame.

Emily stretched her arms overhead, her fingers trailing along the posters stuck to the wall. 'What language do they speak in Belgium?'

Freya frowned. 'Dutch. I think.'

'And Flemish,' Imogen said.

Emily giggled. 'Flemish?' She mimed coughing up phlegm.

'Don't be gross.' Freya flicked Emily's calf, which was slung over her lap. Emily stuck out her tongue. 'And French, in Brussels at least.'

'Oh, *s'il vous plaît*! Le waffle, *monsieur*!' They burst into laughter at Emily's terrible accent, at the way she put her thumb and forefinger together to make an o.

Freya leaned back against the headboard, staring up at the map. This was it, their plans were finally coming together. Their collective dream of travelling the world, just the three of them. Imogen, with whom she'd shared a womb, a cot, a mind. And Emily, the girl next door, their best friend since early childhood when her brother Jamie had kicked a football into their garden, and Dad had kicked it back, before inviting them round for a barbecue. That was his way, their Dad. He loved a full house, the busyness of family life. Kids giggling in the living room, stretched out on the sofa, hidden beneath blankets; winter coats and boots discarded in the hallway; a bath full of toys, bubbles blown into the air. That was life, their life together, a childhood full of noise and laughter and love. Until he died, taking the happiness with him. Most of it, anyway.

Freya felt Imogen's hand on her knee, and she knew her sister could hear her thoughts. They missed him, they all did, and, not for the first time, guilt flooded through Freya as she thought about leaving their mum alone. She imagined their mother drifting from room to room, silence filling the air.

She shook the thoughts away. She was getting ahead of herself. They didn't have enough money yet, and Emily hadn't even received her passport. They still had time.

6

IMOGEN

I stare down at the woman in front of me, the girl I've known almost my entire life. She's kneeling on the grass, her head bent as if waiting for the executioner's blade to fall. Her mother, Agnes, is hovering behind her daughter, a small child clinging to her leg.

I shift from one foot to another, confused and uncomfortable. 'Emily. It's me, Imogen.'

She lifts her head, her eyes wild, strands of reddish hair falling in her face. I hold out a hand and she stares at it for a moment, before taking it and allowing me to pull her to her feet.

'It's been a long time,' I say, blowing out a breath. I'm aiming for light-heartedness, but it falls flat. Emily just gazes at me, her eyes wide, her mouth a tiny o. I want to shake her, turn her upside down and watch the secrets of the past five years tumble out. *Where have you been?* I want to scream. *Where is Freya?*

Instead, I take her in. Her eyes, though somewhat bloodshot and carrying some carefully concealed bags beneath them, are unchanged. She looks stronger, her body held differently to how I remember, and her hair is lighter, but still thick and full. She doesn't look as if she's been chained up in a basement somewhere, or that she's suffered the deluge of horrors I've imagined in the years since she and my sister disappeared. She looks... normal. And scared. But of what?

'Where have you been?' My words are a whisper, but they hit her with the force of a blow. The child cries out and Emily's head snaps to the side, as if attached to the little girl by a string. I follow her gaze. 'Is she... Is she yours?' Emily is still looking at the child, her eyes glazed over. 'What's her name?'

'Ella!' the child cries happily, and I look closely at her for the first time. Her hair is bright and her eyes, a dark blue, glitter in the sunshine. She looks like Emily, her little rosebud lips identical to my childhood friend's. But there's something else, someone else she...

As if reading my thoughts, I see Emily's eyes widen, and, in a rush of movement, she turns and grabs Ella by the hand, pulling her along. Agnes is glued to the spot, staring at me. I open my mouth to speak, but Agnes gets there first. 'We don't want any trouble, Imogen.'

I frown, confused. Trouble? I want to say something, want to ask what she means, but I realise then that she looks so very ill. This woman I've known my whole life, who was almost like an aunt to me and Freya. She babysat us when Mum and Dad went out, which happened rarely, but she was often found in our back garden, handing out plates of sausages and burgers Dad cooked on the barbecue. And, when we were teenagers and her vile husband did everyone the favour of disappearing one night, never to be seen or heard from again, we were often allowed to take over her living room with duvets and cushions, lounging around and eating popcorn and watching movies that scared us silly. She'd come in with a tray of hot chocolate topped with cream and marshmallows, and those little pink finger biscuits. The memory overwhelms me, the smells reaching me from the past as I watch this woman watch me, her eyes ringed with purple bags, lines carved into her skin.

'Mum!' Emily calls, and Agnes snaps to attention, tugging her cardigan around her shoulders.

'We don't want any trouble,' she repeats, and hurries after her daughter. I want to follow, to grab Emily and demand she tell me where she's been, what happened to her. What happened to Freya. Five years ago, I lost my twin sister, my reflection, an entire part of me. She and Emily disappeared, and only Emily has returned.

~

Waiting. Pacing.

'You have reached the voicemail of 0778…'

Waiting. Pacing. Fingers flying over the keyboard.

Freya, where are you?? Ring me! X

Waiting. Pacing.

'You have reached the voicemail of…'

Emily, have you seen Freya? She isn't here. We have to leave soon!
Ring me x

Silence.

'You have reached the…'

Where the hell are you?! Answer your phone!

Pacing. Heart racing. Mum's face filling my vision, the words stuck in my throat.

Freya. Freya is gone.

I wake with a gasp, the dream ending at the same point it always does, when I fell to my knees and buried my face in my hands, the tug of Freya pulling me down into despair. I could *feel* it, feel her calling out to me. But I couldn't reach her.

Sunlight is trickling through the curtains, the air already hot and stuffy. Just like that day, the day Freya went missing. The day we were supposed to leave.

We'd booked a train to Edinburgh. Freya had changed our plans at the last minute, wanting to explore different parts of England and Scotland before heading over to Northern Europe. Why had she done that? I didn't really question it at the time. Emily had agreed with Freya, said she wanted to visit Loch Lomond, and that we could get to Iceland from Inverness. Pins were ripped out of the map and stuck into different places, strings criss-crossing the world. We had so many dreams; there were so many possibilities open to us. But we never saw any of those places. Not together. Emily followed Freya three days later, disappearing into thin air. And now she's back.

I rub my eyes, frustration building. How could Emily run away from me for a second time? She owes me the truth about what happened all those years ago. About what happened to my sister.

7

EMILY

Ella is curled up like a cat, her warm body tucked up against my stomach. Her hair is escaping its plait, curling around her ears and the nape of her neck. I gently run my fingers through the loose strands, relishing the smoothness of it. She fidgets, trying to roll back and face me, her eyes opening slowly. I smile.

'Good morning,' I whisper. She blinks a few times, her little face puffy. 'Did you sleep well?' I know she did. She's always been a good sleeper, even as a newborn. When she was tiny, I would wrap her in a knitted blanket and lay her down on the bed beside me, and just watch her. Her little hands would always escape the blanket while she dreamt and reach up to touch my face. She was beautiful, perfect. My little sunshine child. She still is.

Ella wriggles away from me and rolls off the bed, landing deftly on her feet. 'I need a wee,' she declares, and rushes out of the room. I laugh, throwing back the duvet and following her.

I hover in the doorway of the bathroom, keeping my face turned away while she's on the toilet – Ella is already very concerned about privacy – then turn when I hear the toilet flush. She reaches out for me to lift her and together we wash her hands, breathing in the fruity scent. She can't really reach the sink in this house – I'll need to think about getting her a step. If we stay.

'What's for breakfast, Mumily?' she asks as we pad down the stairs, still dressed in our pyjamas. I smile. *Mumily.* The name I gave myself, the name that hides the truth.

'What would you like?'

'Pancakes!'

I suppress a sigh. I doubt Mum thought to get gluten-free flour. We'll have to go shopping soon. Anxiety grips me. We haven't ventured further than the park since we got back. I can't face seeing Imogen again, or Deb, or anyone else I used to know. Will they recognise me, remember what happened? What they think happened, at least. *Local Girls Missing.*

'We might have to make do with toast, sweetie,' I say, grabbing Ella around the waist and swinging her down the last step. She giggles.

'With jam? No, peanut butter!' She takes my hand and pulls me towards the kitchen. That's another thing I've learned about Ella – she's *always* hungry.

'Let's see what we've got, hmm?' I don't tell her that she probably can't eat the jam or peanut butter Mum has, as it'll be contaminated with gluten. But, to my surprise, a new jar of strawberry jam is sitting on the middle shelf of the fridge, with a Post-it note saying *Special Jam* stuck to the lid. I smile. She did her research, then.

While Ella is munching away, I make a cup of coffee and sit at the table opposite her, turning on my phone for the first time since we got back. I flick mindlessly through Facebook, then switch over to Instagram, but all I can think about is Imogen. Is she sitting in the kitchen next door, trying to find me on social media, trying to figure out where I've been for the past five years? Or is she gearing up to come round, bang on the front door until I let her in?

I shake myself. I have to get out of here. Claustrophobia is closing in and I can't deal with Imogen right now.

'Come on, you, let's go and get dressed,' I say to Ella, putting her plate and my mug into the dishwasher. Mum is still in bed; she sleeps late these days, the pain troubling her worse during the night. Lying in bed beside Ella, I can hear her moving around, the floorboards creaking under her weight, and I feel the walls pressing in on me. It will be good to get out for some fresh air today. At least I'm still insured on her car. A pang of guilt at the expense, the sadness of Mum renewing the insurance every year, in the hope I would come home.

'Where are we going?' Ella asks, racing up the stairs ahead of me and sliding out of her pyjamas. 'To the beach?' Her little face lights up at the prospect.

'Sure, why not? But first to the supermarket. We can have a picnic.'

'Yay!' Ella jumps up and down, her arms lifted above her head. 'A picnic, a picnic!'

'Get a move on then, slowcoach!' I tease, throwing a T-shirt over her head. She giggles and wriggles into it as I change my own clothes, quickly so she doesn't see the scars.

I push Ella in the trolley around Asda, picking up bits for our picnic. Our trolley is full of strawberries and bananas, cheese and crackers, some Ribena and a magazine for Ella. I try not to think of my bank balance as I select a bottle of wine to share with Mum later. An olive branch.

I need to start making more of an effort with her. She's the reason I'm here, after all. The reason I brought Ella back to the home I grew up in, with its shadows and memories that sometimes threaten to swallow me whole. And, if I'm honest, the fact that my bank account is almost empty helped make the decision. I suddenly regret selling my laptop to buy the train tickets to Plymouth. I need to earn some money. Maybe I could borrow Mum's ancient PC and download the software I need. I've taken on commissions over the years, mocking up book covers and setting up websites under another name. It's kept us fed and clothed, just.

At the checkout, Ella sits contentedly as I scan our items through and touch my card against the reader. We're heading back out into the relentless heat when a voice calls my name.

'Emily?' I whirl around to see a face I haven't thought about in years.

'Rachel, hi.' I hand Ella her magazine to keep her busy, pushing the trolley into a corner so we're out of the way of other shoppers. Rachel is grinning as she approaches, her arms held out for a hug. I reach out with one arm, awkwardly patting her back, before stepping away. I haven't seen Rachel since university, those long days spent in the library or the studio, sharing our artwork. 'How are you?'

'How am I? How are you, more like!' Her Cornish accent is strong, reminding me of my mother. 'Where have you been?'

The dreaded question. The expected question. The only one that could be asked, in the circumstances. I lift a shoulder, attempting to appear nonchalant. 'Around. All over.'

'On an adventure!' Ella pipes up behind me, and I close my eyes for a fraction of a second. It's the response I've told her to give when asked that question, and I should've known she'd be more interested in the woman in front of me than the magazine in her hands. Rachel peers around me to smile at Ella.

'Well, an adventure, eh? Must've been a bleddy massive one.'

Her last words are directed at me, and I cringe. 'Anyway, I bet your mum's glad you're back. She was worried sick.'

You have no idea what you're talking about, I think, bristling. I turn back to the trolley, preparing to make my excuses, when Rachel speaks again.

'Have you seen Jamie yet?'

The name freezes me in my tracks. *Jamie.* The name I've been running from for five years. The shadow in the corner of the room. She promised he wouldn't be here. *Come home, Emily. Come home before I die.* She promised.

I look at Rachel and shake my head. Her eyebrows rise to meet her too-short fringe. Does she look... smug?

'We'd better be going.' I turn on my heel and push the trolley out of the shop without looking back.

'Who was that woman, Mumily?' Ella asks, peering over my shoulder. I move to block her view.

'Nobody. Just someone I used to know.'

We go straight home, all thoughts of the picnic on the beach forgotten. Ella must sense my disquiet; she straps herself into the booster seat Mum dug out, burying her nose in her magazine for the drive home while my mind is fixed on Jamie.

Jamie. The brother I've been running from for five years.

8

IMOGEN

I'm in Freya's room, running my fingers over the map which is still plastered to the wall. The plastic creaks under my touch, dust particles billowing in the breeze from the open window.

Mum hasn't changed a thing, not in all these years. Freya's suitcase is still standing by the door, where she left it the day before she disappeared. YOU LOOK FINE is still written across the mirror in faded red lipstick; the bedside table still strewn with jewellery and hairbands, her lamp coated in a thick layer of dust. Her favourite ring hangs on the trunk of the elephant holder I bought her for Christmas one year. If I open the wardrobe, I'd be able to see her clothes still hanging up, her collection of ankle boots lined up neatly at the bottom. I open the drawer to see her passport sitting on top. She wouldn't have run away without these things, would she? Her ring, her clothes, her passport. Her sister.

I stand and catch a glimpse of myself in the mirror, the word YOU stamped across my right cheek. Accusatory.

I turn my attention back to the map. A train up to Edinburgh, stopping at towns and cities along the way, then across to Glasgow, up through Loch Lomond and the Cairngorms, to

Inverness, then a flight to Iceland. To Norway, a tour of the fjords, taking us across to Sweden and Finland. Denmark, Germany, Belgium, France, then a flight to New Zealand, and, finally, Australia.

It took me six months to leave. Six months of waiting for them both to come back. Six months of grief, of watching Mum deteriorate before my eyes, until I finally snapped, emptying our joint account and boarding a train to Exeter. I stuck to our route religiously, watching the crowds, waiting for you to materialise, Freya. But you never did. You weren't in Edinburgh, you weren't in Reykjavik. You weren't in Berlin or Auckland or Sydney. You were nowhere, and you were everywhere. I saw you in shop windows, in the gait of a woman who walked like you, in my dreams. Oh, and the papers. Our faces were splashed across the front pages, in almost every country I went to. The looks people gave me, the questions clear in their eyes, wondering if I was you. I couldn't escape you, not even in the mirror.

'Imogen?' Mum's voice floats up the stairs, breaking me out of my reverie. 'Do you fancy some lunch? I've made soup.'

Soup. Sweat prickles on my forehead and I wipe it away, dreaming of a Caesar salad. 'Coming,' I call, and wince. I hear your voice every time I open my mouth. You will never leave me.

I set down my spoon and wipe my mouth with a napkin. 'Mum,' I begin, choosing my words carefully. 'Don't you think we should go and see Emily?'

Her hand freezes in mid-air, spoon loaded with soup, her mouth open. She lets the spoon clatter to her bowl and looks at me, eyes hard. 'No, I don't.'

I blink, surprised. 'Why not? She must... She must know where Freya is.'

Mum sighs. 'And why would she know that? They didn't go together.' I stare at her, open-mouthed. 'Imogen, Emily left later. I don't believe she went to meet Freya. That's not what happened.'

I stare at her as she gets up and starts loading the dishwasher. 'How could you possibly know that? You can't know that, Mum.'

I watch her back as she stands erect, hands pressed against the counter. 'Because Emily got on the train. And Freya didn't.'

An image flits into my mind, CCTV released by the police in an appeal to the public for information. Emily at Plymouth station, her face in profile, her body turned away from the camera, boarding a train bound for London Paddington, two days after Freya disappeared. But there's no footage of her getting off. She disappears as the doors close behind her, her hair tied back in a messy bun, her rucksack slung over one shoulder. *Local Girls Missing.*

'That doesn't prove anything, Mum!' I explode, and Mum turns to face me, one eyebrow raised in the way that used to mean I was in for a telling off. 'Freya could've been waiting for her, they could've arranged to meet somewhere. I know CCTV didn't pick Freya up when she left, but she could've boarded anywhere! She could've caught a taxi or hitch-hiked or walked. Anything could've happened to her! And Emily knows, I *know* she does.' I pause for breath. 'She went to meet her, she must have done.'

Mum takes a deep breath. 'I think we should leave the girl alone,' she says quietly. 'Poor Agnes has been through hell, wondering where her daughter was. And the cancer. She–'

'And we haven't been through hell?' I interrupt, fury bubbling through me. How can she say these things? In the years since I've been gone, during our snatched conversations on Skype and WhatsApp whenever I could get Wi-Fi, we never mentioned Freya. Not once. I realise now what a huge mistake that was. 'Haven't *we* been worried sick all these years? I went to find her, to find them! I never stopped looking, never!'

'You went to escape.' I freeze at the accusation in her voice, stunned. 'You ran away, just like Emily did. Just like Freya probably did. And I don't blame any of you.' She sits down heavily in the seat next to me, reaches out for my hand. Her skin is warm and dry. 'It was awful here, Im, after your father died. God knows I tried my hardest to do it alone, I really did, but I couldn't fight the sadness, the loneliness.'

I remember that time well, what Freya and I called *Mum's dark days*. She and Dad had been in love, had always kissed each other goodnight, always held hands while out walking. They sat together on the sofa, she reading a romance novel, he with his police procedurals. They rarely fought, and when they did, it was in hushed tones in their bedroom, rarely lasting longer than an hour. And when he died, Mum's world fell apart.

Before that, our home was a happy one, full of love and laughter. Unlike next door. Emily's dad's rants would boom through the walls, shattering our peace. The thuds, the cries. They kept us up at night, those cries. One night I caught Dad sitting on the bottom step, face in his hands, the only light cast by the full moon filtering through the front door. He was crying, his shoulders moving up and down, and I knew it was because he felt powerless to stop whatever was happening next door.

Mum tried to help in her own, quiet way. She'd take casseroles and stews round while he was at work, sit with Agnes and let her cry while we played with Emily and Jamie upstairs, pretending not to notice the bruises.

Mum's voice brings me back to the present, snapping me out of the rabbit hole.

'Those poor kids,' she says, shaking her head, and I know her thoughts are mirroring mine. 'What a horrible man Sam was. Agnes was a wreck, constantly terrified. She tried to shield those children – no, Imogen, she did,' she protests as I pull a disbelieving face. 'I saw the bruises as proof. The cuts across her arms when he threw her into the oven door. That one was because Jamie had been home late, I'll never forget it.'

I close my eyes. Agnes wasn't the only one who tried to shield her children, I realise. We hadn't known the half of it. Dread pools in the pit of my stomach. In my mind, I see Freya leave again, the last time I saw her. She looked furtively behind her as she descended the steps, as if expecting someone to be following her. Then a shadow cutting across the grass, over the low wall that separated our house from next door, and grabbing her by the arm, dragging her into the night: Jamie.

Like father, like son.

9

EMILY

Mum finds us in the bedroom, Ella snuggled under the blanket, watching a TV show on my tablet. I slip off the bed and follow Mum downstairs, where she puts the kettle on. I have to ask her about Jamie. She has to tell me the truth. For once.

'Mum,' I say, as she pours water over the teabags. I can see the tension in her back as she adds milk and stirs. 'Where's Jamie?'

She turns, slopping tea over the side of her mug onto her hand. Swearing, she sets the mug down and stares at her injured hand.

'Come here,' I say, getting up and guiding her to the sink. I run the cold tap and hold her hand under the stream. Her hands look so old, I realise with a jolt. Like she's an elderly woman, not in her fifties. 'Mum,' I say again, and she sighs. I let go of her and step back, leaning against the counter.

'He's here. Well, I mean, in Plymouth. He lives in Mutley, in a shared house.'

I close my eyes. *He's here.* 'Why did you lie to me, Mum? You said he wouldn't be here. You promised. You said you wanted to

35

see me and Ella, not...' I trail off. Not what? Not lure us into the lion's den.

She looks at me, grief written across her face. I hate to see her in pain, but nausea is rising and all I can think about is escaping. We should leave. I should grab Ella now and run, like I did all those years ago.

'I just want us to be a family again,' Mum says quietly, and my heart begins to hurt. Oh, Mum. What a life she's had. Tormented and broken down by *him*, our useless excuse for a father, then the constant anxiety about Jamie's increasingly worrying behaviour: staying out late, drinking, drugs, anger. Anger to rival *his*. I remember sitting in the living room one evening, watching TV with Mum, when Jamie came in, his bulk filling the doorway, and the fear that flashed across her eyes matched the fear that engulfed me. The past was repeating itself. *Like father, like son.*

'Mum, I can't. You know I can't. It's not safe. He's not... He shouldn't be around Ella.'

Mum is still watching me, the water still running over her hand. 'He's your big brother, Emily. He loves you.'

'He doesn't know the meaning of the word,' I spit, memories flooding me. Memories from that night, what he did. What she did. What they made me do. I set my mouth in a line, and Mum sighs again, turning off the tap and drying her hand on a tea towel.

'All right, Emily,' she says wearily, 'he won't show his face yet. You need time, I can see that. And I need time with you, and little Ella. I can't lose you again.'

I relent, blowing out a breath. 'Fine. Okay. We'll stay a bit longer. But he's not coming anywhere near her. Okay? Not until I say so.' *And I will never say so*, I finish silently.

Mum nods, sadness in her eyes, and as we sit back down at the kitchen table, I think again of the night I left everything I'd ever known, the night I ran for my life. For Ella's life. It's all for her. Everything I've done has been for her. I have to remember that.

'You've done a good job with her,' Mum says, looking up at me with watery eyes. 'She's such a bright little girl. I don't know how you've done it.'

The sincerity in her tone makes me uncomfortable. For years it's just been me and Ella, nobody else to watch, to judge. 'It isn't always easy, but she's a lovely child,' I say. 'And she's pretty much always slept well, which helps.'

Mum smiles. 'You were the same, rarely made a peep from the minute we brought you home. Such a quiet, content child.'

Because I didn't dare to be anything else, I think but don't say. 'I'll give you something to cry for' was one of *his* favourite sayings. I learned from an early age not to make a fuss, to blend into the background. A lesson Jamie never learned. No, Jamie learned to be just like *him*, believed it was the only way for a man to be.

The scars on my back itch and I try to force the memories out of my mind. Being back here, in this house, is getting to me. It's engulfing me, pressing down on me. Dragging me down to a deep hole, the hole I've buried my past in. The hole I've buried Jamie in. But he seems intent on digging himself out.

The next morning, Mum wakes me with a cup of tea, and shares her news. I wonder how long she's been keeping it to herself.

'You've done what?'

My words come out in a hiss as I follow Mum down the stairs, mindful of Ella still asleep in the spare bedroom. I can never think of it as *mine*, never again. A few days ago, the first time I set foot in this house in five years, I wondered if Mum would've left my room how it was, like I imagine Deb has done with Freya's. But of course she hadn't. She'd needed space for her ridiculous hoarding. My – *the* – wardrobe is stuffed with boxes now, full of newspapers and other junk. When did she get like this? Why didn't Jamie stop her?

I shake my head. It's not my problem. Except it is because, apparently, I'm staying here forever. Because Mum's got me a job.

'You'll be working for Flo, love. You remember Flo? Poor woman, her sister was in a car crash recently so she needs help with the kids, which leaves Flo in a bit of a tricky position, bless her, but, you know Flo, she–'

I put up a hand to cut off her nervous rambling. 'Mum, did I tell you I wanted a job?' I realise that I sound like a petulant child, throwing a tantrum about having to do the dishes or clean the bathroom, but I can't seem to stop myself. 'What makes you think I want to do this?'

'Oh, Em, really,' she says, and for a moment I'm taken aback. Em and Im, the nicknames Imogen and I gave one another. Freya always called her Immy. The memories are flooding back and I take a deep breath, trying to centre myself. Mum raises an eyebrow at me. 'I thought you'd be thrilled. What else are you going to do with your days, now you're here?'

Now you're here. I knew she'd be like this. I knew she'd expect us to come back and stay forever. But that wasn't my plan – it isn't my plan. Though what my plan actually is, I'm not quite sure yet.

'Come on, love,' Mum says, taking my hand and squeezing it. 'It would be wonderful for me to spend some more time with little Ella. You know I don't have...' She trails off, the rest of her sentence unspoken. Her death sentence. She doesn't have much time left; we both know it. Months. Weeks. Barely any time at all.

Sadness floods me. How did we get here? Despite *him*, Mum

and I had been close when I was growing up. We regularly sat together on the sofa during the evening when he was out drinking, her plaiting my hair so I could have curls like Imogen and Freya, watching some rubbish soap on the telly. And then after he disappeared, we would drink hot chocolate together, painting our toenails bright yellow, garish face masks tightening our skin. I've spent years wondering how it all went so wrong. But I know. We both do.

'Mum,' I begin, and now she holds up a hand, cutting me off.

'It'll be good for you, to get out of this house and see other people. Do something with your day, other than look after me and Ella. You have your whole life ahead of you.' She smiles sadly, reaching out and brushing a lock of hair behind my ear. 'Don't let it slip away. Don't let what happened ruin your life.'

I shudder. It's the first time she's mentioned it, however tentatively, in all the years since… *what happened.* Is that all we're going to say about it? Is that all she deserves?

I look up at my mum, at the woman who is wasting away before my eyes. She's let what happened ruin her life. What she did. What she helped Jamie do. Nausea rises and I have to look away.

If I were to be completely honest with myself, I would admit that looking after Ella all day, every day, for years has taken its toll. There were weeks when I wouldn't have an adult conversation, save with the postman or someone on a supermarket checkout. I went through life in a daze, focused only on Ella and her needs – and our need to stay hidden. To stay safe.

'It's only part-time,' Mum continues, as if following my thought process. 'Monday to Wednesday, nine till three. I can look after Ella. I'd love to look after her.' She smiles again.

I pause, considering. 'But what about your appointments? And she's not always so easy – you haven't seen her have a tantrum.' I try to remember the last time she actually had a tantrum. Mum raises an eyebrow and I can tell she's seen through me. 'All right,' I concede, 'but she can be tiring. She has limitless energy. Can you really handle her?'

Mum takes my hand again. 'Don't you worry about us, love. We'll be just fine. I have a thousand things I want to do with her, things I've always dreamed of doing with my grandchild.' I wince internally. Things she couldn't do, because I took her away. Mum notices my discomfort and rubs my hand. 'We'll make up for lost time. It'll be fun.'

I try to think clearly for a moment, about the logistics of this arrangement. Could this really work? Can I leave Ella for such a long time? I've barely been apart from her since she was born. I swore to protect her with my life, the words whispered into her ear as we boarded the train that would take us away from here, away from what we had done.

But maybe it's time to let go of the past, to finally move on. Maybe we can build a life here. Maybe Ella can start nursery, make friends with other children. I try to picture myself at the school gate, making small talk with the other parents and guardians, watching Ella run out of her classroom, her bright curls bouncing around her head, full of stories about what she'd learned that day, the friends she'd made. Showing me her artwork, a painting of the two of us maybe, one I'd put on the fridge and stare at with pride as I made her tea.

Is this the life I could have? Is this the life I've never dared dream about?

'All right, Mum,' I finally agree with a sigh. I *do* need the money, especially if we're going to leave again. When we leave again. 'Do I have to ring Flo or something, to make arrangements?'

Mum flashes me a wicked grin. 'She's expecting you on Monday, 9am sharp. Smart casual.' I give her a look and she laughs. 'No time like the present, Emily.'

~

I'm in the bedroom with Ella, trying on a pair of black trousers I dug out of the wardrobe. They're too tight, the button almost falling off. I think they used to be my school trousers. I blow a lock of hair out of my eyes in frustration.

'What about this?' I turn to see Ella holding up a navy-blue dress, short-sleeved, knee-length. It's plain, but there's a black blazer I brought with me which could work well. I take it from Ella's outstretched hand, planting a kiss on her head, before stripping off the offending trousers and throwing the dress over my head. I wriggle into some black leggings and the blazer, then turn back to the mirror.

'You look like a princess, Mumily!' Ella declares, and I laugh. She's obsessed with princesses at the moment, declaring that anyone we see wearing a dress or with long hair, regardless of age or gender, is a princess. *I suppose that's something I could learn from her*, I think, picking her up and twirling her round. *You just have to believe.*

'Will I do, my queen?' I ask, setting her down and dropping into a clumsy curtsey. She giggles and nods, reaching out for the hem of my dress.

'What will I be doing when you're at work?' she asks, suddenly serious. I sit down, pulling her into my lap.

'You'll be with Nanny,' I say, using the word that has been forbidden for so many years. What else can Ella call her? She is her nan, after all. 'You'll go to the park and do jigsaws and eat ice cream and paddle in the sea! While I sit in a horrible, stuffy office.' I pull a face and Ella giggles again before frowning.

'That doesn't sound like fun. Why are you going to a stuffy office?'

I laugh. 'To earn money, so I can buy you ice creams and

magazines.' I tickle her tummy and she squirms in my lap, laughing. 'And so I can talk to adults.'

'I like adults,' Ella declares, wriggling out of my arms and flopping down on the bed.

'Oh you do, do you?' I raise an eyebrow at her, but she's staring at the ceiling, arms and legs flung wide, pretending to be a starfish. I get up and sit next to her as she starts to wiggle her fingers and toes.

'You're an adult, and I like you,' she says, 'and I like Nanny. And the man who sells ice creams at the beach. He's nice, even though I can't have any.'

I know it's wrong, I know I shouldn't let my mind go down such dark alleys, but Ella's innocent declaration about the ice cream man makes me shudder. Have I taught her well enough about stranger danger? Does she know not to go off with strange people, even if they offer her sweets or ice cream?

No. I suppose my focus has always been on one person and the danger he posed – poses – to us. But he isn't a stranger. He used to live here, in this house. He shared my childhood with me, protected me.

Oh, Jamie. You just couldn't protect me from yourself.

10

IMOGEN

That evening, I'm surprised to find Flo in the living room, sat on the sofa next to Mum, glasses of white wine in their hands. Flo stands as I enter, her arms spread wide. I step into them, breathing in her musky perfume.

'Imogen,' she breathes, taking me by the shoulders and leaning back to look at me. 'Oh, how long has it been?'

'A day or two,' I joke, and she chuckles, pulling me back in for another hug. 'How are you?' My mother's best friend finally releases me, sitting back down and patting the space next to her.

'I'm good, I'm good. Busy, as always. It's looking like a crazy year.' Flo shakes her head as she takes a sip of wine. 'I'm having to hire a few more people to help with the workload.'

Flo is the managing director of a medical device manufacturer over in Plympton. I did my work experience with her back when I was fifteen, and, though most of that time was spent cleaning shelves in the warehouse, I had a good eye for symbols, and pointed out several labels that were incorrect. So I stayed on part-time while I was at uni, to save up for our trip. And it was Flo who helped me get a job in Australia last year, working for a notified body, by providing a glowing reference. A better reference than I deserved, considering the way I'd abandoned Mum.

'Imogen's looking for a job,' Mum pipes up, and I look at her in surprise. It's the first I've heard of it. She raises an eyebrow at me and I realise guiltily that I haven't thought about contributing since moving back home. But getting a job? It makes it feel permanent, that I'm here to stay. I haven't stayed in one place for longer than a year since I left. I rest a hand on my stomach and Mum, noticing, speaks again. 'Ah, but, well. She's expecting, aren't you, Immy?' Her eyes are sparkling, and I fancy I can see a sadness in them.

Flo's mouth drops open. 'My little Imogen, pregnant? When did you get old enough?' She laughs. 'How old does that make me?'

Mum nudges her shoulder. 'Or me. Granny Deb.' She makes a face and they both giggle. I can't help but smile.

'Oh, what wonderful news,' Flo says, raising her glass in a toast. She drains it, setting it on the coffee table beside her. 'But of course you should come and work for me! It can be on a temporary basis if you want?'

I smile at her, this woman who has known me my whole life. She knows me too well, can sense that itch in the back of my mind that's constantly telling me to keep moving, to keep searching for Freya, or at least the truth about what happened to her.

'She's not due until January, isn't that right?' Mum says. I nod.

Flo claps her hands together. 'Perfect! We can get you in as a consultant.'

'A consultant? Are you sure?' I find myself getting excited. I hadn't considered what I was actually going to *do* once I got back from Australia. I hadn't considered coming back from Australia at all. Not yet, anyway. But I'd reached the end of the line, the last place we were due to visit as a trio, and I still hadn't found them. It all happened so fast: the test, Mum's phone call. Her words reverberate around my head. *It's Emily. She's back.*

'Oh, it'll be wonderful, having the girls back together again!' Flo declares, reaching out to refill her glass. I stare at her, and her eyes widen over the rim of her glass as she registers the look on my face, the look that says *there's one girl missing.* 'Well, what I mean is... You and Emily worked so well together when you were younger, do you remember?' Shock hits me like a wave of cold water at the mention of Emily.

'Emily?' I manage after a moment. 'What do you mean?'

'Emily's working for me. Didn't she tell you? She's helping redesign the labelling, bringing them up to date. You'll be working closely together, actually. Isn't that great?'

I watch Flo's face, trying to work out if she genuinely believes I would want to work with Emily again, as if we've both come back and we can just pick up where we left off. As if Freya never disappeared. As if she never existed.

I look at Mum. Her fingers are twisting in her lap – her tell. She set this up, for both me and Emily I'd wager. I give her a look before turning back to Flo.

'Sure,' I say, forcing a smile to my lips. 'Sounds great.'

It only occurs to me later as I'm lying in bed, listening to the sounds of Mum and Flo laughing at a TV show, that this is exactly what I wanted. The opportunity to get close to Emily again. To claw at her until her secrets come spilling out.

11

EMILY

I arrive at eight thirty, early as always. The car park is almost empty as I pull in, just two cars parked beneath the shade at the far end. No sign of Imogen yet. Switching off the engine, I pause for a moment, closing my eyes and breathing deeply. The air is shimmering in the heat, the sun already high in the sky. I can do this. I have to do this, for Ella. She needs a normal life. Getting out of the car, I try to walk confidently across the car park and ring the bell on the front door. A harassed-looking middle-aged man opens it, and I smile brightly.

'Hi, I'm Emily,' I say, and he just frowns. I falter. 'Is Flo available?'

He grunts and turns on his heel, which I assume means to follow him, so I do. He leads me into Flo's office without a word, and I stare after him as he trudges down the corridor.

'Don't worry about Jim,' Flo says from behind her desk, her eyes creasing with amusement, 'he's always like that.' I give her a smile as she stands, holding out her arms. I let her hug me, feeling only slightly strange. I'd forgotten how touchy-feely Flo is. I remember her sitting in the back garden with Mum and Deb, cocktails in their hands, while I pushed Freya on the swing, and Jamie splashed Imogen in the paddling pool. All of these tiny memories, barely worth remembering, are coming back to me now I'm here. The afternoons I spent in the warehouse here with Imogen, her explaining the labels and symbols to me when I first joined. I remember the divide I felt between us then, how she and Freya were adults now, off to university, to party and make new friends, and I still felt like a kid in school uniform. That divide used to bug me at the time, but I suppose it is much wider now.

Flo is taking my arm and leading me through the corridor and into the office, which is so different to how it used to be. A few people are already here; they lift their eyes and smile as we walk past. I try to return the smiles, listening to Flo as she explains the job.

'It's part-time, as I told your mum, Monday to Wednesday, leaving lovely long weekends with that precious girl of yours.' Flo smiles warmly. 'You'll be helping the regulatory team update the labelling. There's some special software we bought in – hopefully it'll be up to the job!'

'Hopefully I am,' I say, smiling to show I'm not being serious. Flo knows me, she knows I'm more than capable, but it won't do to show any weakness. I need to be confident, professional. I need to remember how that feels.

My hand accidentally brushes Flo's hip as we walk, and I suddenly realise the lack of Ella. Her warm little hand isn't in mine like it usually is, and my hand tingles with loss. *Concentrate.*

Flo chuckles. 'I have absolutely no doubt. This will be easy-peasy for you. It's a relaxed place, no suits in sight – except for the sales guys, who insist on it.' She rolls her eyes. 'Everyone else is chilled out. Well, you remember. There's a new warehouse manager, but he seems to have inherited the old one's dress sense along with the role.'

'Shorts in December? Socks and sandals?' I grin, remembering. Flo laughs.

'That's it. Though at least this guy has tattoos on his legs – makes them a bit more bearable to look at in the middle of winter.'

I look down at the tattoo on my arm, at the vines creeping along the inside from wrist to elbow. Flo notices.

'Oh, that's pretty,' she exclaims, stopping and taking my arm to inspect it closer. She traces a leaf, the newest one, with her finger. 'For Ella?'

I stare at her. 'How did you know?'

She winks, tracing a second leaf. 'One for you, one for her. And then...' She stops, turning my arm to find two more leaves, identical, sitting opposite one another. Flo smiles. 'Imogen and Freya. The three musketeers, you were. Inseparable.' I try to smile, but my face is frozen. I can hear my heart beating in my ears. 'Doesn't Im have the same tattoo?'

I nod. 'We got them at the same time. We all did, I mean. All three of us. I got Ella's leaf added later, of course.' I realise I'm babbling and stop abruptly, looking up at Flo.

'Where did you go, Emily?' Flo's voice is barely a whisper. I blink, wondering if I've misheard her. Her eyes are searching mine.

I pull my arm away from her grip, avoiding her gaze. 'A lot of places. All over.' My default answer. *On an adventure.* And we were, we were on an adventure, by the time Ella could understand what was happening. It's all she knew, living each day as it came. Never knowing when we might have to pack a bag and flee into the night.

'You're lucky to have such a special girl in your life,' Flo says, reading my mind. Her voice is soft.

I flush, force myself to nod. There's nothing I can say. Because she isn't mine. Not really.

12

IMOGEN

My alarm clock blares and I groan, reaching out to snooze it. Why did I agree to take this sodding job? My eyes drift to my wardrobe and I groan again. The dress code is smart casual, but I have no idea what that means anymore. It was all about comfort in Australia, long skirts and vest tops. I don't even know if I've got anything in my wardrobe that will be suitable.

'Immy!' I hear Mum's voice float up the stairs. 'Are you up?'

I roll my eyes, tempted to shout back that I'm not a teenager, and I'm quite capable of getting myself up, have been doing so without her help for almost five years – but stop myself just in time, realising that it would make me sound just like a teenager.

'Yes, Mum,' I say instead, flinging back the covers and padding into the bathroom. It's so hot here. Why is it so hot? I was expecting grey skies and rain, not constant sunshine and thirty degrees. And the humidity. The heat in Australia is different, not so... oppressive. Or maybe that's the memories, the past creeping in, making itself known.

In the shower, I quickly wash my hair, scrubbing at my scalp and squishing conditioner into the ends. I need a haircut, I decide as I fight my way through some particularly nasty tangles before rinsing and applying curl cream. I squeeze out the excess water, shake my head to let the curls fall, and decide to let it air-dry. I can't face a hair dryer in this heat.

Clean, I stand in front of my wardrobe, towel discarded on the floor. Turning my head, I catch a glimpse of my stomach in the mirror, wondering if I can see a slight curve. My mind flits back to the day I took the test, trying not to pee on my hand and failing, then the agonising two minutes as I waited for the result. It was during those two minutes that I realised I had to go home. I had to stop running from the past.

I reach into the wardrobe and take down a pair of loose patterned trousers. I pull out a black vest and a chiffon black blazer, throwing them onto the bed, before sitting at my dressing table to do my make-up. I barely wore any in Australia, the combination of good weather and sea water clearing my skin, leaving it fresh and in better condition than it's ever been. And darker. I note the tan lines on my shoulder from my bikini straps, remembering the last time I spent the day on the beach. The last time I saw Max.

Shaking myself, I start on my face. Cleanse, tone, moisturise. I dab concealer beneath my eyes and apply a coat of mascara, then tidy up my eyebrows and coat my lips in a pinky-peach colour I bought last year, blotting with a tissue. There, that'll do. *No make-up make-up*, Freya would say.

I catch her glint in my eye in the mirror, and smile. She's still here, still with me. I just have to find her.

My old car still smells the same, like perfume and cigarette smoke. And something sweet, like a spilled drink. Memories of road trips on sunny days float back to me; Emily in the back, head poking between the front seats, Freya next to me, long curls blowing in the breeze, mingling with mine. Laughter, music, the sound of seagulls and the rushing of the Tamar under the bridge. Exams and dissertations forgotten. It was just us, the three of us, always together. Until we weren't.

I start the car and pull out of the space. The air is already hot, the promise of another scorcher. I've never seen weather like this in England. Mum will start waxing lyrical about the summer of 1976, the benchmark for British heatwaves, if this continues. I smile. Good old Mum. She kept my car ticking over while I was gone, renewing the tax and MOT, even cleaning it. Guilt floods through me as I wonder what she's been doing all these years. Has she just been here, ticking over, waiting for one of her daughters to return? Am I the daughter she wanted to come home?

It doesn't take long to drive to the office. I pull into a space next to a Mercedes – Flo's, I bet – and turn off the engine. I open the car door and step out into the sunshine. Sweat immediately prickles on the back of my neck, and I regret leaving my hair down. Maybe I should cut it short, like Emily's long bob. But my curls would never sit nicely like her soft waves do.

Emily. I wonder if she'll be here today. Will she run away again, like she did at the park? Or will she finally face me? My skin thrums with anticipation as I walk up the steps and into the building. The foyer is blessedly cool. I sign in and make my way to Flo's office, walking along the corridor I still remember well, and tap lightly on the door.

'Ah, Imogen!' she says, getting up and walking around her desk to greet me. She takes my hands. 'How are you? This heat, huh?' She blows out a breath. 'Though I suppose you're used to it?'

'It's a different kind of heat in Australia,' I say, and she smiles.

'*Australia*,' she parrots. 'You've got a slight accent. I didn't notice it before.'

'You sound like Mum. She was worried I'd become a native.'

Flo laughs. 'And what would be wrong with that? Australia is a beautiful country. Except for all those bloody spiders.' She shudders. I decide against telling her about the time I found five huntsman spiders in my wardrobe. 'And you got on all right at the notified body?'

I nod. 'It was great, actually. I learnt a lot. Though they're a lot more relaxed out there. It often took a while to convince them that some of these things do have to be fixed immediately.'

'Well, they do say they're more laid-back in Australia!' Flo chuckles, before clapping her hands together. 'Right! Let's get you set up. I've got you a laptop so you can take it home or to our other site – you remember the facility in Wiltshire?' I never visited, but I remember its existence, so I nod. We begin walking along the corridor. 'You'll probably have to pop over there a couple of times, make sure everything's running smoothly.'

'Is John still running things up there?'

'Oh, yes,' Flo laughs, 'he'll never retire. I think he'd like to be buried on the grounds. Silly man still works ridiculous hours, and nothing I say ever makes a blind bit of difference, but he knows his stuff. He'll be glad of the company when you visit.'

'I've only ever spoken to him on the phone,' I say, remembering the broad Cockney accent he never lost, despite moving down to the West Country over thirty years ago. As we walk, I remember my first weeks here, when I was still a kid in school uniform, and Flo gave me an after-school job to help us save up. We had our dreams of travelling since we were at school, ever-changing, but it was always going to be the three of us. Freya started working at Starbucks, and Emily, a couple of years younger than us, joined me here when she turned sixteen.

'It's open-plan now – different to when you were here last, I think,' Flo is saying. We're standing in what used to be the corridor; now the room is bright, with desks lining both sides beneath the large windows where my new colleagues sit, flashing me a brief smile above their computer screens. I follow Flo to the end towards the kitchenette.

'Is that the same coffee machine?' I laugh.

Flo rolls her eyes. 'It's had so many spare parts, it's probably technically brand new, but yes, it's the same. And yes, it's still disgusting.'

I make a face. The coffee truly was awful here. Though I probably can't drink much of it now, I realise, placing a hand on my stomach. I'll have to make do with water. Thank God it's so hot.

'You're over here,' Flo says, gesturing to a desk in the corner, facing the rest of the large room. 'Customer care are here – she points to the left-hand side of the room – 'and they usually get questions they need to ask you about, so it'll be handy having you within shouting distance.' Another desk sits at a right angle to mine.

'Who sits here?' I ask, half hoping, half fearing it will be Emily.

'Lucy. She's a recent graduate, studied microbiology.' I incline my head, impressed. 'She assists our consultant with the sterilisation side of things – bioburdens, dose ranges, all manner of things I don't understand.'

I grin at her. Flo likes to pretend she doesn't understand every aspect of her business, but she does. She's worked in almost every department, starting with the warehouse when she was twelve – '*Child labour laws were different back then,*' she'd said when she first told me, winking – and moving up through customer care, marketing, and purchasing, before taking over the managing director position when her dad retired.

'She also does some internal auditing. Things are constantly changing in this business,' she continues, leaning against my desk, 'especially in your department. And this new regulation isn't making things any easier.' She sighs, catches my eye and holds it. 'I won't lie to you, Im, there's a lot to do here. Our technical files are in a bit of a state. The previous regulatory manager left, well, let's just say he left under a cloud.' She gives me a look. 'You'll understand what I mean soon enough.'

I nod, bracing myself. I've seen some atrocious technical files in my time, ones I've been astounded that the manufacturer had deemed acceptable for review by their notified body.

'Right, I'll leave you to get set up. Your laptop should be connected to the server, but give me a shout if you have any problems. I'll come back later and give you the proper tour, let you meet everyone. There's a lot of new faces since you were last here.' Flo squeezes my shoulder. 'I'm so glad you're back, Im. So is your mum. You have no idea...' She trails off, the rest of her sentence hanging in the air between us. *You have no idea what she's been through.* But I do.

I give her a weak smile. 'Thanks, Flo. I'm glad to be here.'

She leaves me then, and I sit down at my desk, my feet finding the footrest. Opening the laptop, I familiarise myself with the server, which is new, thankfully, and swiftly locate the technical files. There are only five, with just one sterile. Easy, I think, clicking through the folders. My heart soon sinks as I realise how much is missing. Sighing, I open a Word document and begin to make a list of what will need to be done. A lot, by the looks of things. A hell of a lot.

Lucy comes in – late due to a dentist appointment – and I'm stunned by how young she looks. She's twenty-one, with short dark hair and a face bare of make-up, eyes bright behind her large, fashionable glasses.

'So nice to meet you,' she says, her Cornish accent strong and lyrical. She lifts her empty mug. 'Want one?' I grimace, and she laughs. 'I know, it's awful, isn't it? But I have my own secret stash.' She opens her bottom drawer to reveal a variety of teabags and sachets of instant coffee.

'Why didn't I ever think of that?' A woman appears behind Lucy and peers over her shoulder. 'Can I pinch a green tea? I've got the worst hangover ever.' She pulls a face, her eyes landing on me. 'Oh, hey. Nice to meet you. I'm Laura.'

'Imogen.' I smile as Lucy hands over a teabag and looks questioningly at me. 'Oh, I'd love a cuppa, thank you.' I can have three cups of tea a day, apparently. I'm not really sure how I'm going to cope. The kettle was always on in our house, a cup of tea was Mum's answer to everything. Had a bad day? Got a new job? Lost your sister? Tea.

I shake myself, blowing on the tea to cool it, and open the gap analysis, working through the medical device regulation to see where the holes are. There are a lot of them, and I quickly lose myself in the work.

'Would you like anything from the shop?' Lucy's voice breaks into my concentration and I look up. It's almost one o'clock. I realise I didn't bring anything for lunch, and I'm suddenly starving.

'Oh, no thanks. I'm going to pop out myself.'

Lucy smiles and raises a hand. 'See you in a bit.'

Stretching, I save my work and lock the computer, gathering up my bag and water bottle. There's an M&S in town, but I'm not sure I can be bothered with trying to find a parking space at this time of day. I decide to go to the supermarket for some fruit – I've been craving strawberries – and to stretch my legs in a place that has air con.

I'm heading back to the car, arms loaded with punnets of strawberries and a bag of apples, when I see her. Emily. She stops in front of me, eyes wide like a rabbit caught in the headlights, keys dangling from her fist. Her hair is swept back from her face.

'Forgot to take a bag,' I say, indicating my shopping, but she doesn't smile. She just stares at me, unblinking. What is she so scared of? I take a step forward. 'Emily, I–'

'What?' Her voice is cold, tight. 'What do you want, Imogen?'

Taken aback, I open my mouth, but no words come out. I want to ask where she's been, what happened to her. Why she's back. Why Freya hasn't come back. But Emily is closed off to me, her mouth pinched into a line, her eyes narrowed. She reminds me of Jamie, I realise suddenly with a jolt, her eyes cold and angry like his used to be.

'Emily.' I hear a voice behind me and turn to find Agnes standing by the entrance to the shop, a little girl clinging to her leg. Emily's daughter. She looks like her, I think, with her wild hair and bright eyes, her voice ringing out across the car park.

'Mumily!' she cries, jumping and waving excitedly. 'Mumily, we're here for lunch!'

'Mumily?' I repeat, laughing despite myself. I look back at Emily, whose features have softened at the sight of Ella. 'Cute.'

She looks at me, as if trying to decide whether I'm taking the piss. The fight appears to have gone out of her; suddenly, she looks like the girl I grew up with, the young woman she became. Fiercely intelligent, fiercely loyal. Fiery by nature, she was more than a match for Freya, whose black moods could engulf us like a storm. Fire on one side, thunder on the other. And me, the voice of reason, the peacekeeper. The *doormat*, Freya called me once.

I realise then that I've been too hasty, backing her into a corner. I've been acting like Freya, too forceful. Who knows what Emily went through in the years she was gone?

'Look,' I begin, trying to keep my voice neutral, 'let's find a time to catch up, okay? It's been a long time.' I take a deep breath. 'I've missed you.'

Emily's eyes are watery now, soft around the edges. She's looking at me in the way she used to look at me when we were younger, when I'd had a fight with Freya or someone at school had picked on me. She was tiny, under five foot and barely a size ten, but I'd seen her stand her ground with her brother, with bullies at school, but only ever in defence of someone else, not herself. So who is she standing up for now?

'I have to go,' she says quietly, and I watch her approach her mother and daughter, bending to scoop the little girl into her arms and striding through the doors to the supermarket. Agnes stares at me for a moment, the breeze catching the scarf tied around her head, making the ends flutter, before she turns and follows her daughter.

13

FREYA

THEN

Freya tied her long hair into a fishtail braid, pulling it over her left shoulder. It was hot; her strapless dress revealed tanned shoulders; her *F* necklace nestled in the hollow of her throat. It was a Saturday, and Imogen was shopping in town with their mum. She needed to buy a new pair of flip-flops, she said, lifting hers by their broken strap. So the day was Freya's. And Jamie's.

She skipped down the stairs, feeling more like a twelve-year-old than twenty-two, and smiled as she caught a glimpse of herself in the hall mirror. She wondered what Imogen would say if she knew. If she told her how the boy next door made her stomach flutter, how soft his lips were. How many secrets she'd been keeping from her.

Donning her oversized sunglasses and stepping out into the sunshine, Freya leapt over the low wall separating the two front gardens and tapped on the door. Emily opened it, her hair in a messy bun on top of her head, wrapped in a dressing gown despite the heat. 'Freya?' She squinted up at her. 'Did we have plans today?'

Freya chewed her lip. 'Oh, no, I... well, Jamie said he'd help me with my car. There's a noise coming from it.' A weak lie, she knew, but it was the best she could come up with on the spot.

'Oh, right.' Emily stood on the threshold, still staring at Freya.

'Is he here then?' Freya asked, leaning against the wall, trying to look bored.

'Oh, yeah, yeah. Jamie!' Emily called his name without turning round. *Why is she staring at me?* Freya thought, anxiety pooling in her stomach. *She can't know anything.* Freya and Jamie kept their blossoming romance to themselves. It was unexpected, the way she looked at him one day, as she had a hundred times before, and felt something pass between them. Since that day, something shifted, and they'd started spending more time together. He always seemed to catch her as she was going out; he was in the front garden pulling up weeds, or down by his car, tinkering away. He took Agnes into the city centre every week to go shopping, and they would pop into Starbucks for a coffee, always during her shift. Everywhere she looked, there he was, with his wide grin and glittering eyes, and Freya wondered why she was only now seeing him in a new light.

Jamie appeared behind his sister, bumping her with his shoulder as he passed.

'All right, Frey?' he said, joining Freya on the wall. 'Hot for September, isn't it?' He turned to Emily, who was still hovering in the doorway. 'Take a picture, it'll last longer.' Despite the immaturity of the joke, Freya laughed, and Emily frowned.

'Let's go,' Freya said, standing up and dusting off the back of her dress. She didn't want to feel Emily's eyes on her anymore, didn't want to know whether she suspected there was something going on between them. 'My car's parked round the back.'

'Bye, sis!' Jamie called, lifting a hand before leaping down the steps. Freya pretended she didn't notice the look in Emily's eyes, didn't recognise the emotion she'd seen in her eyes a hundred times before. Fear.

14

EMILY

I dream of Scotland, of the cabin in the middle of the woods. Ella crying, her tiny hands balled into fists, her red mouth open, her eyes screwed up in anguish. I tried singing to her as I prepared her bottle, a lullaby half-forgotten, my voice shaky with nerves. Nobody had taught me how to feed a baby, or how to sterilise a bottle.

I read and reread the instructions on the box of formula, the words blurring before my eyes and Ella's screams filling my ears. My hands shook as I spooned out the formula, spilling across the counter, then swirled it around in the bottle of water. Was the water cool enough? I tested it against my wrist; droplets splashed across my shirt. And all the while, Ella kept screaming.

I picked her up, cradling her hot little body against my chest. Her face was wet from tears and snot, her limbs rigid with rage. I tried to steady my hand as I picked up the bottle and presented it to Ella. The teat nudged against her lips and she howled again, furious that I would try to trick her with a bottle. She turned her face into my chest, her eyes still closed, feeling her way like a newborn kitten. But I had nothing to give her.

I wake to Ella flexing her bare feet against my back, her little toes needling my skin, reminding me again of a kitten. I take a deep breath, trying to slow my racing heart. I've tried to forget what it was like then, right at the beginning, when Ella and I didn't know each other. When she couldn't tell me what she wanted, or how I could help her, comfort her. But, after months holed up in that little cabin, learning how to feed and bathe and play with her, which lullabies she liked, how she liked to be held before she went to sleep, we finally clicked together. As the years went by, I discovered how much she loved water, splashing through puddles in her purple wellies, almost giving me a heart attack by jumping into a pond and trying to make friends with the fish. By the time she was three, Ella would read to me before bed, putting on voices for different characters, performing for me, as if I were the child and she the mother. She loved jumping into huge piles of leaves, bringing spiders home to keep as pets, and braiding my then waist-length hair. She didn't like carrots but loved cauliflower, preferred eggy soldiers over scrambled egg.

And then she started to get ill, and I had to learn all about her again. I had to learn again that she was the most important thing in the world, the reason I'd made that promise five years before.

I turn over and look at her, this sunshine child of mine, remembering how she would curl up on the floor, knees tucked into her chest, moaning with pain. How the weight dropped off her, her curls hanging limp, her eyes ringed with purple. I remember the trip to the doctors, the fear gripping me as we ventured into the wider world for the first time in years. The GP remembered us from Ella's last vaccinations, gently scolding me for not bringing her for her boosters when I was supposed to. The shame that flooded me, heating my cheeks, as I realised I'd let her down. Ella's calm curiosity as her blood was taken. The leaflet pressed into my hand, covered in pictures of food she could eat. The word *hereditary* sending a jolt of fear down my spine.

Hereditary. What else has she inherited from us?

~

The rest of the week passes without incident, though my insides clench whenever I see Imogen at the sink in the toilets or outside in the car park. But she doesn't speak to me. She only smiles and looks away.

I focus on my work, spending hours sizing and resizing the symbols Imogen sent to me via email with very little in the way of instructions. *The CE mark needs to be 5mm.* So I take my time mocking up new designs, making sure the symbols all line up, that there's enough space for the text.

Before I know it, it's Wednesday afternoon, and the end of my first working week. Flo drops by just before three, perching on the end of my desk.

'Just checking in,' she says, smiling down at me as I save my work. 'Will you be back next week?'

I smile back. 'Of course. It was fun, actually. Good to get my brain working again.' Not that Ella doesn't exercise my brain; with her enquiring mind and startling intelligence for her age, I sometimes feel like I'm trying to keep up with *her*. But, and though guilt shoots through me at the thought, it's been nice to have some time away from her too.

Flo is nodding. 'Good. I'm glad to hear it. Any nice plans for the next few days? The weather is meant to hold.'

I look past her and out of the window at the river of blue without a cloud in sight. 'How long has it been since it rained?' I wonder aloud. It feels like years. 'I saw a fire on the side of the road yesterday. Probably someone flicking their cigarette butt out the car window.'

Flo shakes her head. 'Imogen said the same thing. Said it reminded her of bush fires in Australia.' Her eyes lock onto mine. 'Did you see many, while you were there?'

The question is innocent, her tone light, but I freeze. Flo is Deb's friend as well as my mum's. What does she know? An image of Deb flashes into my mind; her standing on the doorstep, the hallway light casting her face in shadow. A bundle in my arms, quiet now, almost hidden in the folds of the blanket. *Go, Emily. Run.*

I shake myself, noticing Flo's raised eyebrow. 'Erm, no,' I manage, my voice barely a whisper. 'I didn't.'

As I'm getting into the car, I notice Imogen walking around the car park, phone pressed to her ear, her eyes hidden behind large sunglasses. I expect to see a cigarette smouldering between her fingers, but then I see her hand move to her stomach, and it suddenly dawns on me. And with the realisation come the memories I've been desperate to forget.

When I get home, Ella greets me at the door, flapping a piece of paper at me. 'Look, look! I did a picture!' Dropping my handbag at the foot of the stairs, I take the paper from her, smoothing it out.

I frown. 'Who's this, sweetie?' I bend down to point out what I mean. Ella beams up at me.

'It's my daddy. I didn't know I had a daddy, but Nanny told me all about him! I can't wait for him to visit.' My blood runs cold at her words, and she peers up at me curiously. 'Do you have a daddy, Mumily?' My vision blurs, darkening at the edges, until I think I'm going to faint.

15

IMOGEN

LOCAL GIRLS MISSING

A second young woman has been reported missing by concerned family members.

Emily Bligh, 21, failed to return home after a trip to the supermarket, her mother, Agnes Bligh, told police.

This comes just three days after Freya Rivers, 23, friend and next-door neighbour to Emily, went missing. Imogen Rivers, Freya's twin sister, told The Herald that the trio were set to go travelling the day Freya was discovered missing.

"Our train tickets were booked," Imogen said. "We were going to Edinburgh. Everything was set. I don't understand what's happened to her." Deborah Rivers, Freya's mother, told The Herald that Freya did not take her passport or any of her belongings.

Footage released by police shows Emily boarding a train the day before she was reported missing, though it is unclear where she was headed. Emily is not thought to be vulnerable or in danger, but police are keen to speak to both young women to ensure they are safe.

Emily's brother told The Herald that he believes his sister has gone *to join her friend. "I always thought Freya just went off travelling by herself," he said. "Emily has probably gone off to join her. I don't blame her. She's young, she's not long graduated from uni. She's off on an adventure."*

I reread the article, skimming over the details. Freya's height and build, her hair, the scar in her left eyebrow. I read the description of Emily – long auburn hair, green eyes, barely five feet tall. What she was wearing – black jeans, red Converse trainers, a leather jacket. I search online for the last sighting of Emily, watch that five-second clip over and over again, watch her board that train at Plymouth station. I'm not sure I'd be able to tell who it was if I didn't know Emily so well. If I didn't recognise the hair curling against the nape of her neck, the way she put a hand to her cheek when she was nervous. The backpack we bought her for Christmas the year before. Those tiny, intimate details, the result of a lifetime of friendship. But it didn't stop her leaving. And it isn't making her tell me the truth now.

I lay down on the bed and stretch my arms above my head, feel my back click. The puzzle of Freya and Emily has haunted me for five years now, the same questions going around in my head. Where did they go? *Why* did they go? If they were going off together, why did Emily wait a few days to follow? Why has Emily come back? Where has she been?

I let out a frustrated groan, pressing my fingers into my eyes. How could Freya have gone anywhere without her passport? Without her clothes, her money? Emily didn't have enough for the two of them; she barely had enough for just her. We were going to pool our money together and split it three ways, cover the cost of transport and accommodation and food. We'd get jobs along the way, applying for visas and never planning too far ahead. We knew where we wanted to go, the map on Freya's wall dotted with pins, but we didn't know when. We were going to *go with the flow*, as Freya used to say, her eyes glittering. Those eyes have haunted me for years too. The same eyes I see in the mirror every day, set in the same face, our differences becoming less pronounced as the years went by. I place a finger on my left eyebrow, picturing the scar Freya had. I can't let her become absorbed by me.

The red numbers on the clock glow 0416. Freya isn't going to let me sleep. I pull an oversized T-shirt over my head and pad downstairs. The night air is sticky as I step out into the back garden, the grass cool beneath my bare feet. I look up into the sky, the stars glittering amongst the deep blue. I close my eyes and breathe in, trying to clear my mind. I can smell the roses Mum tends carefully every year; they must be struggling without rain. I can smell the sea, that salty tang that will forever remind me of home. And then the smell of cigarette smoke drifts over to me.

I open my eyes, try to peer down the length of the garden. Everything is in shadow, the sun still minutes away from rising, but I can't see anyone. The house to my left is dark, curtains drawn against windows flung wide open. I hear the crackle of a cigarette and turn to my right, to Emily's house. And there, through the square holes in the top of the fence, I see her. She's standing in almost the same spot as me, though beneath her feet will be paving slabs instead of grass, Agnes never being fond of gardening. Her eyes are closed, her hand lifting the cigarette to her lips. The tip glows red in the gloom.

I go to move closer and her eyes snap open, meeting mine in an instant. I freeze. Will she run again? Will she think I'm spying on her? The aroma of her cigarette drifts towards me again and memories flood my mind. Their house always stank of cigarettes, her father chain-smoking every evening in the living room. Emily's hair would pick it up, its reddish colour reminding me of a bonfire.

'Imogen,' she says now, eyes still locked on mine. 'Can't sleep either?'

I shake my head.

'Jamie is coming.' Emily takes another drag on her cigarette, blowing the smoke into the brightening sky. 'My brother.' She lets out a snort.

I take a step closer, breath ragged. There's so much I want to ask her, so many things she hasn't said, but she's talking now and I don't want to scare her away.

'Is this the first time you've seen him? Since...' I trail off, holding my breath. She isn't looking at me now; her face is turned towards the rising sun.

'Since I left? Yes. Five years doesn't seem as long now.'

'What do you mean?'

Emily looks at me, pinning me in place with her gaze. Those eyes that have seen so much; her father's violence, her mother's terror, her brother's transition from ally to monster. A memory hits me suddenly, of an evening not long after her dad disappeared. Emily sitting in her garden, knees drawn up to her chest, picking clumps of long grass. When I called her name through the holes in the fence, her face was tear-streaked, mascara running down her cheeks.

'What's wrong?' I asked her, pushing my face as close to the fence as possible. 'What's the matter?'

But before she could speak, Jamie appeared, standing outside the back door with his feet apart, arms crossed over his chest, and for half a second, I thought it was Sam, returned from wherever the hell he'd disappeared to.

'Emily,' he said gruffly, and her head swivelled round at his voice, her eyes wide, a hand pressed to her cheek. 'Come on.'

That was the first time I saw Jamie for what he was. For what he is. Until I saw his shadow cut across our front garden and pull Freya into the night.

'Why did you come back?' I ask her, watching as she stubs out her cigarette, tossing the butt into the grass. She turns to me.

'I shouldn't have,' she says, running a hand through her hair. 'And neither should you.'

16

EMILY

I tiptoe around the room, stuffing clothes into a bag as quietly as possible. I fold Ella's favourite blanket, tucking it in next to her *Frozen* pyjamas. It was a mistake coming back here. I knew Mum couldn't be trusted. Jamie has always been her favourite, ever since we were children. It was always Jamie she protected, stood up for, took the punches for. Never for me. She never stood vigil outside my room, putting herself between me and *him*. She never saw what Jamie became, refused to see what he was capable of. And then she did it again, helping him, protecting him. Blowing the shreds of our family apart for good.

And now he's coming here. Today. To take her away from me. My sunshine child, the bright-haired girl fast asleep on the bed, her tiny frame curled up in the middle. No. He can't have her. I won't let him.

I shove my make-up bag into the rucksack, snatch my contraceptive pills from the bedside table. I need to pack light. The folder is still tucked into the second compartment, kept safe from Mum's prying eyes, but I check it anyway. Passports, birth certificates. Newspaper clippings. And a small box, a box I have kept for almost five years, in the hope that I will never have to open it and release its secret.

I gently shake Ella awake, watch her blink away the remnants of a dream. 'Good morning, sleepyhead,' I whisper, pushing her hair away from her head. She's warm, her forehead slick with sweat, but there's no time for a shower. We have to go. 'Come on, let's get you dressed.' I hold out a T-shirt and skirt, watch her wriggle out of her pyjamas. They can stay here, I decide. The rucksack is almost full, and I still need to pack Ella's snacks.

I heard Mum on the phone last night, her whispered pleas that he *wait, please wait, she isn't ready yet*, followed by resignation. She conceded, as she always does with him. I waited until almost two o'clock, lying next to Ella in the dark, counting her breaths. Mum stays up late these days, the pain keeping her awake at night, so I waited until she went to bed before starting to pack. I decided to let Ella sleep until five; we would walk into town, hop on a train and be gone before anyone noticed.

I remember the conversation in the garden with Imogen, wonder why I told her Jamie was coming. Maybe I wanted someone to know the reason I'm disappearing this time. Maybe a part of me wants her to know the truth.

Now Ella is dressed, I realise her hair is in desperate need of a brush, but it's already packed. I press my finger to my lips as she opens her mouth to speak. 'We're going on an adventure,' I whisper, and she grins.

I open the bedroom door as quietly as possible, and together we creep down the stairs. Ella stops halfway down, tugging on my sleeve. 'I need to pee,' she says, crossing her legs to emphasise the point. I sigh and give her a gentle push back upstairs.

'Go on now, quickly! Don't flush. You don't want to wake Nanny up. Use the step to wash your hands.' Guilt floods through me as I remember Mum coming home with it a few days ago, a small step covered in sea creatures, just for Ella. How can I take her away again? But no, I have to. I'm doing this for Ella. Mum knew the rules. She made her choice.

Ella scampers back up the stairs and I continue down into the kitchen, rummaging through the cupboards to find her snacks. I slip into my trainers and sit on the bottom step to lace them up, then shoulder the rucksack and wait for Ella, leaning against the bannisters. She appears at the top, a tiny shadow flitting out of the bathroom, taking the stairs painstakingly slowly to avoid making noise. As she nears the bottom, I reach out and take her hand, still damp from the sink, smelling vaguely of aloe vera.

'Come on,' I whisper, swinging her down from the last step, 'time to go!'

As we turn to the front door, the handle shifts down, a key scraping in the lock from the outside. I freeze, the breath catching in my throat as the door opens.

'Hello, sis,' Jamie says, grinning boyishly. He hasn't changed, his hair still ash blond, curling slightly at the edges, his eyes still grey like the troubled sea. The years haven't aged him; his past hasn't haunted him. His eyes shift to Ella, taking her in, and his smile widens. Then he notices the bag on my back, the shoes on our feet, and his eyes harden. 'Where are you taking my daughter, Emily?'

17

FREYA

THEN

Freya sat on the swing, her skirt lifting in the breeze as she went higher and higher. She watched Jamie approach, saw his grin widen as he got closer.

'I could see your knickers from my house,' he laughed. Freya stuck out her tongue.

'Come on!' she called, indicating the seat next to her. Jamie shook his head. 'What are you, a chicken?'

He laughed again, that deep, hearty laugh she loved to listen to, before running behind her and grabbing her around the waist, bringing the swing to a stop. She giggled, squirming, trying to kick him away. His lips brushed her neck and she felt heat rise up her cheeks.

'Not here,' she whispered, and he smiled against her skin.

'Now who's the chicken?' He reached down and put his hand on her skirt, tugging down the hem. 'Isn't this a bit short? You don't want to give the wrong impression.' Freya looked down at his hand on her thigh, his fingers digging into the flesh, and she closed her eyes, feeling the colour rush to her cheeks. Before she could speak, Jamie moved his hand to her chin and, turning her face towards him, kissed her. He grinned when they pulled apart, taking her hand and leading her out of the park and under the cover of the trees.

As they lay in the grass, limbs tangled, leaves in her hair, Freya wondered what Imogen would say if she knew. What Emily would say. Could this work? She glanced down at him, his head resting on her chest, their fingers intertwined. *Is this what I want?*

She didn't know. They were meant to be going off and exploring the world soon. Did she want to get involved with someone now? Did she want to get involved with *Jamie* now? She watched his face, his eyes closed, flickering beneath their lids. She thought of the boy she knew, of the shadow that would pass across his eyes when his dad shouted across the garden fence for him and Emily to come home. She used to hear his cries through the wall separating their house, their bedrooms mirrored, his pain infiltrating her calm, loving home.

The crying stopped when Jamie was about fifteen. When he suddenly grew six inches, put on weight, turning from boy to man. When his head reached his father's shoulders, and his fists could inflict damage on the man who had damaged him. Was he beyond repair? His dad was gone, had disappeared one night when Jamie was nineteen. 'Done a runner,' Agnes said when Freya's mum had gone round the next day. 'Good riddance.' She'd shut the door, left the curtains closed for days, Jamie and Emily trapped inside with her, beyond reach. They saw the police turn up a couple of times, and heard them talk to Mum on the doorstep, but nothing seemed to come of it. When they finally resurfaced, Emily emerging from that house like a phoenix rising from the ashes, she didn't mention him, not once. And nobody asked.

18

EMILY

Memories of that night flood my mind, clouding my vision. Jamie's face contorted with rage, his hands covered in blood. Mum collapsed on a chair, head in her hands, her whole body shaking with sobs. The sheets stained red; ragged strips torn from the bottom. *Get her out. Please.*

My grip tightens around Ella's hand. I feel her looking up at me, confusion coming from her in waves. *Who is this strange man?* I can almost hear her saying. *Why did he call me his daughter?* I remember her words from earlier, how excited she'd been at the prospect of having a dad. But right now she looks young and afraid and vulnerable, and I realise that I have failed her again.

'Mumily?' she whispers, and Jamie snorts.

'Mumily?' he echoes. 'Cute.' But he doesn't mean it. I bristle at the derision in his voice. 'Don't you have anything to say to your big brother? It's been a long time.'

He takes a step forward and I feel my body turn away, automatically pushing Ella behind me. Jamie holds up his hands and stops, his eyes pinning me to the spot.

'Emily?' A voice behind us but I don't move, don't take my

eyes off him. Mum comes down the stairs, leaning heavily on the bannister like she always does. 'Emily? Where are you going?' She must see Jamie then, because she stops, a few steps from the bottom. 'Jamie. You're here early. Didn't we say nine o'clock?'

'I couldn't sleep. I was too excited.' His eyes are searching for Ella, who is pressed up against my legs. 'I wanted to see her. You've kept her from me for so long.'

'With good reason,' I spit, finding my voice. Jamie laughs.

'There's no good reason to keep a father away from his daughter.' He crouches then, peering around me. 'Come on. No need to be shy, little Ella.' Her name in his mouth makes me feel sick. I shift away, moving backwards into the kitchen. I hear Ella whimper and reach behind me to take her hand. *You're safe*, I want to tell her, but it would be a lie. Neither of us is safe now.

He stands up again, looking over my head at Mum, who is still frozen on the stairs. 'You told her I was coming, didn't you?' His tone is accusatory, and I risk a glance at Mum. Her eyes are closed as if in pain. 'She's a flight risk,' Jamie hisses, and Mum flinches. 'I told you not to tell her. I *told* you she'd try to run away again.'

'She didn't tell me,' I say, and even as the words leave my lips, I'm unsure why. Didn't she betray me, betray Ella? But the violence in Jamie's eyes are dragging me back to the past, bringing back the terror.

I take another step back. Maybe we can make it to the back door, I could lift Ella over the fence into Imogen's garden. *Imogen.* I picture myself banging on glass, crying to be let in, Deb's worried face peering out at me through the gloom. Just like all those years ago. The past is replaying itself.

'Don't even think about it,' Jamie says, his voice a low growl. 'You won't get away this time. This time I'll go to the police. I'll tell them exactly what you are – a child snatcher.'

I almost laugh. A child snatcher? Is that the narrative he's been telling himself this whole time? The lie he's told himself until he believed it? I risk another glance at Mum, who is looking fearfully at Jamie. Can't she see that this is another piece of our past come back to haunt us? The dominant male, casting a long shadow of fear and torment. *Like father, like son.*

I want to argue with Jamie, tell him that I'm no longer afraid of him. That he can't hurt us. But he's taking something out of his pocket, and my stomach lurches. *No.* He can't do this. He can't take her away from me. I won't let him, I *won't.*

He's smirking now, holding the necklace aloft. The necklace bought before Ella was born. No, it can't be. I rummage through my bag, pulling out the small box. It's empty. I glare at Mum and she shrinks back, guilt written all over her face. How could she?

I try to think. Who will help me? I've kept this secret close to me for so long, kept Ella hidden away from the world, that we have only each other. I could go to prison, and then she would be alone with him. *No.*

I take a deep breath, try to slow my hammering heart. I need a different plan, a plan that will work. A plan that will get us away from Jamie forever.

'All right,' I say, my voice unsteady. I unpeel Ella from my legs, turn to kiss her on the top of her head. 'Let's do this slowly, okay?' My words are directed at Jamie, but I bend to look Ella in the eyes. Those wide, fearful eyes. 'There's nothing to be afraid of,' I tell her, the lie tasting sour on my tongue. 'Your dad...' The word almost chokes me, but I carry on. 'Your dad is here to meet you. He hasn't seen you in a long time. Can you say hello?'

And Ella, oh Ella, my brave sunshine child, peers around me and looks at Jamie, her gaze steady. 'Hello,' she says, and I close my eyes to stop the tears falling.

I sit on the sofa, knees pressed together, Ella snuggled against my hip. She's watching a programme on TV, and the repetitive music is making my head hurt. Jamie sits in the armchair across from us, one ankle crossed over the other knee, his eyes fixed on us. But I don't look at him. I won't.

Ella is falling asleep. I can feel her little body slackening beside me, her limbs turning to jelly. I turn to look at Mum, sitting on the other side of Ella, her eyes on the TV but her mind far away.

'Mum,' I whisper, and she jumps before looking at me. 'It's time for Ella's nap.'

Jamie leaps out of his chair. 'I'll do it.'

'No!' The word bursts out of me, too loud, too sharp. Ella stirs and I put a hand on her hair, stroking her like a kitten. 'Not yet.'

Without looking at him, I scoop Ella into my arms and take her upstairs, depositing her gently on the bed. She opens her eyes and smiles sleepily, stretching her arms overhead. Love tugs at my heart as I watch her curl up like she always does, cheek resting on her hands, knees tucked up to her chest. I brush her hair away from her face, listen to her breathing deepen. She needs a haircut, I realise, twirling a strand between my fingers.

'Mumily,' she says, surprising me.

'I thought you were asleep,' I whisper, tugging gently on the strand of hair. She smiles, opens one eye. It looks almost purple in the dim light, the curtains shut tight against the afternoon sun.

'Mumily, when are we going on our adventure?'

Dread pools in my stomach as the events of the day hit me. I bend down and kiss her on the forehead, breathing in her scent. 'Soon, my darling. Soon.'

Downstairs, I shut the living room door and turn to face my brother. Anger courses through me, fury at what he has done today, what he did all those years ago. An act he has made me pay for again and again.

'We need to get something straight,' I say, planting my hands on my hips. I will show him that I'm not afraid of him; I will show myself. 'Ella has been with me for all this time. I have fed her and clothed her and loved her. You cannot just turn up and expect to be a part of her life.'

Jamie rises from his chair, his eyes blazing. 'I would've been a part of her life if you hadn't taken her from me.' He jabs his index finger at me.

'You know why I took her. You know what you did.' I glance at Mum. 'We all do. All of us in this room know exactly what happened that night.' The threat is clear, but Jamie only scoffs.

'It was a long time ago. Isn't there a statute of limitations or some shit?' He shakes his head. 'The police won't listen to what you have to say, not after I tell them what you did.'

I decide to call his bluff. 'Do you honestly believe that?' I glare at him, folding my arms across my chest. 'It would be my word against yours, wouldn't it?'

Jamie glares back at me before turning to Mum. 'You'll back me up, won't you, Mum?'

Panic grips me as Mum stares up at him, her eyes wide with fear. No, she wouldn't. Would she? *Say no*, I want to scream at her. *Tell him you won't.* But she doesn't speak. Instead she closes her eyes as if he hasn't spoken, as if we're not standing here in front of her. As if she doesn't hold our future in her hands.

I turn back to Jamie, trying to mask the fear snaking through me. 'It won't get to that. You can play a part in Ella's life, but I won't give her up. Not to anyone, and certainly not to you.' I see anger flit across his features again and attempt to soften my voice. 'We're family, aren't we? We can make this work, but only if we work together.' The word leaves a sour taste in my mouth. *Family.* It means nothing, not in this house.

Jamie's face falls then, his eyes dropping to the floor between us. 'All right, Em,' he says, his voice tight. 'I'm sorry I came on a bit strong, all right? I just... I just wanted to see her. Ella. I want a relationship with her. I'm turning over a new leaf, I swear. I want to do better, for her.'

I stare at him. He's not serious, he can't be. A new leaf? I open my mouth to speak but Mum's voice cuts in, startling us both.

'Jamie's right.' She sits forward in her chair, looking at me and then at Jamie. 'I don't have long left. That's why I called you home, Emily. I wanted to meet my granddaughter. I want her to have a relationship with her father. Family comes first.'

I grit my teeth at her words. I know, have always known, that she will take Jamie's side. But would she send me to prison for him? Would she tear Ella away from the only parent she's ever known? And would she trust him to keep her safe?

I have to believe the answer is no.

19

IMOGEN

Despite the encounter with Emily replaying in my mind, I must manage to drift off to sleep, because I dream of Liv. Liv, who reminded me of Emily, with her red curls and fiery nature. I dream of Byron Bay, Liv's wide smile, her thick, melodic Scottish accent. I dream of the party on the beach, the music pounding through my body, Liv's hand in mine, and I dream of closing my eyes and pretending she was Freya.

Liv stuck out her thumb, turning it downwards. I laughed at her.

'Whit?' she protested. 'It's how you do it here. A guy in Sydney told me.'

'I think he was having you on.'

She stuck her tongue out at me, then raised an eyebrow as a dark truck pulled up alongside us. 'See?' Her laughter cut through the hot air and I shook my head. Liv was the most colourful person I'd ever met, from her sunny disposition to her stripy, multicoloured knee socks.

Nirvana was blaring out of the window of the truck; the driver turned it down as Liv leaned through the passenger side window.

'Where you headed?' the driver asked. He was an all-Australian guy – tanned skin, sandy-blond hair, wearing aviator sunglasses and smoking a cigarette.

'Byron Bay,' Liv said, resting her forearms in the gap. I hovered behind her, always in the shadow of Liv's light. Where I liked it.

'Hop in,' he said, and Liv turned to grin at me. She climbed into the front seat; I sat behind her, rucksack resting on my legs. 'I'm Liam.'

'I'm Liv, and this is Immy,' she said, jerking a thumb at me. I smiled warily. I hadn't managed to get used to jumping into strange cars with strange people, especially not strange men – no matter how attractive Liv found them. There was something about her that radiated confidence and strength, and I felt safer with her, but I never felt *safe*. Not out here, not without Freya.

'Nice to meet you,' Liam said. 'How long have you been in Australia?'

Liv continued to chat with Liam as I stared out of the window, watching the bushland fly past. We'd hitch-hiked all the way from the Gold Coast, and now we were on the last leg. Byron Bay, the place almost everyone we met along the way had told us to visit. And as the coast began to come into view, I could see why. It was breathtaking. Shimmering blue-green waters, golden sand. Ocean as far as the eye could see.

Before long, Liam was pulling into a space. He turned off the engine, twisting to grin at me, pushing his glasses on top of his head. 'Here we are! Where are you girls staying?'

I bristled at the word *girls*, but Liv jumped in. 'At the hostel,' she said, flashing me a smile over her shoulder. 'We heard there are some jobs going. You know of any?'

Liam rubbed his cheek, his fingers rasping against the stubble. I grimaced.

'Come on, Liv,' I said, grabbing my rucksack and reaching

out for the door handle. I knew what she was up to, even if Liam didn't. She wanted him to offer us a place to stay – or, at least, somewhere for her.

Perhaps sensing my wariness, Liam grinned. 'Try the Bay Leaf, they're usually looking for pretty young things.'

I rolled my eyes and pushed open the door. 'Thanks for the lift.' I could tell I sounded stiff, too British, too unlike what a carefree twenty-something travelling around the world is supposed to sound like. But I wasn't carefree. I had been searching for my sister for almost four years, and I still hadn't found her.

Liv eventually hopped out of the vehicle, blowing a kiss to Liam as he reversed out of the space. I turned to her, prepared for her judgement of me and my behaviour, when I heard him call out, 'There's a silent disco tonight, down on Main Beach. You girls should definitely go. It's meant to be a riot!'

'See you there?' Liv called back, and Liam just grinned before pulling away. She turned back to me. 'A party! See, this is exactly the place we need to be!'

As always, her energy was exhilarating, infectious, and I felt my black mood lift. I grinned and took her arm. 'Let's go and get settled, then.'

'And start drinking!'

'You're so Scottish.'

Liv punched my arm. 'Yer gettin' skelped, ya wee bawbag.'

We didn't see Liam there, not that night. Not for a week or two, after several late nights partying and early starts cleaning the hostel and cooking breakfast in return for free lodging. I took the latter job, Liv unable to face cooking sausage and eggs.

'Ah cannae even look at that shite,' she said, pulling out a vegan cereal bar. But she had to scrub the toilets, so I thought I'd been let off lightly. Plus, I could make sure I could actually eat the food.

The next time we saw Liam, the beach was heaving with people, fires burning all along the coast. Music blared out of speakers, bottles of beer chilling in buckets full of ice. Liv had her long red hair tied back in a braid; her tiny body engulfed in a kaftan. She had glitter stars stuck on her cheek, and her lips were a bright pink. She passed me the spliff she was smoking, leaning her head back and blowing rings, her nose piercing glinting in the firelight. I laughed and copied her, blowing smoke into the bruise-coloured sky.

I was *alive*. For the first time in years, since Freya and Emily disappeared, I was able to forget, to live. I could almost pretend that Liv was Freya, with her fingers interlocked with mine as she led me through the crowds. My long skirt was brushing the sand, my purple toenails disappearing as we stumbled across the beach. I bumped into a woman and apologised, laughing, but my voice was lost in the din.

The noise was overwhelming. I could feel the music pounding through my body, beating in time with my heart. My skin prickled with sweat despite the late hour, my hair, loose around my shoulders, blowing in the gentle breeze. Still I followed Liv, focusing on her bobbing braid as we passed groups of people, some dancing, some with limbs entangled, lying together on huge towels. I felt my cheeks burn, wondering what Emily would have made of all of this. Wondering if she had made anything of it. Had she been here? Was I walking in her footsteps, in Freya's?

I shook my head, finished the spliff, threw the butt into the sand. Liv's fingers slipped from mine and I grabbed for her, suddenly afraid of losing her in the crowd. Then hands grabbed me around the waist and I screamed as I was lifted off my feet and spun around.

'Liam?' I choked out as he set me down. I stumbled and he caught me, his hands firm and dry on my bare shoulders. I turned around to find Liv, but she was gone. Panic caught in my throat. Where was she? I couldn't lose her. Not again. Not like Freya.

'There she is!' Liam's grinning face filled my vision, and I took a step back, trying to look for Liv. 'I knew we'd meet again.'

'Liv is–' I started, but he cut me off.

'It was you I wanted to see. Come on, I want to show you something.'

He took my hand, and, just like Liv had done, started pulling me through the crowd. I wondered when I would stop following others – Freya, Emily, Liv – and start walking my own path. I tried to pull away but his grip was firm. He turned and grinned at me, then stopped, producing two small pills in the palm of his hand.

'What is it?' I shouted, trying to make myself heard.

'The feel-good hit of the summer,' Liam laughed, putting one pill into my hand and throwing the other into his mouth, swallowing it dry. I stared down at the pill, my mind hazy.

Don't be so fucking stupid, Im! I heard Freya's voice in my head and tried to shake it away. *You don't know what that is!* Liam was looking at me expectantly.

Fuck off, Freya. You're not here. You haven't been here for a long time.

I tilted my head back and washed the pill down with a swig of cider from the bottle Liam handed me. His eyes glittered as we started moving again, pushing through the crowds, until we got to the water's edge. Liam threw himself onto the sand and I followed, my legs stretched out, my feet just touching the water. I leaned back on my hands and stared up at the sky. The moon was bright overhead, the darkness full of stars.

'Wow,' I murmured, and Liam laughed.

'Beautiful, ain't it?' He copied me, leaning back on his elbows, legs crossed in front of him. His eyes were looking past me; I turned to see Liv stomping across the beach, her eyes blazing.

'Get it up ye, ya bastard!' she shouted, and I felt Liam move, scrambling to find purchase in the sand. I stayed lying down, looking between them as Liv marched up to him. 'What did ye gie her?' she cried, placing both hands on his chest and pushing. He stumbled, almost losing his balance. 'Was it the same shite ye tried to gie me the other night?'

I stared at her, trying to remember if she'd mentioned seeing him since he dropped us off. I take in her fists clenched against her sides, her shoulders squared. What had he given me? Anxiety prickled along my skin as I remembered swallowing the pill. *Don't be so fucking stupid, Im!*

Liam took a step back, his hands held up in submission. 'I don't know what you're talking about,' he said, forcing a laugh. He looked at me. 'She's nuts.'

Liv moved like a cat, striking him in the jaw with her fist. He staggered back towards the sea. 'Aye, we lassies are all mad, is that it?' She glanced around and picked up a rock from the shallow water pooling around their feet. 'I'll only tell ye once more. Get tae fuck.' Raising her arm, she took aim, hurling the rock at Liam. But he was gone, lurching away into the crowd.

My heart was pounding in my chest, the ocean filling my ears. Liv bent down beside me, put a hand on my shoulder.

'Awright, Im?' Her Glaswegian accent was so much thicker – with the drink, or anger, I wasn't sure – and it took me a moment to understand her. Tears clouded my vision and she put her arms around me, her sweat and perfume filling my lungs. 'Ah know, ah know,' she murmured, and I laughed, but it came out as a sob. I pulled away from her, rubbing my eyes.

'I'm okay,' I said eventually, trying to breathe deeply to calm my beating heart. 'I don't know what he gave me, but I'm all right.'

Liv took my arm, guiding me back to the hostel, tucking me into the bottom bunk and placing a bucket and a glass of water on the floor. She climbed in, her arms wrapped around me, reminding me of Freya, of how she would clamber into my bed whenever I had a nightmare and woke her up with my screams, her face pressed into my hair, one arm tight across my chest. It was how we used to sleep, she would say, in the womb, and although it was impossible to know, it always felt right.

I didn't ask Liv what happened to her a few nights before. I didn't have to. I knew.

I left Byron Bay the next morning, getting a bus to Ballina and flying to Melbourne, the next stop on our planned journey, leaving Liv behind. I had been in Australia for almost two months by that point, and I was tired of wandering, of wondering if I would find Freya. I think I knew, deep down, that I wouldn't.

I wake, bleary-eyed, to the sound of my phone ringing. Max's name flashes up on the screen. I hit the red button and reject the call, dropping back against the pillows with a sigh.

I wonder where Liv is now. Is she still in Australia, hitch-hiking her way across the continent? Or is she back home in Edinburgh, her multicoloured socks replaced with sensible black tights, sitting behind a desk, her wild curls straightened into submission? I smile at the idea. Definitely not.

I face the wall, wondering if Emily is in her room beyond, if she's asleep. Or has she disappeared again?

20

EMILY

Jamie surprises me by backing off. He tucks his anger away, but I know it's only a matter of time until it comes spewing back out.

On Sunday, I cook a roast and Ella spends the day in the garden, making a fort, apparently. With a glance at the sky, I go to call her inside for more sun cream, when I see Jamie slathering it on her shoulders and arms, before reaching down to get her bare feet. Fear grips me as he crouches in front of her. Ella's little face is bright with happiness; she giggles as he dabs a blob of cream on her nose. A mixture of relief and anxiety floods through me as I realise she isn't afraid of him. But maybe she should be.

On Monday, he makes Ella's breakfast to my instructions, grilling her gluten-free bread separately and keeping her food away from ours.

'There's a lot to this, eh?' he says, placing Ella's plate in front of her. I look up at him, certain I've mistaken his tone, but his eyes are soft as he watches Ella eat.

I nod, taking a sip of coffee. 'There is.'

'Where did she get it from, I wonder?'

My mug freezes halfway back to the table. I stare at him, willing him not to say it, not to speak of it. His back is to me as he wipes down the kitchen side, something I never saw him do as a child. Ella drops a piece of bacon onto the table and looks up at me, breaking the tension in the room.

'Five-second rule,' I say, grabbing it and popping it into my mouth. She giggles.

'That was mine!' she protests, but she picks up another slice of bacon and snaps it in half, offering me a piece. I open my mouth and she lays it carefully on my tongue, before doing the same with her own half.

'We're the same,' she says, mouth open, words distorted. I laugh and wiggle my tongue around, almost dropping the bacon.

'You're so good with her,' Jamie says, and I feel the air shift around us, Ella's tongue still hanging out.

I quickly chew the bacon and swallow before turning to him. Is he taking the piss? He's leaning against the counter, eyes on Ella; I hear her start to chew and turn back to her plate.

'I've had a long time with her,' I say carefully. Mum bustles in before I can say anything else, a plastic bag dangling from her wrist.

'I thought we could bake a cake today,' she says, smiling warmly at Ella. I see her wince as she lifts the bag onto the counter. 'I've just been to get eggs and lemons. What do you think, munchkin?'

Ella claps her hands. 'Yay, cake!'

Mum turns to look at me. 'Aren't you going to work today, Emily?'

I frown at her. She can't be serious. I'm not leaving Ella here alone, with *him*, no matter how good he is at play-acting. Because this is surely an act.

'Work?' Jamie asks, taking out the cake ingredients and laying them on the counter. 'Where are you working?'

'For Flo,' Mum says, easing into the chair opposite me. 'Designing labels and the like. You enjoyed it last week, didn't you?'

My mouth suddenly feels dry. I *did* enjoy it last week, but that was before Jamie came back into our lives. Before he shattered our carefully constructed walls.

'I'm not going back,' I say after a moment. 'I've already told Flo.'

Mum's face creases into a frown. 'Oh, Emily, whyever not?' I raise an eyebrow at her, and she sighs. 'I can look after Ella, you know that. And Jamie has to go back to work tomorrow, don't you, love?' Jamie nods, his face blank. 'Besides, I bumped into Jane at the shop earlier, and she said a space has opened up at her nursery. Wouldn't it be nice for Ella to mix with kids her own age?' She smiles at Ella, who has finished her breakfast and is lining up her crusts along the edge of the plate. 'She can start next week.'

I look between them, my mother and brother, trying to catch them in a lie. But if there is one, if they have concocted this tale to manipulate me, I can't detect it. I look at Ella, who is now beaming up at me.

'Look, Mumily, they're soldiers!' She gestures to her plate. I smile back at her.

'Well done,' I say, kissing the top of her head.

'Ella,' Jamie says, crouching down beside the table and catching her eye. I hold my breath. 'Would you like to go to nursery?'

Ella screws up her face. 'What's nursery?'

Jamie laughs. 'It's a place where kids like you can play and learn. Does that sound like fun?'

'What are you doing?' I hiss, but Mum shoots me a look. Ella is smiling again now – always smiling.

'Yes!' she exclaims, wriggling in her seat. 'I like playing. Can I go, Mumily? Will you come with me?'

I glare at Jamie as Ella turns to face me. I take her hands and bring them to my lips, kissing the palms. 'It's not a place for me, darling,' I say, hating Mum and Jamie for putting me in this position. Put like that, what kid wouldn't want to go to nursery? 'And I'm not sure it's the right time for you to go. You're too little.'

Instantly, I know I've said the wrong thing. Ella frowns. 'I'm not little, I'm big!' She tears her hands out of mine and stretches them above her head. 'I'm big! I want to play!'

Ella never has tantrums. I've seen other kids in supermarkets and at the park, screaming and throwing their little bodies on the ground, their legs kicking furiously. Ella has always stared at those kids with wide, curious eyes, perhaps wondering, as I am, why they are so upset. She has her moments, those short flares of defiance, determination in her eyes, but if she sleeps like a cat, she lives like a dog, happy to go with the flow. The saying shoots through me, Freya's voice running through my head.

'I know, I know,' I say quickly, high-fiving her hands. Her face brightens a fraction. 'Let me have a think about it, okay?'

'Okay!' Ella cries happily, reaching up to high-five me again. 'Can I go read a magazine now?'

I nod my assent and she climbs down from the chair, running upstairs to lounge on the bed, as she always does, legs in the air, nose in a magazine, looking for all the world like a fourteen-year-old, not a four-year-old.

I turn to my brother, who has moved away to lean against the kitchen counter again. 'Look,' I say, trying to keep my voice down, 'I'll decide when Ella goes to nursery, all right? Not you.' I look at Mum next. 'And not you.'

Mum reaches across the table for me. I snatch my hands

away and clasp them in my lap. Her eyes fill with hurt. 'Oh, darling, I was only trying to help.'

Jamie is busying himself with the washing-up, pretending not to listen. But he is. Of course he is. If he thinks I'm falling for this 'new leaf' bollocks, he truly has underestimated me. Just like he always has.

21

IMOGEN

Flo has tasked me with preparing a presentation for her and the other directors on the implementation of the new regulation. I nibble on a ginger biscuit to calm the morning nausea and start transferring the information I've gathered into small, easily digestible slides.

I haven't seen Emily since the night in the garden. *Jamie is coming.* The name makes my heart lurch, brings back the memory of that night I last saw Freya, his shadow dragging her away. I told the police about it, told them that if something happened to Freya, it involved Jamie. Jamie, the boy next door, the one with bruises and black eyes, the one we heard crying at night. Jamie, who always seemed wary of me, holding himself at a distance, but he would let Freya hold a pack of frozen peas against his shiner. Fiery Freya. She was always gentle with him.

I shake my head and force myself to focus on my work. I have to get this right. I realise I've slipped easily back into my own skin, confident in my work. I enjoy it, always have, and I'm grateful that Flo has given me this job.

My phone vibrates but I ignore it. Max hasn't stopped calling since I came back. But I can't answer, I can't face what happened. I have to put it behind me.

Concentrate. I put together a few slides, condensing the main parts of the regulation and typing out a sheet of extra notes. Not that I think I'll need them. I've barely put the regulation down these past couple of weeks, constantly reading and trying to understand what I'll have to do here. It's a big job; a lot has been left to stagnate, and several of the clinical evaluations haven't been touched in years, but I can do it.

An email from Flo pops up and I click to open it.

Hey Im, can you come into my office at 10am on Monday? We need to book your trip to Wiltshire!

I realise I'm looking forward to travelling. I haven't left Plymouth since I got back, and although I'd been in Melbourne for almost six months, we often took day trips out along the coast or into the national parks. Max could never sit still for long.

I look over at Lucy, who's poring over the shelf life validation reports. She catches me looking and grimaces.

'You were right, there's no traceability here. Looks like we'll have to do these tests again.'

I sigh heavily. Those tests will cost thousands of pounds. I'll have to find some good news to give Flo when I tell her about this, to soften the blow.

'Thanks for checking. Could you make a note of the batch numbers used so we can figure out when they were made, at least?'

Lucy makes another face. 'As far as I can tell, these batch numbers are made up. They're not like any of the others on the system, all the way back to... well, the year dot.' I sigh again, and Lucy chuckles. 'I have to say, it's good to have someone here to commiserate with. Tea?' She opens her drawer and lifts up a teabag.

'Lovely, thanks.'

I turn back to my computer as Lucy makes us both a cup of tea. I wonder what the hell the previous regulatory manager was doing for so many years. Maybe he had another business on the side. Maybe he used to fall asleep at his desk.

By midday, my eyes are tired, and I decide I need a break. I remember I told Mum I'd return a top for her, so I lock my computer and head out for lunch, taking my sandwiches with me. There's a bakery next to the post office, one I can eat precisely nothing from, but that doesn't stop me from being tempted by chocolate eclairs.

I step out of the post office and into the bright sunshine, closing my eyes against the glare. It is so hot. The radio this morning said it would get to thirty-two degrees today; my maxi dress is sticking to my skin as I cross the car park and slide into the car. I'm about to pull out when I see them; three figures walking together, plus a small one just in front. It's Ella, skipping ahead of Emily and Agnes. And... Jamie?

I freeze, hands on the too-hot steering wheel. Jamie. He's laughing as he walks beside his mother, her hand on his arm, sunglasses covering his eyes. Emily is watching her daughter, a child's rucksack dangling from her hand.

Why is Jamie with them? I watch as they enter a café, Jamie holding the door open while Ella skips through, Agnes leaning on Emily now. I remember the fear in Emily's eyes when I caught her crying in the back garden, when Jamie came outside and called her in.

A memory flashes into my mind. The night Freya disappeared, when I walked into her room to find it empty, her bed made, her desk chair slightly pulled out. The tug in my stomach telling me that something wasn't right. That she hadn't come home. We used to laugh when people asked us if we had the 'Twin Thing', but that day, I realised how strong it was. I could almost hear her calling for me, crying my name over and over again.

The police took my statement with barely-concealed impatience. She was twenty-three after all, a grown woman. But I knew something wasn't right.

'Have you spoken to Jamie yet?' I asked as the officers stood to leave. 'He lives next door. Jamie Bligh.'

'Why do we need to speak to him?' one officer, a woman, almost as tall and broad as her male colleague, asked, one hand on the door handle.

I blew out a breath in frustration. 'I just told you – I saw him with her last night. I don't think she came home.'

'You saw' – the male officer glanced down at my statement – '"a shadow in next door's garden, grab Freya and drag her down the street".' He looked at me. 'Did she go unwillingly?'

I paused for a moment. Did she? I wanted to say yes, of course, why would she have wanted to go off with him? But something stopped me. I was remembering whispered conversations, loaded glances. Secrets filling the air between us. The things Freya was hiding from me.

'I... I think so. I don't know.' The officers raised their eyebrows in unison, and I deflated, realising they didn't believe me, or if they did, they didn't think it was worth pursuing.

'We'll be talking to everyone who may be able to help us with our enquiries,' the female officer said after a moment, nodding to Mum, who was stood behind me, one hand on my shoulder, before letting herself and her colleague out.

Watching Jamie play happy families now, that feeling of unease rises within me once again. Jamie knows something about what happened to Freya. I can feel it. And I'm going to find out exactly what he did.

22

EMILY

My week off flies by, spent with one eye on Jamie and the other on Ella. But she seems to have taken everything in her stride. Maybe she doesn't fully understand what's going on. Maybe she doesn't really care. I've learnt that Ella will always go with the flow.

Mum takes me aside on Saturday night, while Jamie is putting Ella to bed. I'm hovering at the foot of the stairs, listening to him read one of her books. He's putting on voices, and Ella is giggling in that tired way, when she desperately wants to stay awake but sleep is dragging her under. It's been quite a hectic week; we've been to the Eden Project and spent the day at the Barbican, even venturing into the Aquarium, which Mum always told us was cruel when we were younger.

'It's the grandmother's prerogative,' she said, winking, as we entered, 'to spoil their grandchildren.' Her eyes had twinkled and I felt a happiness I hadn't expected.

Now she looks tired. Her eyes are puffy and her mouth is drawn down at the corners, a sign she's in pain but fighting it.

'Mum, let's sit down,' I say, taking her elbow and leading her into the living room. I throw a glance back up the stairs but all is quiet now, Jamie's soft murmuring the only noise drifting down.

I get Mum settled on the sofa then perch next to her, hands fluttering in my lap. 'Mum, are you feeling all right? Do we need to make an appointment with the GP?' I wonder again why she has refused all treatment, even stubbornly going without pain relief unless it gets really bad. I wonder why she feels the need to suffer.

Mum waves a hand at me. 'Don't worry about me. I want to talk about Ella.' She sits back, resting her head on the sagging cushions, and looks at me. 'Have you made a decision about nursery yet?'

'Not this again, Mum,' I sigh, turning my face to the ceiling. 'I'm really not sure about it. You said you could–'

'I know very well what I said, Emily.' Mum's tone is clipped and I look at her in surprise. 'And I can. But I really feel that nursery would be good for her. Give her the chance to mix with kids her own age. To learn and explore. Broaden her mind.' She fixes me with her gaze, her dark grey eyes the mirror image of Jamie's. 'You loved school when you were younger. Do you remember?'

A memory flashes into my mind: a tall woman, dark-skinned, with intricate drawings on her hands. 'Henna,' she said, taking my hand and drawing a pattern on my skin with a marker. 'Now we match.' I remember a feeling of affection flowing through me, relaxing into the warmth of her earthy-brown eyes. And then *he* had seen it, the drawing on the back of my hand, and ranted about immigrants and foreigners while Mum furiously scrubbed it away with a flannel.

'Yes,' I say, blinking back the memory, hating that every good one is cast in *his* shadow. 'I remember.'

'It would only be for the mornings to begin with, love,' Mum says. Her eyes are closed, a hand resting on her stomach. I picture the cancer moving through her body, spreading like a dye through her veins and her organs. I imagine her turning black from the inside out. 'She should be starting school in September anyway. Why not give it a go?'

I realise suddenly that maybe this is her way of telling me that she can't handle Ella for three full days a week. I open my mouth to tell her that I'll quit the job, that I don't need it, then close it again. Mum hasn't worked in years, has been living off *his* pension since she had to give up being a midwife. First it was rheumatoid arthritis, seizing and swelling her joints. She fought against it for years, going to appointment after appointment, trying every medication there is. Then the cancer hit, starting in her ovaries, then moving to her breasts and her bowel. The weight fell off her, except for her stomach which swelled like Ella's does when she eats gluten, and all her energy left her. She stopped fighting, then. That's when she called me home.

I wasn't there to see any of this. I was gone before her health started to decline, and a part of me knows that I am to blame for it.

I let out a sigh. 'All right. We'll give it a go. But if she doesn't like it, she's leaving, okay?'

Mum smiles, reaches out to pat my hand, her eyes still closed. 'There's a good girl.'

Later, in the kitchen, I find Jane's number and call her, asking what time Ella needs to be there on Monday. She says she'll email me the forms to complete, and then it's done.

I place my phone on the table and rest my head in my hands. Am I doing the right thing? At least if Ella is at nursery, she won't be in Jamie's clutches, but I feel an almost physical pain at the thought of leaving her with strangers. I wonder if this is normal, if *I* am normal. I want Ella to have a normal life, to make friends and learn and play, even if that doesn't involve me. I want to help set her up for life, for adulthood, for school and university and the working world. I want her to fall in love with the right person, to notice the signs of a bad relationship, to hold herself with confidence and to know that she is worthwhile. That she is safe and loved and precious. That she is smart and fierce and kind. But I don't want to let her go.

A rustling behind me makes me jerk my head up, the hairs on the back of my neck standing on end.

'I wouldn't recommend sleeping at the table, Em,' Jamie says, moving into the room and filling the kettle. 'It's bleddy uncomfortable. I should know, I've done it a few times.' He laughs and flicks the kettle on, turning to face me. I feel my features turn to stone. *Em.* I don't want this, this pally-pally nonsense. This nice-guy act. I don't want him in our lives.

I stand up, refusing to even look at him. He sighs.

'Come on. I thought we'd moved past this. It's been a good week, hasn't it?' I meet his gaze then, and I'm not sure what I see there. Nerves? Frustration? 'Ella has enjoyed herself. I have too. You need to loosen up a little bit. Dad always used to say so.'

The breath hisses through my teeth. For a moment, I wonder if I've heard him right. 'Loosen up?' I feel my eyes widen, my back straightening. If I were a cat, my ears would be flattened against my head. 'Loosen up? You really don't have a clue, do you? Or, no, you do. You know exactly why I can't *loosen up.*' My words are sharp, like daggers, thrown across the room at him, this brother of mine. The brother I can never forgive.

'Not this again?' Jamie throws up his hands. 'It was such a long time ago, Em! We have to move on, all of us. Together.' He exhales sharply through his nose. 'Ella is my daughter. I've lost so many years with her. Five years. It's torn me apart.'

I try to laugh, but it comes out like a grunt. 'Torn you apart?

Have a word with yourself, Jamie. I'm not buying this bullshit. Mum might believe you, you might have convinced her that you've "turned over a new leaf".' I make air quotes with my hands. 'But I don't. All right? I know who you are. I know *what* you are. And I know what you've done.'

'And what did you do?' He's in front of me now; I can feel his breath on my face and I draw back, fear coursing through me. 'You weren't totally innocent, were you? I know you like to pretend you were. Always *poor little Emily*.' He makes a face. 'But you knew exactly what you were doing.'

I shove him then, placing my hands on his chest and throwing all my weight behind it. Years without a car, having to walk miles to and from our cabin, lifting and running around after Ella have made me stronger, stronger than the little sister Jamie remembers, and his eyes widen in surprise as he stumbles backwards. 'Get out of my face,' I hiss. 'We might be playing your game right now, *brother*, but one day, the rules will change. And you'll be out of our lives for good.'

'Is that a threat?' I can see his chest is heaving, the muscles in his arms quivering with pent-up rage. I feel a slow smile creep across my face, and something flickers in his eyes.

'No,' I whisper, feeling the legacy of our father shoot through me. 'It's a promise.'

23

IMOGEN

Monday morning dawns bright and hot, the sun piercing through a gap in the curtains and scorching my bare legs. It's almost six thirty and it already feels like thirty degrees in here.

I push back the damp covers and pad to the bathroom, stripping off the oversized T-shirt I've been sleeping in and throwing it into the washing basket. I catch sight of myself in the full-length mirror hanging behind the bathroom door and I pause, turning to look at myself in profile. My stomach is protruding slightly, a small curve that wasn't there before.

'Hello, baby,' I whisper, cupping the bump with my hands. I remember that I need to book a scan; I'm coming up to twelve weeks now. 'We need to see how you're doing in there, don't we?'

I look up at my reflection, and, for a split second, I see Freya there too. Her face next to mine, her hand stroking my stomach. I feel her loss then, so keenly it almost splits me in two. Standing there on the bathroom mat, chipped polish on my toes, stretch marks spreading up the inside of my thighs like the stripes of a tiger. I wish she was here with me, to go through this with me. I wish I wasn't so alone.

~

I drop the towel as soon as I'm in my room; my skin is so prickly, I can hardly bear to have anything touch me. I do my make-up and scrunch some cream into my hair before finally getting dressed, opting for a long skirt and a vest top. Flo hasn't remarked on my dress sense, despite her preference for dark, muted colours. I leave my feet bare and go downstairs for breakfast.

Mum is already sitting at the table, hair still in the messy plait she always wears to bed. Her curls have always been more unruly than ours, resisting all efforts to tame them, though she does insist on blasting her hair with a dryer twice a week. I pat her on the shoulder as I pass.

'Morning,' I say, filling the kettle and flicking it on. 'Cuppa?'

'Oh, yes ta. Did you sleep well?' I make a face, and she laughs. 'I don't think I got one full night of sleep when I was expecting you two, especially towards the end. It's like you were preparing me for motherhood. And then when you were born, wow!' She continues as I turn to make the tea. 'You were an angel, but Freya, lord did that child test me.' I hear her chuckle, and I'm amazed at how effortlessly she can mention Freya, as if she's only popped out to the shops and hasn't been missing for five years. 'Always screaming blue murder, she was, all through the night. It's a wonder the police weren't called. It sounded as if I was...' She trails off, the smile dying on her lips, the rest of her sentence unsaid. *Killing her.*

I force a smile, trying to skip over the moment. 'Remember that Christmas, when she ate all the strawberry creams from the Quality Street tin?' I laugh then, the memory flooding back. 'She was violently sick all over the living room carpet.'

'Oh yes, and it was tinged pink!' Mum is smiling again now. 'Your father was furious; they were his favourites, you know.'

'And mine!'

'I wonder if she was coeliac too.' Mum's tone is wistful. 'Maybe that's what made her so ill.'

I shake my head, still smiling. 'No, Mum, I can still eat strawberry creams. She was just a greedy pig.'

Laughter fills the room as we share the memory of Freya, how she laid on the sofa afterwards, refusing to eat her Christmas dinner. Until I threatened to pilfer her pigs in blankets, that was. She soon found her appetite then.

I sit down at the table and blow on my tea to cool it, remembering the coeliac disease diagnosis after a blood test and an unpleasant endoscopy. I'd still been in the UK then, holed up in a hotel in Edinburgh, believing it to be a bug, before finally calling 111.

'Aren't you hungry, love?' Mum asks, breaking into my thoughts. 'I quite fancy a bacon sandwich now.'

I laugh and shake my head. 'Ugh, no thanks. I can't stomach anything first thing.'

Mum smiles and pats my hand. 'I'll try to pick you up some more ginger nut biscuits when I'm in town later. I can't believe how expensive they are!'

I lift a shoulder. 'The joys of being gluten-free.'

She harrumphs, getting up to make her breakfast. The smell of bacon fills the room and I feel nausea rise in me.

'No offence, Mum, but I'm gonna head off. It bleddy stinks in here.'

Mum sniffs her armpit, grinning. I laugh again and lean in to peck her on the cheek.

'Have a good day, love!' she calls as I slip my feet into my sandals and grab my bag. I lift a hand in goodbye and step out into the fresh air, fumbling for my sunglasses. It's a bit too early to leave, but I'm glad to be outside. I can nip to the supermarket first, pick up some fresh strawberries. I remember Freya and the strawberry creams and smile again, eyes closed against the bright blue sky.

The slam of a door startles me, and I turn to see Ella on the other side of the wall, her hair in lopsided pigtails. Her eyes are wide as she smiles at me, a curl escaping by her left ear.

'Hello,' she says, her face bright and open. Emily bustles out after her, carrying a lunch box. She stops dead when she sees me, mouth slightly open.

I find my voice, directing my greeting to Ella. 'Morning.'

I feel Emily staring at me for a moment, perhaps remembering, as I am, our last conversation, whispered through the fence in the twilight. I wonder why she wasn't at work last week, wonder if it had anything to do with Jamie turning up. Just then, he steps out behind her, his eyes meeting mine. I feel a coldness take root inside me, a mixture of fear and disgust, and my stomach turns as he smiles at me.

'Hello, Imogen. Long time, no see.'

Not long enough, I want to say but don't. I manage a tight smile, then open my bag and dig out my car keys. I can still feel his eyes on me; my skin prickles under his gaze.

'See you at work.' Emily's voice surprises me and I look at her, take in the telltale circles under her eyes. I see Jamie beside her, his wolfish grin, and I wonder whether she's happy to see him again. Whether she suspects him as I do. As I always have.

I throw myself into my car and slam the door. My heart is racing. I take a deep breath, closing my eyes and counting to three. In – one, two, three. Out – one, two, three.

I'm pulled back to the memory of that night, when I saw Freya disappear into the gathering dusk. 'I'm just nipping out,' she said, flipping her hair over her shoulder. I checked my watch, and she gave me a look. 'I won't be long, *Mum*.' She rolled her eyes, her lips turned up in a faint smile. She'd been happier in those last weeks, seemed to be excited about our trip, constantly chattering about our plans. She was already packed; her suitcase stood beside her bedroom door. It's still there, still packed. Waiting for her to come back.

But I'd noticed the dark circles beneath her eyes, heard her pacing her room late at night, and caught the furtive glances she shared with Emily. Suddenly, I was on the outside looking in. She had a secret, a secret she was keeping from me, and I hated how hurt I was.

'Don't wait up,' she said, and I stood up from my chair, slamming a hand on the desk.

'Why would I bother?' I hissed at her, and she took a step back, surprised. I was surprised too, surprised by the venom in my voice. 'You've barely spoken to me in weeks.'

'What are you on about? We do nothing but speak.' She stared at me as if in exasperation.

'What are you hiding from me, Freya? What's your secret?'

She opened her mouth, words on the tip of her tongue, then shook her head. 'I don't have time for this,' she said, disappearing down the stairs and out the front door, slamming it behind her. I rushed over to my bedroom window, peering out into the gloom. I saw a shadow appear behind her on the path, grabbing her by the arm and pulling her onto the street below, beyond my vision. Beyond my reach.

The last words she said to me. *I don't have time for this.* I'd pushed her away, and then she was gone.

At five minutes to ten, I make my way to Flo's office. The door is open and I raise my fist to knock, but I notice she's on the phone, so I hover in the doorway instead, feeling like a schoolgirl summoned to see the head teacher. After a few moments she beckons me in.

'Sorry, sorry! Come on in, Imogen.' She looks harassed, her normally sleek bob looking as if she's been running her fingers through it. She checks her watch. 'Emily should be here in a moment, and we'll begin.'

I'm just about to sit in one of the chairs opposite her desk and freeze, hands planted on the armrests on either side. 'E-Emily?' I manage, forcing myself down into the seat. 'Is she coming to Wiltshire?' I'm surprised she'd leave Ella, especially with Jamie back in the picture. But maybe I've got it all wrong. Again.

'Yes, I thought it would be a great opportunity to get a second pair of eyes on the place. An artist's eyes.' She smiles warmly at me, then flicks her eyes to the doorway. 'Ah, speak of the devil.' I hear Emily enter behind me, closing the door with a soft click. She clears her throat as she sits next to me, her eyes on her hands folded in her lap. 'I was just saying how good it will be for you both to visit our other depot. You were brilliant at spotting design flaws on labels, Emily.'

Emily's cheeks flush; I watch the pinkness creep up her neck. She's wearing a too-small blazer, the cuffs barely reaching her wrists, and a plain black playsuit underneath. For a second, I think I recognise it from nights out when we were younger. A memory flashes before my eyes: Emily, still underage, dancing in the student union with a girl with long black braids, huge smiles on their matching red lips. I remember that Emily saw her for a while – what was her name? Liana? – but she never took her home, even though her dad was long gone. I suppose his presence never left, his shadow constantly looming over her.

'Imogen?'

I shake my head to bring myself back to the present. Flo is looking at me expectantly.

'Sorry. What did you say?' Now I can feel the blush creeping into my own cheeks. *Pay attention.*

'We were just discussing dates. How does this Wednesday sound? You can stay overnight, visit the site on Thursday, then come back that afternoon. You should be home at a decent time if you leave there by two-ish.' I nod and Flo sits back in her chair, looking at Emily. 'Does that work for you? Can Agnes have Ella overnight?'

'Oh, y-yes. I'm sure she can.' Emily's voice is small. She still hasn't looked at me. 'I'll sort it.'

'You could take the following Monday off instead, since you'll be working an extra day?' Flo smiles at Emily, then glances at me. 'No such luxury for you, I'm afraid! Though you're welcome to work from home on Friday if you like. Organise your thoughts in the peace and quiet.' I nod again, shift uncomfortably in my seat. 'You can present your findings next Wednesday, if that works?'

I take a breath. This is moving faster than I expected. Though I know better than anyone the pressures the company is under, how swiftly the changes will have to be made.

'Sure,' I say, trying to sound confident. 'I'll put something together by then.' A thought occurs to me, and I feel a flutter in my stomach. 'Why don't I drive us both down?' I say, turning to Emily. 'Saves fuelling up two cars.'

Emily looks at me then, though she doesn't meet my eyes. 'I have Mum's car,' she says. Flo waves a hand.

'No, Imogen's right. Save the planet and all that. We pay forty-five pence per mile, so you'll get it back and then some. For the wear and tear.' She winks at me, then claps her hands. Out of the corner of my eye, I see Emily flinch. 'Right then, that's settled! Thanks, ladies.'

Dismissed, Emily and I rise, and I indicate she should go first. She stalks out of the room and up the corridor, pushing through the double doors with more force than is strictly necessary. I've rattled her. I'll have to tread carefully on our trip. I don't want to push her away entirely.

24

EMILY

I sit down at my desk, my mind reeling. An overnight trip with Imogen. Fantastic. Fan-fucking-tastic. How can I leave Ella for so long? We've never been apart longer than a few hours, not once in her entire life. She's never gone to sleep without me there, watching over her, keeping her safe. Will Mum be able to cope? Will I?

I snatch up my phone and find Mum's number. She answers on the fourth ring.

'Hello, love.' She sounds tired, and I realise that I've probably woken her up. That this could've waited until this evening.

'Sorry, Mum, did I wake you?'

'Oh, no, of course not.' I hear the rustling of her duvet, the telltale creak of her mattress exposing her lie.

'Just a quick one. Flo's asked me to travel up to the other site, in Wiltshire.' I swallow. 'It's an overnight trip.'

'It's only a couple of hours away, isn't it? Up past Bristol?'

'Yeah, that's it. But we need a full day really.' I pause, considering. 'I suppose I could leave here at five or six in the morning, beat the rush hour.' And it would mean not having to travel with Imogen.

Mum clears her throat. 'I bet the M5 is a nightmare at that time of day. No, no, you go up the night before. Spend the night in a luxury hotel, courtesy of Flo.'

I laugh despite myself. 'I think it's a Premier Inn, Mum.'

'Well, whatever it is, it'll be nice to have a night to yourself, won't it? Have a meal, a glass of wine. Sleep in your own bed.'

I can't sleep alone, I think, chewing my lip. I haven't slept alone for five years. But I know she's right. 'Are you sure, Mum? Are you sure you can cope with her for that long? Alone?' I emphasise the last word. I don't want Jamie there with her, not while I'm away.

'Yes, love, don't worry about me. I'm a big girl. And Ella is no trouble at all. She's such a lively maid, always smiling.' I can hear Mum's smile as she speaks, feel the pride emanating from her. 'It'll be fun. We'll have a sleepover, drink hot chocolate under blankets like we used to when you were younger.' A tightness in my chest at the memories, the bittersweet childhood we had. So much sadness, so much pain, interspersed with tiny fragments of light. And even when the release came, with our tormentor finally gone, we still couldn't escape what he left behind.

I take a deep breath. 'All right. I'll tell Flo to book the hotel. See you later.' When I hang up, I feel the overwhelming urge to cry wash over me. Regret at coming back here, guilt for feeling that way. *You came back for Mum*, I tell myself, *because she's had enough sadness in her life. She doesn't need you adding to it.*

A favourite saying from our childhood, hushed words between Mum and Jamie when he was a teenager. *Your dad is stressed enough, without you adding to it.* What she really meant was: *Please stop making things worse for me.*

I breathe out, pushing my shoulders back. *Fake it till you make it.* Another childhood saying, this time from Deb. Her sad smile when she looked at me and Jamie, the knowledge in her eyes of what went on behind closed doors. Behind our closed door, behind the wall that separated our houses. Night and day, light and dark. Rivers and Bligh, bound forever by secrets.

∼

That evening, while Ella is splashing around in the bath with her beloved, if a little creepy, toy octopus, my phone pings with a message. It's Imogen.

Hey, just wondering what time you want to leave on Wednesday night? I've got a scan in the morning so I'll be working from home. Should I pick you up from work or home? X

So simple, so innocent. A text from one colleague to another. One kiss on the end, so friendly colleagues. But that's not what we are. Not all we are.

I glance up at the wall, picture the house next door. Our houses are mirrored; behind Ella and the bath is their shower cubicle, fancier than our over-the-bath job, put in by Jamie when he was eighteen, and showing its age. When their dad died, his work had some kind of death-in-service thing in place, and Deb got a nice chunk if Mum is to be believed. But Deb didn't care about the money, anybody could see that she was heartbroken. Deb and Tom, Tom and Deb. They'd been together since they were fourteen, had gone to school and grew up together. Childhood sweethearts, Mum used to say. How could they have known at such a young age? Did Deb look at Tom when they were teenagers – children, really – and think, *yes, he's the one*?

Ella splashes me with water and I flinch. 'Mumily, when are you going on an adventure?'

I'd told her about my trip away when I got home, purposefully refraining from using the term *adventure* in case she got jealous that she wasn't coming. But, as with all things, she doesn't seem to mind.

'Wednesday evening. Two days from now.' I hold up two fingers. 'And then I'll be back on Thursday, three days from now.' I hold up an extra finger. 'So I can give you your bath then.'

'Who will give me a bath in two days?' She screws up her face, blinking the bubbles which have managed to congregate on top of her head out of her eyes. I laugh and wipe her face.

'Nanny will.'

'Not Dad?'

I freeze. I know I called him that when he first met her – I hadn't known what else to say – but I haven't heard him or Mum use the term since.

'No, darling. Not Dad.'

Ella splashes again, dunking her octopus under the water. 'I like him. I like it when he reads my stories.' That's what she calls books, *her stories*. As if they were written just for her. Though isn't that what every reader believes, that they are the first to turn the page, the first to immerse themselves in a story? The only ones to truly understand it, to imagine they see themselves in the characters, or to see themselves reflected from the page, as they truly are. Or, rather, better versions of themselves.

I reach out and pick up a bottle of conditioner. 'What story do you want today?' I massage the conditioner into her scalp, breathing in the coconut scent.

'Lions!' Ella bares her teeth at me and I laugh.

'We had lions last night! Don't you want something else?'

She shakes her head, splashing me again, this time with conditioner as well as water and bubble bath, and when she stops, her hair is standing on end like a mane. 'Lions! Lions! Lions!'

'All right, little cub,' I laugh, 'all right. Lions it is. Now sit still while I rinse your hair. And let's get poor Octopus out of the water, before he drowns.'

'Oh, Mumily,' Ella sighs, looking at me with despair, 'octopuses can't drown.'

A fist raps against the front door as I'm coming out of the bedroom, Ella fast asleep in the middle of the bed. I freeze on the stairs, eyes glued to the shape beyond the frosted glass. The knock comes again, louder this time, banging in time with my heart. I hear Mum come out of the kitchen; she glances up at me, but before I can tell her to stop, she's pulling open the door.

'Hello, can I–' The words die on her lips as she takes in the figures before her. Two uniformed officers stand on the doorstep. I feel myself sway and clutch the banister. Sensing the movement, Mum opens the door wider and turns to me. 'Emily,' she says quietly, her face a mask of anxiety, 'it's the police. They want to talk to you.'

25

FREYA

THEN

Christmas. The tree in the living room window sparkled with lights, the scented candles filling the air with cinnamon. Freya stood in the doorway watching her sister braid their mother's hair, noting the grey streaks woven through the strands. They were watching TV, some terrible Christmas movie they both loved, and, for a moment, Freya was filled with envy.

Her phone vibrated in her hand and, as she unlocked the screen, she saw Jamie's name pop up.

Come outside. I've got mistletoe.

She smiled and pocketed her phone, slipping her feet into her boots and grabbing her coat from the hook behind the front door. Jamie was sitting on the wall, legs kicking like a toddler, mistletoe dangling above his head.

'You're such an idiot,' she laughed, stepping up and kissing him quickly on the lips. He tasted of peppermint. 'Have you been eating After Eights?' She checked her watch. 'At seven o'clock? That's a hanging offence, you know.'

Jamie chuckled, the sound low and deep, sending a thrum of excitement through her. How did it take her so long to notice him, this boy next door? The boy who climbed trees with her when she was nine and he was twelve, cleaning her grazed knee with a wet piece of kitchen roll. The boy who used his last pound to buy her another ice cream when a seagull swooped in and nabbed hers after just one lick. The boy whose father cast a long shadow, even after he was gone.

The boy who had grown into a man, who had a tender side she hadn't seen in years. Not until six months ago, when he first kissed her in the long grass of his back garden, one hand in her hair, pulling her so close she thought they would merge into one.

'Come on,' he said, leaping up and grabbing her hand. 'Let's go before Emily sees us.'

Freya knew that part of the thrill of their relationship was that it was forbidden, secret. Hidden from his sister and hers, the twin she knew inside out. She'd never had a secret from Imogen before, and it felt delicious.

They giggled as they ran down the front steps, narrowly missing a patch of ice. They made their way to the park, where all young lovers went to drink and kiss and gaze out across the sea.

'I wish it would snow.' Freya sighed, linking one arm through his. Jamie grinned down at her.

'I can't remember the last time it snowed down here. Can you?'

Freya wrinkled her nose, something she always teased Imogen for doing. 'No. I vaguely remember building a snowman with Dad, but I can't remember when that was.' Sadness crept into her voice and Jamie nudged her shoulder.

'One day, we'll go to Canada, and live in a log cabin surrounded by snowy mountains. We'll build an army of snowmen!'

'And snowwomen!' Freya laughed. 'Imogen wants to go to Canada, too. But it's not on our list.' She remembered how easily Imogen had accepted that they wouldn't make it to Canada, despite wanting to go so badly. She was always better at accepting things, going with the flow. Freya could only pretend to be so easy-going.

Jamie opened the gate to the park, bowing elaborately and holding out an arm to let Freya go first. He put an arm around her shoulders as they made their way to an empty bench. 'Ah, the list,' he said, sitting down and drawing out a packet of cigarettes. He offered one to Freya and she took it. Another secret she was hiding from Imogen.

She thought she sensed an edge to his voice. She knew he didn't want her to go travelling next year, and that he couldn't afford to go with them, but it was a topic they tended to avoid. Not tonight, apparently.

'How long are you going for again?' Jamie asked, his voice falsely casual. He took a drag on his cigarette and blew the smoke into the sky. The stars twinkled above them, the cold air sharp on their cheeks. Freya sighed.

'I don't know. Probably about two years. We're just going to go with the flow.' It was the same answer she'd given every time he asked. The answer he already knew, the length of time they'd all agreed on. But then, as always, he turned to her and said:

'Two years? Why so long?'

And so on the script went, the same argument going around and around. Freya stood, suddenly frustrated. 'Stop asking me the same question over and over again! You know the answer.'

Jamie stood too, his face half in shadow, the street light glowing behind him. 'Freya, don't we have something here?

Something special?' He reached for her, pulling her closer to him. 'I think we do.'

She sighed again. He was still reading from the same script; he'd just jumped a few lines. 'Jamie, come on. You know I do. But we've been planning this for years. *Years.* It's our dream. Imogen and Emily are so excited, and so–'

'It's not all about them, Freya.' His voice had turned cold, his words sharp. 'What about me?'

His fingers were digging into her arm. Freya blinked, surprised. 'You're hurting me,' she said, but he didn't let go. Fear bloomed in her chest and she tried to take a step back, but his grip tightened. 'Get off!' She threw her arms up, knocking his hands away, and without hesitating, ran past him and out of the park.

'Freya!' His voice rang out through the night, her heart pounding in time with her footsteps as she ran away. 'Freya!'

26

IMOGEN

Freya. Freya!

I wake, gasping into consciousness. Every night I dream of Freya, of the last time I saw her. Her long hair bouncing behind her, shining in the fading light. The shadow cutting across the grass, grabbing her and pulling her into the night.

In my dream, I cry out. I run down the stairs and wrench open the front door, the sultry air prickling my skin. In my dream, I run out into the garden, the grass prickly on my bare feet, and I scream Freya's name.

But in truth, I didn't do any of those things.

That night, five years ago, I let my sister disappear into the darkness. I let him take her. Because I was hurt. I was upset with Freya for keeping secrets from me. I knew she was seeing Jamie, had noticed the looks exchanged between them, watched them steal away when they thought we weren't looking. I'd let her go, and she never came back.

I heave myself up and sit on the edge of the bed, grimacing as I try to peel the sticky sheets away from my skin. The heat is oppressive, pressing in on me from all angles. The breath tightens in my chest and I sit forward, resting my head in my hands.

'Im?' Mum's voice calls from downstairs as I try to get my breathing under control. 'Are you up?'

I fight the nausea that has plagued me since the day it happened. Since the day I took the test. Though I'd already known.

I get up, calling down to Mum that I'll be ready soon, and climb into the shower, turning the temperature all the way down, the water like ice on my skin.

'Slow down, Im.' Mum puffs as we rush through the entrance to the hospital, almost late after driving around the car park for twenty minutes in a futile attempt to find a space. We hovered behind an elderly couple who seemed to take forty years to get into their car and leave, and now we're half jogging through the hospital, Mum out of breath beside me.

'You need to give up smoking,' I joke, and she whacks my arm.

We pull up short at the sight of the full waiting room. 'Oh. It's a popular day for a scan, it would appear!' Mum says, attempting to make her voice bright. I sigh and check my watch; hopefully we won't be hanging around for too long. The waiting room is unbearably hot, and I see several women fanning themselves with pamphlets taken from the table between the rows of chairs. I take one and, folding it in half, begin fanning the air in front of my face.

'Did you know that makes you warmer?' Mum whispers from the seat next to me. 'You create more energy and so more heat by wafting your–'

'When did you become an expert?' I snap, and immediately

regret it when I see the pain in her eyes. 'Sorry,' I whisper, avoiding the eyes of the women around us, 'it's so bloody hot in here. And my bladder is about to burst.'

Mum smiles and nudges my shoulder. 'I'll order you one of those handheld fans from Amazon, I've got Prime now, you know.'

I laugh. 'Okay, seriously, when did you become an Amazon Prime member?'

Mum is fiddling with her phone, searching for the app. She tuts at my tone. 'I signed up a while ago, I'll have you know. Jamie installed one of those Fire Stick things for me, he said it was better with...' She trails off, the colour draining from her face. *Jamie.* I stare at her, barely registering that my mouth is hanging open, shock momentarily making me speechless.

'Imogen Rivers?' I snap my head up as my name is called. A nurse about my age smiles from the end of the corridor. 'Imogen? Follow me, please.'

I stand, the pamphlet flying from my lap and floating to the floor. I sense Mum behind me as we trail along the corridor, following the nurse with her neat bun and squeaky shoes into a room. The sonographer smiles as we enter, Mum closing the door behind us with a click.

'Hi, Imogen,' the sonographer says, indicating for me to sit on the bed. 'How are we feeling today?'

I look up at her and notice she has a scar in her left eyebrow, just like Freya did, and my heart skips a beat. 'F-fine,' I manage after a moment. She smiles again.

'No need to be nervous. Just lie back and lift up your T-shirt for me.' I do as she asks, exposing my small bump. It really is tiny, I realise with a jolt. Is this normal? Is my baby normal? I want to ask, but my mouth is too dry, my heart too sore. Freya should be here with me, I realise with a pang. She should be clasping my hand as we meet my child for the first time.

Eyeing the bottle of ultrasound gel she squirts onto my stomach – not a brand I recognise, but at least it's CE marked – I try to relax back onto the bed. I stare straight up at the ceiling, trying to avoid Mum's tearful gaze.

The sonographer places the probe onto my stomach, pressing uncomfortably on my bladder. 'Ah, here we are,' she says after a moment, her voice hushed. 'Shall we have a look at the little one?'

Mum moves closer and gasps, reaching out to grip my hand as I turn my head towards the screen. I hadn't known what to expect when I first saw her, this baby I didn't ask or plan for, but who has come into my life regardless. And there she is, her heartbeat filling the room, beating in time with mine, and I feel my eyes fill with tears.

'I'd say you're about twelve weeks along, Imogen.' *Eleven weeks and four days*, I think but don't say. 'I think a due date of the seventh of January is likely.'

'The seventh!' Mum gushes, squeezing my hand tighter. 'The day after your father's birthday!'

'All ten fingers and toes, all present and correct. She's roughly the size of a lime,' the sonographer says with a little laugh. 'Some people like those facts. You're a little on the small side, but nothing to worry about.' I breathe a sigh of relief. 'Now, shall we go ahead with the combined screening test, Imogen?'

I tear my eyes away from the screen, trying to take in her words. 'Oh, yes. Go ahead.'

'Your midwife will have explained everything,' she says, and I wince internally. I really need to get myself organised. 'I'm just going to measure the fluid on the back of baby's neck.' The sonographer busies herself with the screening and I turn my eyes back to the ceiling, wondering what the result will be. Wondering what my reaction will be. In truth, I haven't put much thought into the possibility that my child might have

Down's syndrome, and I feel my mind turn down a dark alley, full of doubt and fear. Would I be able to cope? Am I capable of looking after a disabled child? Am I cut out for motherhood at all?

'All done,' the sonographer says, and I release the breath I'd been holding. 'You should receive your results in a few weeks.'

'Can't you tell us now?' Mum asks, her brow knitted. The sonographer shakes her head.

'I'm afraid not. You'll need to pop along to get your blood taken on your way out.' She looks at me with what I think she believes is a reassuring smile. 'Try not to worry, baby is looking good in there.' I nod and her smile widens.

Mum chats with the nurse as we wait for the scan photo; I hear the words *Australia* and *twins*, but I tune out, staring at a spot on the wall where the paint is a slightly different colour. My head should be full of her, of my baby, the child I've already fallen in love with.

But all I can think about is how my mother can bear to be anywhere near the man who took my sister away from me.

27

EMILY

I'm waiting outside the office when Imogen pulls up, music blaring from the speakers. Mum dropped me off earlier, taking her car back in case she needs it while I'm away. I blow out a breath, trying to ignore the anxiety pooling in my stomach. I feel a tug on the line that binds me to Ella, and I realise how alone I feel when she isn't with me. Is this normal? I wonder. Am I normal?

The memory of the night before slams into me, and I reach out for the low wall, resting my back against it. How could I have been so stupid? I should have expected the police to come knocking someday. I was a missing person: girl, lost. I couldn't just reappear five years later without questions being asked.

'Can you tell us where you've been, Emily?' one of the officers asked. He was older than his colleague, with greying hair and eyes that crinkled as he smiled and told me their names. PC Alan White and PC Jack Hunt. PC Hunt was younger, his piercing blue eyes full of suspicion.

I swallowed, my mouth suddenly dry. 'Just around. I went travelling.' I couldn't meet his eyes as I spoke, certain he would see the truth written across my face.

'Travelling? Alone?' PC Hunt said, a slight sneer on his face.

I tried to picture Freya, the way her face would harden at this question, at the hidden meaning. *A woman alone.* I tried to draw on her strength as I answered, sitting up straight and finally lifting my gaze from the table. 'Yes. Alone.'

The officers exchanged glances before PC White spoke again. 'And you didn't think to tell anyone?'

'They knew,' I said. 'They just didn't want me to go.'

He looked at Mum then, who was sat beside me, chewing her thumbnail. 'Is that true, Mrs Bligh?'

She glanced at me before nodding quickly. 'Y-yes. Yes, it's true.'

'And that's why you didn't continue to look for her?' he asked. I felt my stomach clench. They *had* kept looking. If they hadn't, Mum would never have found us. I wondered again whether it was Ella they'd wanted to find, not me.

'We were concerned,' Mum said carefully, dropping her eyes to the table. 'She was so young to be going off alone. But we knew she'd be okay.'

'And Freya Rivers?' PC Hunt said, one eyebrow slightly raised. 'Did you see her on your travels?'

I shook my head. 'No. I didn't see her. I haven't seen her for five years.'

A noise from the doorway made me turn. Ella. I stood, almost knocking the chair over in my haste, and crouched before her. 'What are you doing up?' I whispered.

'Bad dream,' she said, her eyes wide. I picked her up and held her close, one hand pressed against her head as I rocked her gently.

'Who's this then?' PC White asked, smiling widely.

I stared at him, panic flooding me. Her birth certificate has my name on it; I registered her once we got to Scotland, telling them I'd had no idea I was pregnant, that I'd given birth in a hostel. I must have looked a state, with my wild, tangled hair and dark circles beneath my eyes. They hadn't pushed me, and we had left quickly afterwards, escaping back to our hideaway. Could the police investigate further? Could they find out the truth? I held Ella close and tried to gather my strength.

'She's my daughter,' I said, lifting my chin, locking eyes with PC Hunt, daring him to question me. I saw Mum flash PC White a tired smile.

'Is that everything, officers?' she asked. 'Only it's past the little one's bedtime, and I'm due my medication.'

PC White frowned. 'Are you unwell, Mrs Bligh?'

'Cancer,' she said simply. 'Terminal.'

I clutched Ella as the officers glanced at one another. I could feel the frustration emanating from them, and I feared their unasked questions. *Go*, I urged silently, kissing Ella's hair, *leave*. After a moment, they stood, thanking us for our time and telling us they'd be in touch if they had any more questions. Mum and I exchanged a look as the front door closed behind them, our fear written across our faces.

She's my daughter. The words make my chest ache. Am I a good mother? I have nothing to compare myself to, no reference point. Mum tried her best, when she could, once *he* left, but before that it had been hell. Deb, then? A memory pops into my head of Deb braiding my hair while Imogen and Freya did cart-wheels in the long grass of their garden. The sun was shining; I could smell sun cream and lemonade and the meat the neigh-bour behind was cooking on the barbecue. A typical British summer.

What kind of mother was Deb? I rarely heard her shout; she didn't even raise her voice to call us in for tea, but rather stuck her fingers in her mouth and whistled loudly. It was her party trick, she said, her eyes dancing with amusement. She let Imogen and Freya have their freedom, back in the time before all kids had mobile phones and were traceable 24/7. We all had to come home when the street lights turned on, an unwritten rule of the summer holidays, and we had to make sure we always had twenty pence on us, in case we needed a lift and had to ring home from a phone box. We put sun cream on in the morning, packed a drink and some snacks, and took off on our bikes, often setting up on the Hoe and basking in the sunshine, watching the sea shimmer beneath us and seagulls soar above our heads.

No, Imogen and Freya weren't tied to their parents. They were normal. They had to do their homework before going out after school, and they had chores to do. They got grounded for staying out late or talking back, and were forced to cut the grass or clean their dad's car as punishment. But they were happy. Next to our house of violence, the Rivers' house was quiet and content. Until Tom died. Until Freya disappeared.

'Em?' Imogen's voice startles me from my reverie. She's turned the music down and is leaning out of the window, huge sunglasses obscuring her eyes. 'You can just throw your bags in the back if you want.'

'Okay.' I wince at how nervous I sound. At how nervous I *feel*. It will be fine, I tell myself firmly. Ella will be fine. I have to start building a normal life for her, for us. I owe it to Ella to do my best for her.

I slide into the passenger seat, grimacing as my bare legs touch the hot leather. Imogen turns and offers me an apologetic smile. I drop my eyes to the dashboard, and a laugh bursts out of me.

'Is this still the same car?' I ask, incredulous. 'What was his name... Percy?'

Imogen shakes her head, a smile on her lips. '*I* wanted to call him Mufasa, but no, you guys decided to christen him with the most ridiculous name ever.' She indicates to pull out of the car park.

'This car is not and has never been a Mufasa,' I laugh. 'Percy suits him.' I look around again, find the rip in the back of my seat. 'I can't believe he's still going.'

'Mum kept him ticking over. Even gave him a clean, which is more than I ever did.'

'Didn't you get him when you passed your test?' I cast my mind back to that day. Imogen passed her driving test first, much to Freya's annoyance, who didn't pass until they were nearly eighteen. Deb bought her this car not long after; I remember us coming home one afternoon to find it sitting outside their house, bright and shiny and just a few years old. There was only one condition: that Imogen had to share with Freya when she passed her test. It didn't seem to faze Imogen, but Freya always hated it, saving up and buying herself an old banger a couple of years later.

Imogen indicates and changes lanes before responding. 'Yup. Do you remember when we got stuck in a ditch up in St Agnes?'

I laugh as the memory comes back. 'Yes! When that old couple in the caravan totally misjudged the space and you had to reverse half a mile.' I shake my head. 'Oh my God, that was hilarious.'

'Bleddy emmets,' she says, grinning. 'They're a nuisance.'

'It was worth it though. I always loved it up there.'

'Wheal Coates? Yeah, it was Freya's favourite place too.'

Silence follows the mention of her twin, the girl who didn't come back, and the past five years suddenly comes crashing down on me. Imogen is no longer my childhood friend, the friend who knew me inside out, someone I could trust, let my guard down with. How could I be so stupid?

I pull my phone out of my pocket and open the messages. 'Just going to text Mum,' I say quietly, keeping my eyes down.

'Is she looking after Ella for you?' Imogen asks, her tone even. She glances across at me when I don't answer. 'Or is she with Jamie?'

My stomach lurches and I glare at her, but her eyes are focused on the road ahead. 'No,' I say shortly, 'she isn't with Jamie.'

Thankfully, Imogen doesn't push it, and we travel in silence for a while, the initial giddiness at being reunited and sharing old memories gone. After an hour or so, Imogen breaks the silence to announce that she's stopping at the next services.

'I'm dying for a pee,' she says, lifting a shoulder as if to say, *what can you do*? I nod and she looks at me. 'Did you have that? Does it ever go away or does it just get worse?'

I stare at her, wondering what the hell she's talking about. Realisation dawns as her expression morphs into a frown and I feel my cheeks flush. 'Oh! Oh, yeah, no. It wasn't too bad for me.' I glance down at her stomach, barely visible beneath her dress. 'How far along are you?'

'Twelve weeks. Had the scan today.' Her face breaks into a smile and I feel the corners of my own lips tugging upwards.

'And the dad? Is he about?'

Imogen's face clouds over as she indicates into the service station. 'No. He's still in Australia.'

'Oh. Does he know?'

'No.' Her answer is short, her voice hard, and I fall silent.

While Imogen rushes off to the toilet, I take the opportunity to stretch my legs. I wander round WHSmith, browsing the paperback chart, and pick up a colouring book for Ella. I buy myself a latte and Imogen a tropical smoothie. I'm leaning against the car when she comes out, sunglasses obscuring her eyes, her mouth in a tight line. I hold out the smoothie.

'Sorry,' I say, as she stops in front of me, head tilted slightly to the left, a gesture that immediately transports me back ten years, Freya mirroring Imogen exactly, as if they had practised it. Their eyes glittering, one eyebrow raised, mouth pulled slightly to one side. The gesture that said, *I know you. I know what you're about.* And they did. They knew exactly what I was about, exactly what I was thinking. What I was hiding. But she doesn't know now.

I watch my old friend as I hand her the smoothie, wishing I could see her eyes. Freya was better at concealing her true feelings, her eyes smooth as a lake, impenetrable. But Imogen's eyes always gave her away. And even though I can't see them, I can hear the unspoken question, see it shimmering in the air between us. *What for?* And what would I say? Would the years unspool between us, the secrets spilling out? I can never apologise for what I'm truly sorry for. I can never speak of it. I just have to hope she doesn't ask.

28

IMOGEN

I manage to find a parking space right outside the hotel, the small car park surprisingly busy for a Wednesday evening. It's almost seven o'clock, and I suddenly realise I'm starving.

Reaching in for the empty smoothie cup, I glance up at Emily through the windscreen. Her arms are folded across her chest, overnight bag dangling over one arm. Her mouth is pinched, eyebrows knitted in that way she has when she's thinking about something. Overthinking.

I deposit the cup in a bin and lock the car before turning to her. 'Shall we check-in then get some food?'

She looks up at me in surprise, as if she'd forgotten I was there. I watch her blink twice, three times, before responding. 'Yeah, all right. Where should we go?'

I jerk my head to the left. 'There's a Lounge here, they do quite a good gluten-free menu.'

'Oh yeah, we've been to one before. They've got them all over.'

I want to ask where, but I remind myself to be cautious. I raise an eyebrow instead. 'You're not one of those "gluten free for fun" people, are you?'

Emily gives a laugh before shaking her head. 'People do that for fun?'

'Yep.' We step through the entrance to the hotel and press the button for the lift, watching the number count down. 'What I wouldn't give to eat an extra-large, greasy takeaway pizza.'

I see a question forming on Emily's face, but as I press the button for the reception, the door starting to close, an arm appears, stopping it with a jolt. 'Sorry.' A man in a crisp white shirt and dark jeans steps inside. 'Room for a small one?'

I smile and move aside, tucking myself behind Emily. As the doors close, I see her reflection, the darkness in her eyes. She suddenly looks younger, so much like the girl next door, the girl whose fiery nature was almost extinguished by her childhood. Not for the first time, I wonder how deeply Emily and Jamie were affected by their father. How much happier they were when he disappeared.

Her gaze meets mine in the mirror and I look away guiltily. But not before I notice the look in her eyes. They are those of a haunted woman, one who is slowly starting to unravel.

The hotel room is basic but clean. I deposit my bag on the bed and, after visiting the loo, text Emily to tell her I'll meet her at the Lounge. I'd kill for a glass of wine, I realise. I place a hand on my belly as I wait for the lift, cupping the slight curve, and as the doors open, I almost miss a step, my eyes finding my own face in the mirror and seeing Freya.

Freya. A wave of sadness washes over me, and I close my eyes as the lift descends. Where would we be if she hadn't disappeared? If we'd stuck to our plan, we would've been back in Plymouth for almost three years by now, probably renting a flat with Emily. Or we might've had partners, people in our lives we loved almost as much as we loved each other. I was the only one who wanted children; both Freya and Emily used to grimace whenever children were nearby, or even mentioned. I smile as my hand finds my bump again. It would appear that Emily changed her mind, but would Freya have? Somehow, I doubt it.

I try to picture Emily pregnant. Her little girl looks about four, so she must have become pregnant not long after she left. Or was she already pregnant? Is that why she ran away?

The endless questions whirl around my mind as I find a table by the door and open the menu. This is one of the few places I can eat fries, so I decide to treat myself. I check my phone, but Emily hasn't replied yet. I order a drink and sit flicking through my emails, catching up on the news, when she appears looking slightly harassed.

'Sorry,' she says breathlessly, 'have you been waiting long?'

I shake my head. 'Not long. Though I have managed to thoroughly depress myself by checking the news on Brexit.'

Emily makes a face. 'That's not a word to use in polite company.' I smile and she sits down, grabbing a menu. 'Have you decided? I'm not very hungry, maybe I'll just have a salad. I like the salads here. Ella does too. She likes a lot of the food here actually...' She's babbling, and I notice the menu trembling in her hands. I want to reach out and take her wrists, ask her what's wrong, tell her that she can tell me anything. But I hold back.

'I've decided. I'll go up and order if you want.'

She settles on a chicken salad and, taking the menus with me, I order our meals, making sure to tuck the receipt in my purse. When I get back to the table, Emily is rummaging through her purse, taking out a ten-pound note.

'How much was it?' she asks. I shake my head.

'I'll put it through expenses – we get thirty quid each for dinner, I think.'

'Oh.' She puts her purse away and looks at me. 'Why didn't I think of that? You always were better at this stuff than me.'

I laugh. 'What? You're talking to the woman who managed to misplace her driving licence twice in the space of three years.' I take a sip of my drink. 'Though I always suspected Freya of stealing it, before she got hers.'

Emily's cheeks redden. 'She definitely did that at least once. We went to a club and she didn't have ID, remember? She'd lost her own somewhere. You were with your mum; I can't remember where.'

'We went up to London for a night,' I say, the memory coming back to me. 'We went to the theatre to see *Grease*. Freya didn't want to come. Her face when I suggested it.' I shake my head, smiling at the memory. 'So Mum and I went alone. I thought I lost the licence in London.'

Emily is grinning too. 'That night was a total disaster. A fight broke out in the club, just two guys throwing punches, but then a third guy joined in by throwing a chair across the room. It was chaos. And a proper dive.' She sits back as our food arrives, smiling her thanks at the waiter. 'They were charging four quid for a WKD. Four quid! We could only afford two each. And then we had to walk back in the pissing rain.'

'Well, I'd say it serves you both right for nicking my ID.' I thank the waiter as he deposits our cutlery and a bottle of mayonnaise. 'What happened to it anyway?'

'That's the thing – Freya lost her purse. It's not even like we were drunk, so maybe someone stole it, but we just couldn't figure out how.' Emily forks a few sad-looking salad leaves into her mouth and chews, looking thoughtful. 'Though I don't see why it serves *me* right; I didn't steal your ID. I didn't even have ID; I wasn't old enough. They didn't check.'

I nibble on a chip, savouring the saltiness. 'You should've known better. You know what Freya was like.'

'A storm,' we say in unison, and I catch the amusement in her eyes as our gazes meet.

'Emily,' I begin after a moment, trying to keep my tone light. I can't push her too hard. Not yet. 'How old is Ella?' The question surprises me; it isn't what I intended to ask. And, judging by the way Emily's eyes dart up to my face, it surprises her too.

'F-four,' she says. 'Well, three and a bit.'

A bit? I nod as if it's the answer I expected. 'So you weren't already pregnant when you left?'

Emily pauses before shaking her head, her gaze fixed on her plate, the fork moving between it and her mouth mechanically. When she doesn't speak, I take a deep breath and ask another question, the question I've been meaning to ask since Mum told me Emily had returned.

'Did you go to meet Freya? Do you know what happened to her?'

Emily's fork clatters against the plate as it falls from her hand. Her eyes are wide, fixed on mine, and I see fear flash across them. Too late, I realise I've pushed it too far.

'I-I need to get to bed. We have an early start tomorrow.' Emily is gathering her things, avoiding my gaze now. She stands and almost knocks her chair over in her haste to escape. 'I'll meet you at the car at eight?'

Before I can respond, she's gone, the door closing with a soft whoosh behind her.

'Shit,' I mutter into my now-cold chips.

29

EMILY

Shit.

Why did I do this, why did I come on this trip with Imogen? I knew she'd start asking questions. Of course she would. Anyone would, in her position. But they aren't questions I can answer. I can never tell her the truth.

I throw myself down on the bed and close my eyes against the bright overhead light, thinking about how I almost slipped up at dinner. I should never have come back. When I got Mum's letter I should have asked her to come to us instead. But no, that wouldn't have been fair. I've watched the cancer ravage her over the past few weeks, the pain constantly etched onto her face. She could never have travelled. A part of me wishes she never found us, never sent that letter begging us to come home.

Jesus Christ. What kind of daughter does that make me? A fucking awful one.

Groaning, I push myself off the bed and pad into the bathroom. I want a bath, but it's so hot. I don't think the temperature has dropped below twenty-five in weeks. I fill the tub with lukewarm water and lots of bubble bath, and as I slide into the water, I picture Ella having a bath, Mum blowing bubbles in the air like she did when we were kids. She'll be asleep now, but I grab my phone from the side and call Mum anyway.

'Hello, love.' I can hear the TV in the background, one of her soaps, no doubt. 'Everything all right?'

'Fine, everything's fine here. How is she? Did she go to sleep okay?'

'Oh, yes. We read a story together – she's quite the pro at voices, isn't she? – and then she was out like a light.' I hear Mum sigh. 'She reminds me so much of you two when you were small. I said I'll take her to the Hoe tomorrow. There's meant to be a funfair on.'

'Don't let her go on anything too fast,' I say quickly. 'She's got a tendency to throw up.'

Mum chuckles. 'Just like Jamie. Do you remember that time he went on the waltzer? He just about covered everyone in his puke. It was disgusting.' I make a noise that I hope passes as a laugh. 'We'll stick to the teacups.'

'I can't wait to hear all about it when I get back. I'll see you tomorrow, okay? Hopefully not too late.'

'Don't worry about us, love. We'll be just fine. I'll try to take pictures. They grow up so fast; she'll be an adult before you know it.'

I grip the phone and try not to cry. I want Ella to remain young and carefree forever, concerned only about her magazines and stories and who will give her a bath. I don't want her to grow up, not in this world of fear and pain. I don't want her to look at me one day and wonder why I wasn't a better mother.

I'm sitting on the low wall in the car park, a latte in hand, a cup of tea for Imogen sitting beside me. The Costa across the way was barely open before I pushed my way inside, desperate for caffeine. I light a cigarette and blow the smoke into a sky streaked with red, wispy clouds like candyfloss drifting across.

'Morning.' Imogen stands a few feet away, hands in pockets, a tentative smile on her face. Last night comes back to me and I cringe inwardly. We just have to get through today.

Grinding out my cigarette, I jump up and hand her the cup. 'Tea, one sugar,' I say, matching her smile, and her eyes meet mine. She knows what this is; a peace offering.

'Thanks.'

Imogen drives in silence, following the satnav. It only takes about ten minutes, despite the hour. Rush hour here doesn't appear to mean the same thing as it does in Plymouth. She parks in front of the building, a sprawling metal construction with a domed roof which reminds me of a farm. Imogen turns to me and smiles before unclipping her seat belt. 'Here we go,' she says. 'Ready?'

'Just about.' I check the clock on the dashboard. 'Time for a cigarette?'

Imogen laughs. 'I wish. You go ahead though.'

I get out of the car and light up, trying to breathe deeply. I need to relax, focus on the day ahead. As I'm finishing up, a man opens the front door, propping it open with his foot.

'Good morning!' he calls, and Imogen gets out of the car.

'John?' She strides across the car park, hand outstretched. 'Nice to finally meet you. I'm Imogen.'

'I know who you are,' he says, grinning as he shakes her hand. 'And this must be Emily.' He turns to me and shakes my hand too. 'Right then, let's get you inside and set up. Kettle's just boiled.'

'You have a kettle?' Imogen asks, hoisting her laptop bag onto her shoulder. 'We're not allowed one. Health and safety.'

John taps the side of his nose. 'The perks of being tucked away up here.' I smile and follow Imogen inside, pausing to coat my hands in the alcohol gel fitted to the wall. John leads us into an office with two tables pushed together, chairs dotted around the edges. 'Plugs are either side,' John says, pointing, and I make my way over to the far side, Imogen settling down opposite me. 'Right. Cup of tea? Coffee?' John rubs his hands together. 'I'm afraid we don't have any gin.'

'Mother's ruin,' Imogen jokes, her hands going to her stomach. I look away. 'Tea please.'

I settle for water and boot up my laptop while John is in the kitchenette next door, and open the plan Imogen and I made for today. I'm going to be checking the distributed products for compliant labelling, while Imogen visits the clean room. I'm not technically trained as an internal auditor, so I'm just making notes and Imogen will write it all up. We used to work together like this when we were younger, when Imogen was training me up to take over her summer job when she went to university and had to drop some hours.

I glance at her over the top of my screen and suppress a sigh. It all could've been so different. If it had remained the three of us, if our plans had stayed the same. If Jamie had never wormed his way in.

30

FREYA

THEN

As winter finally blossomed into spring, Freya made a decision. She was going to break it off with Jamie. She spent the evening with Imogen, her phone turned to silent as the messages from Jamie became too much. As they walked along the seafront, Freya reflected on the conversation she would have with him. She looked at her sister, her face turned toward the sea, and wished she could confide in her, could ask for her advice. But she was in too deep now, and she had to deal with this alone.

He was waiting for her when they got home, the tip of his cigarette glowing in the darkness. Imogen's fingers tightened around Freya's, and for the first time in months, Freya heard her sister's thoughts as if they were her own. *Don't.* Imogen was always the cautious one, always the voice of reason. And this time, Freya intended to listen to her.

'I'll just be a minute,' she whispered, giving Imogen a little nudge. 'Make me a hot chocolate, yeah? With cream.' She forced a bright smile, and, after a wary glance at Jamie, Imogen went inside.

'I'm glad you're here,' Freya said, stepping closer to Jamie. She felt bold, strong. She was doing the right thing. 'I wanted to talk to you.'

'You've been ignoring me all day,' he said, refusing to look at her. 'All week, actually.'

She took a deep breath, sitting down on the wall running between their houses. 'I wanted to spend some time with my sister. I feel like I don't see her anymore.'

Jamie scoffed. 'What are you talking about? You live with her.'

Freya shook her head. 'You know what I mean. Ever since...'

'Ever since *what*?' His tone of voice startled her. He had always been quick to anger, but now it seemed as if any little thing could set him off.

Freya blew out a breath, avoiding his eyes. She stared up at the darkening sky, the stars visible overhead. 'I think we should call it a day.' Jamie's eyes widened at her words. 'It's been fun, but–'

'Fun?' He was on his feet, his bulk towering over her. She shrank back, remembering his fingers gripping her arm, the bruises he left on her body. She wasn't sure when the first time was; she wasn't even sure he meant to do it. But anger radiated from him that night, and she flinched away from his touch.

'Get off me!' she cried as he grabbed her chin, forcing her to look at him.

'What has Imogen been saying?' he hissed, bringing his face close to hers. 'What poison has she been dripping into your ears?'

'N-nothing,' Freya whispered, tears stinging her eyes. *Poison?* She wondered what he was so afraid of, why he was clinging so tightly to her. And why was she so scared of him? She felt fury bubble up inside her and she knocked his hand away. Her jaw ached from where he had been gripping it. His eyes widened and he took a step back.

'We'll talk about this tomorrow,' he growled, then turned on his heel and disappeared inside, slamming the door behind him.

Freya sat for a moment, massaging her jaw, trying to make sense of the conversation she'd just had. Trying to make sense of him, of his behaviour. He had always been possessive, she realised now, always trying to monopolise her time, prone to sulking if she said she was busy. But it had all been new and exciting, and she hadn't listened to the warning bells. Now they were ringing loud and clear, and Freya knew what she had to do.

Glancing up, she saw the shadow at Emily's window, the curtain fluttering as the figure moved away, leaving Freya alone.

31

IMOGEN

The day flies by, and before I know it, we're getting in the car, ready to travel home. Emily sits on the wall opposite, smoking, while I fiddle around with the satnav. I think about the work left to do when we get back to the office, the report I'll have to make to Flo, and sigh inwardly. She's not going to like what we've found.

Emily opens the car door, bringing in a whiff of cigarette smoke. I'm about to put the car in gear when a twinge makes me gasp. Emily turns to me, her face pinched with worry, but the pain is already subsiding. I take a deep breath and force a smile. 'I'm all right,' I say, pushing my anxiety aside. My baby will be fine. She *is* fine. I'd know it if she wasn't.

We drive with the radio on, the windows down to let in the breeze. Emily is frowning down at her phone.

'Everything all right?' I ask, indicating and moving around a caravan. Emily grimaces.

'Bloody emmets,' she says, nodding towards the caravan. I notice then that her accent is almost gone, the West Country vowels rounded out during her time away. 'Aren't they a bit early?'

'Grockles,' I correct her. 'We're not in Cornwall. And you know tourist season runs from April to October. We've got a while until they clear off.'

Emily smiles. 'Mum still calls them emmets. I guess it's rubbed off.'

'How is she?'

Emily is silent for a moment before speaking. 'Not good. She tries to hide it, but she's in a lot of pain every day.'

'Is she taking anything for it?'

'She could open a pharmacy with her stash,' she says, laughing bitterly. 'I don't think she has long left.'

I glance at her, surprised at her candour, noting the purple under her eyes, her pursed lips.

'I'm sorry,' I say. 'Is that why Ella is going to nursery now?'

Emily shoots me a look. 'No,' she snaps, then sighs. 'Yes. Partially. Mum thinks it's a good idea, and Jamie...'

I hold my breath, my stomach jolting at the mention of his name.

'Jamie does too,' she finishes.

'And you?'

'Ella seems to love it. She's always been sociable, always made friends with animals and people alike. She's just one of those kids.' A brightness has entered her voice now. 'I think it's good for her,' she says with a firmness that makes me wonder who she's trying to convince.

'You must miss her. Did you work while you were... away?' I try to keep my voice light, but I feel the tension creep back in. I pass another caravan, this one with a Scottish flag stuck in the rear window.

'Yes,' Emily says after a moment. 'Though nothing as structured as this. And we haven't spent a night apart before.'

I glance at her again. 'What, never?' I place a hand on my

stomach. 'I can see why. I don't think I'll ever want to be parted from this little one.'

'Do you know what you're having yet?' Emily asks, turning towards me.

I shake my head. 'Not for certain. But it's a girl, I know it is.'

A motorbike speeds past, the sound filling the silence between us.

'I'm happy for you, Imogen,' Emily whispers. 'I really am.'

The words tumble out before I can stop them. 'You know you can talk to me, don't you? We were so close when we were younger. We all were. What happened?' Emily is silent, staring out of the passenger window. I grit my teeth in frustration. 'Come on, Em. We were like sisters. Sometimes I thought I was closer to you than I was to Freya.'

She looks at me then. 'Really?'

I nod, overtaking a lorry. 'Yeah. Freya could be so... distant. Especially after Dad died.' I sigh. 'She seemed to change overnight.'

'I know what you mean. Freya was such a difficult person to understand sometimes. She could be so caring, so thoughtful.' She gives a laugh. 'Remember when she let me use her brand new bike, that summer mine got broken? She used that old rusty thing your dad left in the shed.'

I laugh too, remembering. 'God, that thing was a pile of crap. Mum told him to take it to the dump, but he was a bit of a hoarder when it came to things like that. He said he'd fix it up, but he never did.'

Emily shakes her head. 'She let me use it all summer, refusing to give me the rubbish one. How old were we then? Ten?'

'I think it was the summer before you went to secondary school, so Freya and I would've been about twelve.' I smile. 'Do you remember when she left our birthday party one year, I think it was our fourteenth or something, to watch a cat giving birth? We found her an hour later in the park down the road, grass stains on her white skirt, just as the last kitten slid out.' I remember Freya's eyes shining in the dusk, a finger pressed to her lips as the cat laid on her side, panting, her kittens nestled up beside her. 'She wanted to take them home, but they belonged to the woman on the other side of your house, what was her name?'

'Mrs Willis,' Emily says. 'That old bat. Do you know she's still kicking?'

'No way! She must be over a hundred.'

'Mum thinks she's a vampire,' Emily snorts. 'She's got about twenty cats now, but they seem all right. Friendly, well-fed.'

'She's probably just lonely,' I say. 'Now you mention it, I think Mum still pops in every now and then, takes her some food.' Guilt shoots through me as I picture Mum sitting in Mrs Willis's kitchen, surrounded by cats and silence. Was she lonely too, with us all gone?

'I always loved your mum's food,' Emily says, breaking into my thoughts. 'Though your dad did the best pancakes.'

I smile, a memory of us all in the kitchen flooding back. Emily beside me, Freya opposite, Dad at the stove, flipping pancakes with expertise. Mum leaning in the doorway, a cup of tea in her hands. The radio playing in the background, the smell of bacon filling the air, the sun shining outside.

'So many memories,' I say, almost to myself, and Emily stiffens beside me.

'Not all of them good,' she snaps, and I glance at her in surprise. She turns from me again, staring out of the window, and I know I've lost her again.

32

EMILY

Imogen pulls up outside our houses, manoeuvring effortlessly into a tight space. 'Thanks for the lift,' I say, heaving my bags from the boot. I grab Imogen's too, dragging them all up the steps and depositing them on the path. I open the front door and call out for Mum, but the house is quiet. Maybe she's already set off to collect Ella from nursery; she likes to walk, says she enjoys the fresh air. If I'm quick, I can meet them there. I dig through my handbag for the car keys.

Imogen is opening her front door, wrestling her suitcase through the gap, when Deb appears from inside, wiping her hands on a tea towel. 'Oh, hello girls,' she says. She tuts at Imogen and takes the case from her, moving aside so her daughter can enter. 'I've made spag bol for tea. Are you joining us, Emily?'

I freeze. 'N-no thanks, Deb,' I stammer, 'I'm going to get Ella.' I almost stumble on the name, and Deb's eyes widen a fraction. 'Maybe another time?' She smiles.

'That would be lovely. Off you pop then, best not keep her waiting.' Her eyes are shining as she closes the door, and I take off down the front path, memories snapping at my heels.

I pull up outside the nursery five minutes later, parking at an angle right outside the gates. I ignore the looks from other mothers and, spotting Ella's teacher, run across the playground. 'Hi Jane,' I say breathlessly. She turns and frowns at me.

'Oh, hi Emily. What are you doing here?'

'I got back early, so I thought I'd get Ella. Is Mum already here?' I look around for her.

Jane takes a step closer. 'She's already been collected, about ten minutes ago? Jamie said...'

The air flies out of me. 'Jamie? Jamie took her?'

Jane is looking at me with concern now. 'Yes, your mum was with him. I thought it was okay, her name is on the list.'

Jamie. Why would he take her? He knows how I feel about it. He *knows*. And so does Mum.

My ears begin to buzz as I run back to the car, dialling as I go. Voicemail. I try again, before throwing the phone onto the passenger seat and tearing away. I use the voice control to ring Mum's landline; maybe they're back home already, waiting for me? But it rings out. Jamie's house is closer; I decide to go there first.

I throw my car into a space outside his house and leap out, barely remembering to put the handbrake on. I raise my fist and hammer on the door, before bending to call through the letter-box. 'Ella? Ella, are you here, sweetie?' My voice is shaky, and I try to stop myself from screaming her name. 'Jamie!'

Silence. I raise my fist and knock again, stepping back to peer through the front window. Through the net curtain I can see the outline of a sofa, a TV hung on the wall. But no movement. I pull out my phone and ring Jamie again. Voicemail. I try Mum next, but it rings out. 'Fuck!' I shout in frustration, kicking the front door. I run a hand through my hair, tugging at the roots. Where is she? Where has he taken her? They can't have gone far; he must have left mere minutes before me. My skin goes cold as I imagine him driving up the motorway, Ella strapped in the back seat, never to be seen again. No. No. He won't have taken her, he can't. He wouldn't do that. Would he?

I lean on the wall, trying to calm my racing heart. I have to concentrate. I have to find her. Mum's name flashes up on the screen and I jab a finger at it. 'Where is she?' I spit at her, barely registering the dirty look an elderly lady throws at me as she walks past.

Mum is silent for a moment, a moment which stretches the length of a year. Finally, I hear her inhale, and brace myself for her words. 'She's safe, Emily. She's with us. At home.'

I hang up, throwing the phone onto the passenger seat and tearing out of Jamie's road. He has her. He took her. I wind my way around Mutley, cursing when the lights turn red outside Goodbody's café. A woman with a pram guides a small boy next to her, his dark curls bouncing as he skips across the road, her bright dress flapping in the breeze. I drum my fingertips on the steering wheel, slamming my foot on the accelerator as soon as the lights change. I take the corner too quickly and my heart leaps into my mouth as I see a fire engine exiting the station ahead. I feel my tyres skid as I brake, ignoring the stares of pedestrians on the other side of the road. I have to get there, to Ella. *How dare he,* I think, trembling with rage. *How dare he take my child.*

I pull up outside the house, leaving my car parked at an angle behind a Corsa which belongs to one of the students a few doors down. The front door opens as I run up the steps and I push my way in, shoving past him.

'Where is she?' My voice is too loud, and Ella looks up from the kitchen table and the picture she's drawing. I feel my heart clench as I take her in, my eyes roaming over her, checking for injuries, for distress.

'Mumily!' she exclaims, holding up the paper. 'Look, it's you!'

She's drawn a woman with ridiculously long arms and a large head. A lopsided cabin is in the background, and the breath catches in my throat. Our cabin. Where Ella learned to read, to walk, to swim. Where I learned her moods, the way she tips her head to the side when she's thinking. How to care for her curls, running my fingers through the tangles in the bath, cupping them in my palm and gently scrunching out the water. Where we learned of her illness, and how to cook for her. Where we curled up together at night, her little toes pressed against my back, her fingers in my hair. Tears fill my eyes as I crouch beside her.

'Thank you, sweetie. It's lovely.' She grins and reaches out to touch my cheek.

'Are you okay, Mumily?' she asks, tilting her head, and I smile, pushing the tears away.

'I am now,' I say, mirroring her and placing my hand on her cheek, 'now I'm with you.' I stand and turn to find Jamie in the doorway. Signalling for him to follow me, I stalk into the back garden, digging in my pockets for a cigarette. Jamie removes an e-cigarette from his back pocket and raises an eyebrow at me.

'You know they'll kill you,' he says as I light the cigarette. I blow the smoke out, the breeze carrying it away, and fix him with my gaze. Rage makes my heart pound, hatred filling me at the sight of my brother's smug face, the glee in his eyes. 'Come on, Em,' he says, his lips turned up in a smirk. 'What's the big deal? She's fine. She's had a great time with me. Her dad.' His words are meant to wound, designed to seek out my weak spots and hurt me enough so I can't fight back. But it's too late for that.

'I'll kill you if you take her again.' The words leave my mouth in a whisper, so quiet I might not have spoken at all, but I can see in his eyes that they register. I drop the cigarette butt and stamp on it, before taking a step closer, our eyes locked, our noses almost touching. 'Do you understand me, Jamie? I will fucking kill you.'

I turn to see Mum leaning against the back door, her eyes wide with shock. 'You are your father's daughter,' she says, and, shaking her head, turns back into the house.

33

IMOGEN

I head into the office the next morning, intending on spending the day writing up the audits. Mum is redecorating the bathroom, which for some reason includes a lot of loud banging and the radio playing at full blast, so I settle down at my desk with a cup of tea, enjoying the relative peace of the office, and skim through my emails, stopping suddenly on one with the subject *Notice of Withdrawal of Services.*

I stare at the email, unblinking. Even as the words burn themselves into my mind, I try to convince myself it isn't real. That I'm misreading. Maybe I'm dreaming. But no. It's happening.

We are writing to inform you that KS Quality Assurance are withdrawing their Notified Body services, effective immediately...

Words, more words, floating before my eyes as the message sinks in.

I knock gingerly on Flo's door, taking a deep breath as she calls out for me to enter. She glances up from some papers on her desk, giving me a warm smile. 'Ah, Imogen, come on in. Are you...' She falters as she registers the look on my face. I've never been good at delivering bad news. That was always Freya. I remember the way her eyes held mine when she told me Dad had died. 'He's dead, Immy,' she said, her voice steady, her emotions carefully controlled. But I could feel them rolling off her like waves, in the way only a twin can. And her hand stroked my hair as I wept, face buried in her shoulder, her perfume filling my nose. The comfort of her, the similarity.

I watch Flo's face drain of colour as I explain the situation to her. I tell her that we have ninety days to find a new notified body, that I will start looking immediately. Unlike Freya, who always stuck to the facts, never giving false promises, I've always struggled to deliver bad news without also presenting a solution. But Flo is shaking her head. I can see her mind whirring, processing the news, considering all the possible options.

'There are only three notified bodies left in the country.' She frowns. 'Two now. Only one of those is designated under the new regulation. And with Brexit coming, there's little point switching to a European one.'

'But the UK will recognise EU notified bodies,' I protest, faltering as I remember the webinar I joined last week. The new requirements imposed by the UK should a no-deal Brexit occur. The additional registrations, the cost. It always comes down to the cost.

'There's no point, Immy,' Flo whispers, and fear floods me as I understand her words. 'It's over.'

Mum shakes her head as I fill her in over dinner.

'Oh, what a mess,' she says. 'Poor Flo. And poor you. Is there really nothing to be done?'

I sigh, laying my fork aside. My plate is still half full, my appetite gone. 'Not really. We have a few options, but the money made from the products wouldn't begin to cover those costs. Financially, it makes sense to discontinue them.'

'But those products were made by Flo's grandfather,' Mum protests. 'Some of them are almost fifty years old!'

'I know.' I cover my face with my hands. 'It's a nightmare. And that's not all of it.' I pause, trying to gather my thoughts. 'Brexit is going to cause even more chaos. So many of our suppliers are based outside of the UK, meaning they'll have to spend a fair amount of money in order to continue to sell to us. The workload just to get them to comply with the regulation is terrifying enough, let alone these new requirements.'

Mum takes a deep breath. 'So, what now, Immy?' I look at her in confusion. She smiles. 'You always have a plan. What are you going to do now?'

I spend the evening checking documentation, making lists, running reports on sales, and drafting up an email to our suppliers. Mum's right, I do always have a plan.

By the time I get into bed, I'm exhausted, the heat of my bedroom causing sweat to prickle along my brow. But I feel more positive than I had this morning in Flo's office. I feel hopeful we can tackle this.

I fall asleep thinking of Freya, of how she would've sat up with me, brainstorming, making endless cups of coffee, dropping biscuit crumbs all over my bed. How she would've laughed off my worries, convinced she could sort it out, no matter the barriers. That was Freya all over; confident, self-assured. Always certain in herself and her decisions, her place in the world. She didn't need anyone, not even me, not really. She was a force of nature, strong and unapologetic, feet planted firmly on the ground, head firmly screwed on. Unlike me, she never seemed to be plagued by anxiety, kept awake by her thoughts racing, unsure of herself. Freya and Emily were the strong ones, the boulders between which I drifted, keeping me tethered, safe. And when I lost them both, I had to become my own tether, force myself to survive without them. Will I ever be strong enough alone?

34

FREYA

THEN

Imogen burst into the room, Emily on her heels. 'What are you still doing in bed?' she cried, dragging the duvet off Freya. 'It's our shopping day!'

Freya groaned. 'What time is it?'

'Not even eight,' Emily sighed, collapsing on the end of the bed in a mock faint. Freya noticed her shirt had ridden up, caught a glimpse of something on her back before Emily pulled it back down, her eyes hard.

Imogen laughed, shaking Freya by the shoulder. 'We need to get a move on if we're going to get the best deals! And we need to get Mum a present,' she added. 'It's her party tonight!'

'All right, all right,' Freya said, swinging her legs out of bed. 'Give me twenty minutes.'

'Ten!' Imogen grinned, bumping her with her shoulder. 'Chop-chop!'

Laughing, Freya shook her head and went into the bathroom. It wasn't often that Imogen got excited; she was usually the sensible one, always calm and clear-headed. But when she did, she always reminded Freya of their dad. With a sad smile, Freya climbed into the shower.

The party was in full swing. Their mum hadn't really celebrated her birthday since their dad died, preferring to order a pizza and sit in front of the telly, but it was her fiftieth that February, and her daughters insisted on marking the occasion. Freya, dressed in a dark-blue dress she'd picked up earlier that day for a fiver, her recently-trimmed curls bouncing around her head, floated through the house with a plate of mini sausages, while Imogen, in her burgundy blazer and black jeans, her hair straightened, offered glasses of Buck's Fizz to the guests.

Emily was sitting on the sofa with her mum, a glass of wine in her hand, her eyes glittering, her laughter slightly too loud. Freya caught Imogen's eye and they smiled; Emily never could handle her drink.

She saw Jamie through the patio door, leaning against the tree, smoking. As if sensing her eyes upon him, he turned, catching her gaze before Emily appeared, blocking their view.

'You all right, Frey?' Emily slurred, leaning against the counter.

Freya smiled. 'Yeah, you?'

Emily laughed and shook her head. 'I think I've had too much to drink.'

'You think?' Imogen said from behind her, depositing her empty tray on the side. 'Come on, Em, let's get you to bed.'

'Do you need a hand?' Freya asked, watching her sister take Emily by the arm. A feeling shivered through her, one she'd tried to ignore countless times over the years. The feeling of being left out.

Imogen shook her head. 'I think Mum's ready to open her presents,' she said, holding Emily close as she led her out of the room. 'Can you tell her I'll just be a few minutes?'

'No worries.' Freya watched Emily loop her arm over Imogen's shoulders, their heads pressed together, their laughter tinkling above the music and voices in the other room. Imogen and Emily had always been close; sometimes Freya wondered if she and Emily should have swapped places, if Emily was more like a sister, a twin, to Imogen. She felt a pang as she saw the distance grow between her and her sister, the girl she grew with, grew *up* with, was supposed to grow old with. Twins were supposed to be close, to stay as close as they were in the womb. What happened between them? Freya didn't know, but she had a feeling it was her own fault.

'Freya!' Flo sashayed into the kitchen, reaching out and taking Freya's hands, bangles glinting on her wrists. 'How beautiful you are! Where have you been hiding?'

Freya smiled. She'd always liked Flo, had even gone to her for advice when she was growing up. When she couldn't go to her own mother, or to Imogen. She wondered if she should ask for her advice now.

'Your mother was just telling that story again. You know, the *birth* story,' Flo said, eyes twinkling. Freya sighed. Every time her mother had a drink, she would start telling anyone who would listen about how Freya and Imogen were born. Freya came first, slipping out after a couple of hours, but Imogen had the cord wrapped around her neck and they couldn't get her out without an emergency caesarean.

'Come on,' Flo said, breaking into her reverie. 'It's time to open the presents!' She looked around. 'But where *is* that sister of yours?'

'She took Emily home,' Freya said, feeling that familiar emotion wrapping around her like a blanket. She tried to shake it off, catching Jamie's eye through the window, seeing his hard eyes and smirking mouth. She looked away quickly.

'Yes, Emily had a glass too many, I think!' Flo laughed,

putting an arm around her shoulders and squeezing. 'Never mind. Come on, let's not keep your mum waiting!'

When Freya handed her mum the gift she and Imogen had chosen, Deb's smile had faltered for a moment, her eyes flicking to the empty space behind her daughter. The words *Where's Imogen?* hung in the air between them, and Freya felt her mood darken once more. She was never enough, not without Imogen.

35

EMILY

Ella is quiet that night, content to let me wash her hair without demanding stories or that I play with her octopus. She's always been able to sense my mood, even when she was a baby. Such a sensitive child. I run my fingers gently through her curls, separating the tangles, feeling myself relax in her presence, as I always do.

When she's out of the bath and standing on the mat, wrapped in a huge fluffy towel, she looks up at me, her eyebrows knitted together. 'Mumily,' she says, her voice quiet and careful, 'I have something to say.'

I stare at her, uncomprehending, as her face slowly transforms into a grin. Then it clicks, and I burst out laughing. Ella giggles, throwing the towel from her shoulders and striking a pose. We sing her favourite song, 'Happy' from *Despicable Me*, as I pat her dry and she wriggles into her pyjamas. We dance down the hallway, her feet on top of mine, her hands gripping my wrists, until we reach the bedroom. She puts her arms around my neck and I pick her up, startled at how much bigger she seems. How quickly time drifts by, taking our children with it.

I swing Ella down and onto the bed, where she bounces,

giggling. When was the last time I saw her cry? Even faced with the prospect of a father, a person she'd never considered before, she was strong and fearless. *Just like her mother.* I push the thought away and sit down next to her, pulling the covers over our heads. It's like an oven under here, but it reminds me of happier days, Ella and I snuggled beneath a blanket, poking our fingers through the holes.

'Mumily, when are we going to the beach?' she asks, her face serious now.

'How about... tomorrow?' I smile and reach out to tap her nose with my finger.

'Yay!' She begins to wriggle, tucking her head under my arm. 'Oh, no,' she says suddenly, and I look down at her. 'What about Dad?'

I feel as though a bucket of cold water has been thrown over me. 'What about him?' I manage.

'Well, tomorrow is Friday, and on Fridays he goes to work.' She screws up her face. 'Or is it Saturday tomorrow?'

'It's Friday,' I say, stroking her cheek. 'And he still has to go to work. But we can go, just you and me.'

'Just you and me?' she repeats, pointing a finger at my chest, then at herself. She looks as if she's considering it, and I don't know whether to laugh or cry. Has she forgotten what it was like to just spend time with me? Has she already lost her memories of those early years, the days spent in the cabin and the woods and the river? The spiders she used to bring me, how she used to brush my hair until it shone?

'Yes,' she says after an eternity, nodding once. 'Just you and me. Like it used to be.' And I feel tears sting my eyes.

I decide to take her to Perranporth. Mum told me about a café which does proper gluten-free meals, and a shop which sells gluten-free ice cream cones. Today is all about me and Ella.

At eight the next morning, Ella launches herself down the stairs, her backpack bursting with a towel and swimming costume. She almost knocks into Mum, who lets out a surprised laugh.

'Someone's full of beans!' she exclaims. Ella jumps up and down.

'We're going to the beach, Nanny!'

Mum catches my eye. 'Oh, really? Well, aren't you lucky.' Ella runs off into the kitchen to collect her bucket and spade. 'It'll be nice for you two to spend time together,' she says to me. I make a noise in the back of my throat, still uncomfortable with her. I should've been able to trust her, but once again she chose Jamie, and once again she chose to see the dark side of me. *You are your father's daughter.*

I catch the hurt on her face as I move past her. 'What time will you be back?' she asks.

I shrug. 'Not sure. Don't bother doing us any dinner, we'll be eating out.' I hold out my hand to Ella, who is still grinning widely. 'Say goodbye, Ella.'

'Goodbye, Ella,' she says, eyes twinkling with mischief.

'Have a lovely time!' Mum says, bending down to kiss Ella's cheek. Without looking at her, I open the front door and stride out into the sunshine.

It's already hot inside the car, despite the early hour. I clip Ella into her seat then slide into the front. 'All right!' I say, catching her eye in the rear-view mirror. 'Who's ready for the beach?'

'I am!' she cries, hugging her bucket to her chest.

The drive is easy, no caravans blocking up the roads, and we arrive in good time. I park next to the Wetherspoons, grimacing at the price as I slot my coins into the machine, then unload Ella and our bags. We stop on a bench to take off our shoes, and as soon as Ella's feet touch the sand, she's off, running across the beach.

'Not too far!' I call, but my words are lost on the sea breeze. The beach is relatively empty at this time, except for a few dog walkers enjoying the early morning air, and I jog after her, smiling as she slows to say hello to a golden retriever. I catch up with them just as the dog licks Ella's face, and the owner arrives at the same time.

'Making friends, are we?' I say to Ella, who is hugging the dog's neck. 'Good job he's friendly!' I look up at the owner, a small woman in her fifties, and smile apologetically. 'I've told her hundreds of times not to go near strange dogs.'

'He's not strange!' Ella exclaims, throwing me a wounded look, and I laugh. The woman smiles.

'It's no problem. But *he* is a *she*. This is Ruby.' She has a strong Cornish accent, and her short grey hair blows in the breeze.

Ella gasps. 'Ruby! Oh, what a lovely name!' She hugs the dog tighter, who seems perfectly content to let her.

I shake my head, still smiling. The woman holds out a hand.

'I'm Robin,' she says, taking back her hand when she realises I'm laden down with Ella's beach paraphernalia. 'Why don't we find somewhere to sit while these two play? I could murder a cup of tea.'

I feel the usual jolt of unease at the idea of spending time with a stranger. But Ella is looking up at me, the dog at her side, her eyes wide with excitement. 'Can I throw a stick for her?' she asks Robin.

'Of course you can,' Robin says, bending down to Ella's level. She reaches out to stroke her dog. 'It's one of her favourite games.'

'Not near the water though, all right?' I add, giving Ella a stern look. 'Toes only.'

'Yes, yes.' Ella sighs in her usual way, which makes her sound far older than her years, and I can't help but laugh. 'Toes only. I know.'

'Go on then! We'll be just here, look for the pink towel.' I set down Ella's bag and lay her towel out in front, before shaking out the beach sheet and settling down on it. Robin watches Ella run across the sand, Ruby at her heels.

'She's a precious girl,' she says, shading her eyes with a hand. 'Now, how about that tea? I'll nip over to The Watering Hole. Sugar?'

'Two please.' I watch Robin make her way across the sand to the café, before turning back to Ella and Ruby. Ella has found a stick almost as big as her, and she's struggling to throw it for the dog. But she's laughing, and Ruby is jumping around her ankles.

Maybe we should get a dog. A little house in Cornwall, close enough for daily walks on the beach. No. This is a dangerous train of thought, one full of memories I've been running away from for five years.

'Here we are!' Robin appears beside me, holding out a cup of tea. 'Two sugars.'

'Thank you.'

She sits next to me and stares out to sea. 'How old is she?' she asks, blowing on her cup.

'Four.' I follow her gaze, catching sight of birds whirling in the distance. Ella has found a small stick now, and is throwing it into the surf. Ruby barks excitedly before diving after it. 'She loves dogs. How old is Ruby?'

'Six.' Robin smiles. 'I rescued her a couple of years ago. Terrible business, she was skinny as a rake when they brought her in. Her fur was all matted, and she had the saddest eyes I'd ever seen.' She turns to me. 'I've volunteered at a rescue place since I retired. She came in and I knew immediately that she was coming home with me.'

I watch the dog playing with Ella, try to imagine her in such a state. 'Poor thing,' I murmur. 'What did you do before?'

'I was a police officer, based out of Truro.' My heart starts to hammer at her words. She's still watching me, her eyes trained on my face. 'Are you local?' she asks, her voice light.

'N-no.' I take a deep breath. 'Plymouth.' There's no hiding my accent, even after all these years. Out of the corner of my eye, I see Robin nod.

'Ah, yes. Now I see it. You're her, aren't you?'

I tear my eyes away from Ella to face Robin, her brown eyes searching. I don't speak. I can't. I daren't. *Local Girls Missing*. I think of the officers who came to our house, the way the younger one looked at me. He hadn't believed a word of my story. Does Robin suspect there's more to it? Did she investigate our disappearance? I try to remember the names of the police officers from the articles, but fear has left me frozen, my mind empty.

'Time to go,' she says, almost wistfully, and I feel my heart leap into my mouth, thinking she means to take me with her, drag me into the police station to answer more questions. But she stands and dusts off her trousers, before putting two fingers in her mouth and whistling. Ruby runs over immediately, Ella on her heels. 'It was nice to meet you, Emily.' Smiling, Robin strides down the beach, Ruby trotting by her side. She turns to wave once, and Ella waves back, stretching her arm high above her head.

I sit, watching them go, willing my heart to stop pounding. Ella drops into my lap and I jump, startled. 'Ruby is a nice doggy. Can I have a doggy?'

I put my arms around her and squeeze. Ella giggles. 'Maybe one day,' I whisper, watching as Robin disappears from view.

36

IMOGEN

I spend the weekend with Mum, both of us dressed in Dad's old T-shirts as we paint the living room walls. 'It's called *griege*,' she said when she dug the tin of paint out of the shed. I raised an eyebrow at her, and she smiled. 'I know, I know. I didn't name it.'

In the living room, we move the furniture into the middle, covering it with dust sheets, and take down the photo frames from the walls. I pause, staring at a collage of Freya and me. It shows us aged four, with wide, gap-toothed smiles, in matching yellow dresses covered in white flowers. At seven, bundled into red coats with fur-lined hoods, blue wellies on our feet, the soles covered in mud. At twelve, awkwardly posing in our secondary school uniforms, my shirt untucked, Freya's odd socks peeking from beneath her trouser legs. At fourteen, our skin coated in a too-dark shade of Dream Matte Mousse, our lips glossy, our hair poker-straight. At sixteen, our GCSE results in our hands, our arms raised, grinning at the camera. At eighteen, sitting in the beer garden of a local pub, sipping from pints of beer. At nineteen, Freya dressed in a long skirt, me in denim shorts, our feet bare as we walked along the beach, hand in hand. At twenty-one, our dissertations printed and bound and held in front of our faces, our eyes just visible above them, tired but crinkled in joy.

On and on they go, documenting our lives together. Freya in her Starbucks uniform, sticking out her tongue; me and Emily in fancy dress, getting ready for a night out. I smile as I remember Emily puking all over my duvet when we stumbled home, before passing out on the floor. I tiptoed into Freya's room, sliding beneath her duvet like I had done so many times before, our limbs used to being close together. I remember her nose wrinkling at the scent of alcohol and perfume and cigarettes as I climbed in beside her, her giggling when I told her about Emily, and the bartender who gave me a free drink because he'd thought I was Freya.

'Oh God, *him!*' she whispered, snorting with laughter. 'He comes into Starbucks every day, at the same time, and orders the same drink – a medium latte with sugar-free caramel syrup.' She rolled her eyes. 'I gave him a free cookie one day – we were giving them out to everyone, I think they were about to go off – and ever since then he's tried to chat me up.'

I smile at the memory of us giggling together in the dark, limbs tangled like when we were kids. Mum comes up behind me and lays a hand on my shoulder.

'Oh, look!' she says, pointing at another photo. 'Do you remember that day? Oh, I was furious with your father when you came back. Covered in mud, all of you.' I peer at the photo, at our white jeans splashed with dark mud, our trainers filthy, smudges on our cheeks and in our hair. Dad standing between us, an arm around us, grinning from ear to ear. We got our hair colour from him, though his has faded to a sandy blond in this photo, and our smiles look identical.

'Not so furious you couldn't take a photo,' I murmur, smiling as I remember the walk Dad had taken us on that day. We were about eight, still dressing the same, still close enough to finish each other's sentences. We'd been to a forest somewhere and got caught in a downpour. Dad took a wrong turn and we had to trek through a muddy field, our trainers sticking as we tried to outrun the rain. I remember how, once across the field, Dad had bent double, hands on his knees, tears running down his face as he howled with laughter. 'I'm gonna need a hand here, Deb,' he called when he opened the front door, all three of us staying out on the porch, and Mum had come down the stairs, the washing basket in her arms.

'For Christ's sake, Tom!' she'd shouted, dropping the basket in the hall. 'What have you been doing?'

'We went on an adventure,' Freya piped up, grinning, and Mum had dissolved into laughter, running to grab her camera to take a photo. This photo.

'So many memories,' Mum says quietly, stroking Dad's face beneath the glass. 'We had such fun, didn't we?'

We were twenty-one when Dad died, barely three months out of uni, preparing for the rest of our lives. It was sudden, the kind of story you expect to read about in the paper. It wasn't supposed to happen, not to us. Not to Dad. He was so young, not even fifty. Too young.

'We were supposed to have more time,' Mum continues, squeezing my shoulder, and I smile sadly. She's right; we should have had years, decades, left. She and Dad were supposed to grow old together, still sitting in the same chairs, reading their novels, sipping tea in contented silence. Freya and I were supposed to go off travelling together, see the world, then come back and start our lives. We should've had careers, loves, birthdays, Christmases, arguments, nights in and nights out. We should've had each other for longer, much, much longer.

I turn and give Mum a hug, tears brimming in my eyes. 'I miss him too. I miss them both.'

She nods, pulling away. 'Oh, Im. There's been so much heartache in this house.'

'There was a lot of fun too,' I say firmly, taking her gently by the shoulders and forcing her to meet my eyes. 'So much fun and laughter and love. We had so many good times.'

'We did,' she murmurs, her gaze unfocused, lost in her memories. 'We did have a lot of fun.'

'What would Dad have thought of this *griege* then, Mum?' I ask, trying to smile. She snaps out of her reverie and laughs, taking the photo from my hands and laying it carefully on the floor.

'He would've said, "What on earth is *griege* when it's at home eating its cornflakes?".' A tear spills out, trickling down her cheek, but she's still smiling. 'And then he probably would've tried to have a paint fight.' She gives me a look. 'Don't get any funny ideas.'

I laugh. 'I wouldn't dream of it.' But when she turns away, I bend down and dip my finger in the paint, smudging it across her cheek. She gasps, batting my hand away.

'You are your father's daughter,' she says, shaking her head. I pull a face and she laughs. 'Get a move on, or we'll be sitting on the floor this evening to watch the telly.'

A car door slams and a voice drifts through the open window. 'Mumily!' Mum looks at me with fresh grief, and I put an arm around her as I watch Ella dance up the front steps, Emily on her heels.

37

EMILY

You are your father's daughter. The memory of those words hits me like a blow, just as they did when she first uttered them. I remember that day clearly, the day I discovered what they had done and sprang across the room, my fist connecting with Jamie's nose, blood spurting across the floor. Mum dragging me off him. Protecting him, always protecting him. Never me.

You are your father's daughter, Emily.

I force the words from my mind as I watch Mum move painfully across the kitchen. She's getting worse, I realise. Guilt floods me as I remember how I shouted at her, pushing past her to get to Ella the other day. To Jamie. He's the one who deserves my anger right now. Not Mum. She never deserved any of this.

'Mum, let me do that,' I say, taking a dirty mug from her and placing it in the dishwasher. She's holding onto the counter with one hand, still bent forward, pain twisting her features. 'Go and have a lie down. I'll get dinner on.'

I expect her to wave a hand at me, to tell me to stop fussing, but she doesn't. She looks up and meets my gaze, her lips pressed together, and nods once. I move to help her up the stairs, but she goes into the living room instead, her steps slow, her breathing laboured. She sinks down onto the sofa, closing her eyes and tipping her head back.

'Em?' she croaks. I take a step closer. 'Could you bring me my pills please? They're upstairs, on the bedside table.'

I jog up the stairs, pushing open her bedroom door, wrinkling my nose at the smell. When's the last time she changed the sheets? I rip the duvet back, stripping off the covers, and throw them into a pile by the door, before opening the window. I rummage through her wardrobe for fresh sheets, knocking down a hanger as I tug a pillowcase free. As I go to put the hanger back, I freeze, realising what I'm looking at. *His* clothes. Why are they still here, all these years later? I push the door wider and stare at the shirts lined up together, all facing the same way. His trousers are folded on the shelves in the far corner, along with his T-shirts, and his jackets hang closest to me. A few blazers, worn at the elbows; he rarely dressed up, rarely had the occasion to.

My eyes find his belts, wound up carefully on the top shelf, and the breath catches in my throat. The scars on my back begin to burn, the memories searing through my mind. No. *No.* I can't do this; I can't go back there, to that day. The day he disappeared. The day Jamie pulled him off me, taking the belt and wrapping it around his throat. The way his eyes bulged as he struggled for air. Mum's scream as she fell to the floor beside me, hands fluttering over the cuts on my back.

'Jamie, no,' she said, her voice shaking. 'Not like this.' Through a haze I saw Jamie step back, heard the crash as *he* fell to the floor, gasping. And then blackness descended, and when I woke up, he was gone.

I snap myself out of the memory, slamming the wardrobe door shut, the mirror beside it quivering. I stare into my reflection, take in the eyes ringed with purple, the greasy hair scraped back into a bun, the pinched mouth. I can see my mother in me, the pain ravaging us both. And I can see him, his legacy, his eyes staring back at me. Consuming me.

I have to get out of here. Grabbing Mum's pills from the bedside table, I run out of the room, slamming the door behind me. I fill a glass of water in the kitchen and stand at the sink for a moment, trying to regulate my breathing.

'You took a while,' Mum murmurs when I go back into the living room. She opens her eyes and struggles to sit up, holding out her hand for the water and pills.

'Sorry.' I sit down next to her, popping two pills into her palm and handing her the glass, before taking it back and setting it on the coffee table. 'Are you able to sleep down here? I stripped your bed; I'll make it again in a bit.' I don't want to go back up there, back to those memories I've spent years trying to bury.

Mum smiles, closing her eyes again. 'That was nice of you. I'll be fine down here, love.' She settles back against the cushions and I leave her there, closing the door behind me. I lean against it for a moment, my eyes closed, counting my breaths.

'Mumily.' My eyes snap open. Ella is standing in front of me, her hair ruffled from sleep. I'd forgotten she was taking a nap.

'Hey, sleepyhead,' I say, crouching down. 'Nanny's having a little sleep too, so we have to be quiet.'

She nods seriously. 'What should we do?' she whispers.

'I'm going to make dinner. Do you want to do some colouring at the table?'

Ella frowns. 'I can help make dinner. I help Jane give out the snacks at nursery.' She always pronounces each syllable – nur-ser-ee – and I smile.

'You're such a good girl.' I reach out and hug her, breathing in her scent, trying to centre myself, bring myself back from the past. 'Let's go then.'

'What are we having?' she asks as she follows me into the kitchen. I stop and turn.

'I don't know, actually. What do you fancy?' I open the fridge door and peer inside. 'There's some mince in here. We could make burgers?' I check the freezer next. 'But it doesn't look like we have any buns.'

'It's okay, Mumily, we can have a naked burger.'

I laugh. 'A naked burger? Where did you hear that?'

'Daddy ordered one when we went out.'

I freeze, hand still on the fridge door. When did they go out? I cast my mind back, trying to remember if he told me he was taking her out. Was I at work? Or was it while I was in Wiltshire? Did Mum lie to me again? I realise suddenly that I'm losing control of the situation, of Ella. I used to know where she was twenty-four hours a day, could see her at all times. She dominated my world. And now?

'Mumily?' Ella steps up beside me, standing on tiptoes to look into the fridge. 'Look, there's a lettuce! I like lettuce.'

She's grown; the top of her head reaches my hip. I'm not ready for her to grow up, to leave and experience the world. But I know that she must, someday. I force myself to smile at her. 'Okay, we'll have lettuce.' I reach in and grab it, passing it to her outstretched hands. I take out the mince and an onion, and set Ella to work ripping up the lettuce at the table while I make the burgers.

After I put Ella to bed that night, I go back into Mum's room, my heart pounding as I push open the door. I quickly make the bed, stuffing the ancient pillows into their cases. I realise I haven't been in here since that day, since I woke up in my own room,

Mum stroking my hair, the room dark and warm. My back throbbed, my head ached, my throat scratchy from crying.

Mum, noticing I was awake, took my hands in hers. 'Don't worry, Em. He's gone.'

'Gone?' I croaked, letting the word settle on my tongue. *Gone.* Was it true? Could he really be gone? 'Gone where?'

'For good,' she said, squeezing my hand. The door creaked open and I saw Jamie silhouetted against the light in the hall. He nodded once, his eyes on Mum, and I felt her exhale.

Gone. He was gone. He never came back, and I never found out where he went. I never asked.

38

FREYA

THEN

She drifted from room to room, following the ghost of her father through their years together. From the front door, where he held her in his arms for their first photo together, beaming from ear to ear. Through to the living room, with the battered Christmas tree as old as she was, bought last minute for half price due to its inclination to lean to the side, its branches brushing against the bay window. To the kitchen table, where they sat and ate together, Emily drawing, Freya writing poetry, Imogen reading. Where they baked cakes and laughed together. Upstairs to Imogen's bedroom, their first bedroom together, matching cots against opposite walls, a large F for Freya, I for Imogen, painted above them. Their parents' bedroom, with the old-fashioned wardrobes he pulled down one summer, smashing them apart in the back garden, and burning them that evening, the flames crackling as they sat on deckchairs, milkshakes in hand, a blanket shared between them all. To Freya's room, where he painted the wall above her bed a deep blue – *to match your eyes* – and then Imogen wanted the same. The white fluffy rug he brought home one day, which she'd promptly spilled nail polish on, the pale coral stain still visible.

And then to the bathroom. Years of splashing, giggling, plastic ducks and bubble bath, all wiped away by the sight of him collapsed on the floor, his cheek pressed against the worn bathmat, his eyes open, unseeing, his mouth a tight line. One arm stretched out, his fingers reaching. Reaching for her, one last time.

Freya fell to her knees in the doorway, hands pressed to her mouth. Even after all these years, she could still hear voices through the open window, her mother and Imogen, friends and family, paying their respects in hushed tones, their hands grasping, eyes watering. *I'm so sorry for your loss.* But it wasn't enough. It would never be enough.

She let her mind drift, let the memories engulf her. Imogen and Emily splashing in a paddling pool in the back garden; his laughter ringing out as they chased each other round with water pistols. Mum shrieking when he shot her from behind, a sausage rolling off the plate in her hand onto the grass.

Take my hand. Words whispered whenever she was afraid. Her first night in her room alone, the shadows seeming larger without Imogen there, despite being adamant she wanted her own room. When she fell out of a tree, grazing her elbow. When she played an angel in the nativity play, Imogen already on stage, her hair shining brighter than her tinsel halo, but Freya had been too nervous to go up and join her. When she fell out with some girls at school, and then when she punched one of them, ripping her hair out, landing her with a two-day suspension and a black eye of her own. When she heard Sam next door shouting, and she cowered on the stairs, listening to Emily cry.

Take my hand. It was his answer to everything. If she could feel the warmth of his palm, his fingers clasped around hers, then nothing bad could happen to her. She was safe.

She would never take his hand again. He was gone, his love, his laughter, his ability to get her through anything. The way his eyes twinkled when he was up to mischief, bringing a finger to his lips as he crept up behind Imogen, placing a plastic spider on the sofa next to her. How he brought flowers home every Friday, making the girls guess the colour before revealing them with a bow, presenting them to Mum, who tutted at the expense, smiling as she filled a vase. How he made pancakes thick and fluffy, covered in maple syrup, the bacon crispy, the strawberry milkshake cold against their teeth.

Now there would be no more Saturday morning trips to the beach or Sunday evenings spent on the sofa, plaiting her hair. No more school plays or sneaky ice creams before dinner. He would miss everything; she would never again turn to see him standing beside her, smiling, not on her wedding day, not at the birth of her children, not when she was upset or happy or lost, as she was lost now.

Now, the world was on fire. Her father was dead, and Freya was alone.

Almost two years later and she was stood in her bedroom, remembering those initial dark days. She wondered if she'd ever have looked at Jamie if her dad hadn't died. If she would've felt the desperate need to be loved, wanted. If she hadn't needed to reach out beyond this house, beyond her small, broken family, to the broken boy next door. Two broken pieces can never become whole, she knew now. She stared up at the map on the wall, at the future she had planned. It was all going to unravel.

She hadn't told anyone about the test, hidden at the bottom of the bathroom bin. She kept it to herself, curling up in bed at night, whispering to the child growing inside her. She didn't tell

Imogen, or their mother. She didn't tell Emily, and she didn't tell Jamie. She knew what she had to do. She knew he couldn't be a father; knew she didn't want him to be. As the child grew, Freya knew she would do anything to protect her. Finally, she had her missing piece, the piece that would make her whole.

39

IMOGEN

Flo calls me into her office on Monday morning, her face drawn and pale. I sink down into the chair opposite, my stomach clenching.

She looks at me sadly. 'You know what I'm going to say, don't you?' She sighs, slumping back in her chair. 'What with my sister still so unwell after the crash, and the kids, I just can't keep this business afloat anymore. Not after this.'

I reach down and pull my phone out of my bag. 'But I've come up with a plan, Flo,' I say, scrolling through my notes. 'I think we can get through this. We'd have to lose a lot of the legacy products, but they were more trouble than they were worth, documentation-wise.' I take a breath. 'If we cull all the higher class products, we won't need to find a new notified body. And then we can...' I trail off as she shakes her head.

'It's not just that, Im. The MHRA have announced new rules for medical device manufacturers located outside the UK if a no-deal Brexit goes ahead. The financial and administrative burden would be... well, I've spoken to some of our biggest suppliers, and it will be too much for them.' She takes a deep breath. 'They're pulling out, Imogen. It's over. I'm closing the business.'

I sit back, reeling. I know Flo wouldn't make this decision easily. The company has gone through four generations, passed down through the family since the 1940s. Now everyone here will lose their jobs. And it's not me I'm concerned about, not really. It's everyone else, the people with mortgages and loans and children... I place a hand on my stomach. Noticing, Flo smiles.

'I'll see everyone right, please don't doubt that. So many people here have been with us for a long time, I'd hate to see them struggle. I'm meeting with the other directors later today, but we're going to draw up a redundancy plan.'

I nod, unable to speak.

'And that will include you,' she continues, holding up a hand as I open my mouth to protest, 'and Emily. You've not been back long, granted, but you were with me when you were younger, and the work you've both done here has been excellent. You've saved us a few times, as I recall.'

A memory of an unannounced visit by the notified body enters my mind. Emily and I were in the warehouse, sticking labels over incorrect CE marks, when an auditor strolled in, clipboard in hand, assistant hurrying along behind him. His shiny shoes squeaked on the floor as he made a beeline for the warehouse manager's office.

'Excuse me,' Emily said, stepping out in front of him. 'Can I see some ID please?'

I remember staring at her in awe, as I always did when this side of her came out. This assertive, confident side. The man indicated the lanyard around his neck and attempted to walk around her, but she moved to block him again.

'I'll need to verify your identity,' she said, reaching out and inspecting the badge closely. 'Follow me, please.' She turned and led them towards the meeting room, mouthing *get Flo* at me.

Flo smiles knowingly, as if reading my mind. I smile back. I get to my feet, holding out my hand for her to shake. She steps around the desk and pulls me into a hug.

'Thank you, Immy,' she whispers, squeezing me. 'Your mum would be so proud of you. Your dad, too.' She steps back, holding me at arm's length. 'I just have one more favour to ask of you.'

~

I head upstairs, the weight of Flo's decision dragging me down. I've been sworn to secrecy for now; Flo is going to make an announcement once her plans are in place. Sitting down at my desk, I slide a USB stick into my laptop, and start to transfer all of the technical files over. They need to be kept for five years after the last sale of the device, so Flo has asked me to back them up.

While the files are copying, I begin drafting a letter to the MHRA, notifying them of the closure. Flo will ask the customer service manager to write to the customers, urging them to buy the existing stock, and Flo herself will deal with the suppliers and subcontractors. It feels strangely easy, to wrap up a business like this, but I know there's a lot more going on in the background. I sigh heavily, attracting the attention of Lucy.

'Everything all right?' she asks, raising her arms above her head in a stretch. I wonder what she'll do next. Maybe I should offer to help her with her CV, or provide a reference. There's not much else I can do.

I smile at her, forcing my anxiety away. 'Just tired. Did you have a good weekend?'

'I did actually. I went to Newquay with my girlfriend on Saturday – I'm still feeling it now. I'm too old to go out clubbing.'

I shake my head. 'If twenty-two is old, I don't know what that makes me.'

'Dead?'

We both laugh.

'What did you get up to?' she asks.

'Oh, I helped my mum paint the living room. She went for "griege".' I raise an eyebrow. 'It looks good though.'

'Where is it you live?' Lucy asks. 'We're looking for a place to rent, get out of our parents' hair.'

'Lipson. In one of the Victorian terraces.'

'We've seen some flats by the park that look quite nice. Is it all right round there?'

I shrug. 'There are some student houses dotted about, and I think teenagers like to frequent the chippy at the end of my road, but it's not too bad. Pretty quiet. The parking can be awful though.'

Lucy makes a face. 'I lived in Mutley when I was a student, near Goodbody's? Glad I didn't have a car then. With the student houses and the doctor's surgery, it was an absolute nightmare.'

'I can imagine.' I take a sip of water. 'What does your girl-friend do?'

Lucy's face brightens. 'She's still studying, doing her Master's. Creative writing. She wants to be an author.'

I try to remember the last time I read a book and inwardly berate myself. I used to love reading, spending an evening curled up on the sofa, a blanket across my legs, a cup of tea at my elbow. And Freya always wanted me to read her poetry, despite my protests that I never really understood it. She had a vague, lyrical way of writing, full of metaphors that were beyond me. I remember her rolling her eyes as she had to explain them to me.

'It's about us, you moron,' she said, her eyes glittering. No matter how frustrated she pretended to be, she secretly loved explaining the mystery behind her poems. 'All of us, how we're ground down by daily life.'

I looked down at the poem again. 'But it's about the sea,' I said stupidly. She sighed.

'Life is the sea,' she said, 'and we are the sand, battered and bruised. And moulded too, shaped into what – into *who* – we are.'

I feel a shiver run down my spine as I remember that poem. What shaped Freya into who she was, led her down the path she took? Was it something we should have seen?

'What does she want to write?' I ask Lucy, shaking myself.

'Historical fiction, with a focus on LGBT characters. Kinda like Sarah Waters.' Lucy rolls her eyes, smiling. 'I told her, she'd better not put any of our sex life in her books.'

I laugh. 'They do say to write what you know.' I wonder if that went for Freya, whether her poems were shaped by her life. Could there be any clues in her writing?

Lucy shakes her head, laughing too. The phone on her desk rings; she glances at it and groans. 'Christ, I'd better get this.'

'No worries. I'm going to pop out. Do you want anything from the shop?'

She shakes her head as she picks up the phone. 'Good afternoon, Lucy speaking.'

Stretching, I grab my bag and head out of the office, wondering how many more times I'll walk down this corridor, when I'll leave this building for good.

40

EMILY

The sky is tinged with purple when I step outside after putting Ella to bed. The air is thick, the concrete slabs still hot beneath my bare feet. Will this heatwave ever end? A cloud passes overhead, its shape reminding me of a leaf. I look down at the tattoo on my arm, the vines criss-crossing from elbow to wrist, the watercolour leaves bright against my skin. I turn my arm over and trace the leaf for Freya with my finger, remembering the day we got them done.

It had been my idea. A new tattoo parlour had opened up round the corner from our houses, next door to the shop, and I'd popped in one day when I was supposed to be buying milk. A hulking guy with a huge beard and leather boots had emerged from the studio, grinning widely as I dithered by the counter. He put me totally at ease, and, before I knew it, I'd booked us all in for a session the following week.

Freya was immediately excited, but Imogen took some persuading. She never liked to spend money, was constantly fretting about our travelling fund, but Freya had recently picked up some extra work in a swanky bar on the Barbican, so we were managing to save more than we'd expected.

'Come on, it'll be fun!' I said, putting my hands together and smiling sweetly at her. When she laughed, I knew I'd won.

We spent hours trawling the internet for a design, something we could all get. We settled on the vines, with three leaves, one for each of us. I drew it up, agonising over it, before sending it to the tattoo studio and, suddenly, I couldn't wait for our appointment. I had just turned nineteen, was still caught up in the excitement of being young and at university and free, free in a way that I'd never imagined before. After that day, when Jamie had saved me from *him*, and *he'd* disappeared, I suddenly found myself able to live without fear, without limitations, except those I chose to live by. It was exciting, and scary, and I felt breathless with the idea that I could do whatever I wanted. That this was my life, and I was in control.

When the day came, I decided to go first. Imogen and Freya sat on a sofa opposite me, squirming as the tattooist started. The pain wasn't as bad as I'd expected, and I watched with fascination as the needle moved across my skin, small pinpricks of blood bubbling in its wake. Before I knew it, it was over, and my arm was cleaned and wrapped in cling film. Then it was Imogen's turn.

I tried not to laugh as she gritted her teeth, her eyes screwed tight as the needle dragged across her skin. Afterwards, she admitted she'd wanted to cry. 'I've never felt pain like it!' She laughed. But I had. The scars on my back itch as I let the memories wash over me, memories I've buried for such a long time.

Freya was brave. Of course she was. She chatted to the tattooist – Imogen later accused her of chatting him up, despite his almost constant nattering about his wife and toddler, who seemed determined never to sleep – and stared up at the ceiling, which was covered in drawings. She pointed out designs like they were stars in the sky – *look, there's a wolf! And there, a teapot! Isn't that a jar of Marmite?* – and our eyes searched, trying to follow her gaze as she jumped from drawing to drawing. That was how it was with Freya, her running ahead, Imogen and me trying to keep up with her. She was always the first to do anything; the first to start her period, the first to kiss a boy, the first to start wearing make-up. The first to disappear.

I shake my head. I can't go there, not right now. Not ever.

41

FREYA

THEN

Freya laid across the bed, watching her sister curl Emily's hair in front of the full-length mirror. It was her first night out with them in ages; she had been focusing too much on Jamie, and she realised just how much her confidence had dipped over the past year. *Enough's enough*, she thought, flicking the page of her magazine. *It's time to get back to the old me.*

'Will you keep still?' Imogen cried, tapping Emily's shoulder with the hairbrush as she reached out for her drink.

'Ouch!' Emily giggled, slurping the bright blue alcopop through a straw. 'I was thirsty.'

Imogen shook her head, meeting Freya's eyes in the mirror. Freya smirked and lifted a shoulder.

'I feel like we're fifteen again,' Emily mused, tapping her feet to the music playing in the background. 'It's been ages since we had a night out like this.'

For some reason, Freya thought she heard a note in Emily's

voice, a note that said it was Freya's fault. *And isn't it?* she thought, her cheeks growing hot with shame. *Isn't it all my fault?*

'I know, we're proper adults now,' Imogen said, laughing. 'Mum even makes us do our own washing!' She tried to catch Freya's eye again, but Freya stared down at the pictures before her without taking them in. 'Do you remember that night you tried to do the Rattler challenge, Frey?'

Freya looked up to find both of them looking at her. She smiled. '*Tried* being the operative word. Didn't I only make it to three before I puked?'

'I thought it was two,' Emily said, taking another sip. 'Immy managed four, didn't you?'

Freya felt that old feeling rise up, the feeling she'd tried to bury for years. The feeling that she was on the outside looking in, the spare part in their trio. She shook herself. They were going to have a good night tonight. She had to get herself out of this funk.

'Are you done yet?' she asked Imogen, who was sliding the hair straighteners through Emily's auburn locks.

'Yep!' her sister replied, picking up the hairspray and spraying a liberal amount over Emily's head. Emily coughed dramatically before beaming.

'Thanks, Im. I've never been able to do my hair like you do.'

Freya suppressed the urge to roll her eyes and jumped off the bed, pulling off her top and rummaging through the wardrobe for her dress. She'd bought it the week before with tonight in mind; a black skater dress with lace sleeves that ended at her elbows. She turned so Imogen could zip her up, then stepped in front of the mirror. With her hair, even brighter than usual after weeks spent in the sun between shifts, and bright red lipstick, she looked striking. Imogen stood behind her, smiling.

'It really suits you, Frey,' she said quietly, giving her shoulder a squeeze. Sometimes, Imogen surprised her by being in tune with her thoughts, despite the distance between them in recent months.

'Thanks.' Freya gave an elaborate twirl before reaching out for her jacket. 'Come on then, let's go!'

They entered the club to booming music, lights flashing across their eyes. Freya watched Imogen's hair go pink, then green, then blue as they walked across the dance floor to the bar. Emily hopped up onto a stool, twisting to shout, 'What do you guys want?' in their ears.

'White wine,' the twins answered in unison, and smiled at one another. Was it the alcohol that brought them closer together? Did it switch off the part of their brains that kept them apart? But Freya had no intention of drinking tonight.

Glasses in hand, the trio turned to face the dance floor. It was packed with women in high heels and short skirts, guys lounging around the edges, watching the women over their pints. Freya wondered if the women realised they were being sized up, analysed for their apparent willingness to get off with a strange guy in a dark club. She suppressed a shudder.

'Wanna dance?' Emily asked, nudging Imogen with her elbow. Imogen grinned and nodded, helping Emily jump down from the stool. She turned to Freya.

'Coming?'

Freya shook her head, and Imogen shrugged. Freya knew her sister inside out, despite the distance that had grown between them over the past year, and she could almost hear her thoughts. Freya did what she wanted, always had. Or so everyone thought.

As she watched her sister and Emily make their way across the dance floor, Freya wondered if Imogen knew how Emily felt about her. If she had noticed the way she looked at her, how Emily's eyes trailed after Imogen as she left a room. She watched Emily draw Imogen close and smiled. Perhaps she did know. Perhaps they were having a secret relationship. How bittersweet that would be. Freya and Jamie, Imogen and Emily. Rivers and Bligh, bound together forever.

Someone bumped into Freya and her eyes snapped to the left, ready to berate the clumsy dickhead for spilling her drink. But the words died in her throat as she realised who it was.

'What the hell are you doing here?' she hissed at Jamie as he leaned against the bar beside her. He raised an eyebrow.

'Can't a man get a pint without the third degree?' He winked at her, and she felt her cheeks flush. 'Of all the places in all the world, and I find you here. Having a good time?'

I was, she thought, almost taking a sip of her wine before stopping herself. *Until you showed up.* She remembered the last time she saw him, the bruises on her arm where he'd gripped her. Again.

She shook her head, placed her glass on the bar and reached for her jacket. Jamie's hand shot out and caught her wrist.

'Where are you going?'

She glared at him, hating him, hating herself for ever getting involved with him. 'Are you my fucking keeper?' The words spilled out before she could stop herself, and she saw the anger flash in his eyes. She turned before he could speak, wrenching her arm from his grip and pushing her way through the writhing bodies towards the back door. Outside, the air was cool, refreshing. She breathed in the cigarette smoke of the people gathered outside and grimaced. The music pumped out of the open door, and she wondered if Jamie had seen their sisters dancing together. Wondered if he saw what she did.

She was just about to go back inside when he filled the door-way, his eyes trained on her. She let out a breath, glancing sideways to check they weren't alone. A small group of guys stood a few feet away, laughing loudly, plastic cups of beer in their hands. Two women sat on overturned crates, sharing what Freya suspected wasn't a roll up.

Jamie stood beside her, leaning one shoulder against the wall. She closed her eyes for a moment, waiting for him to speak, but he was silent, staring at her.

'What do you want?' she said after a moment, her voice quiet. She felt anger swell again at her weakness. At the power he seemed to have over her.

'I wanted to talk to you, before you go,' he said, his mouth close to her ear. She felt his breath tickle her cheek and she shuddered. 'You've been like a ghost lately. Have you been avoiding me?' He reached out and tucked her hair behind her ear, and she flinched. 'Are you afraid of me, Freya?' he whispered, and she closed her eyes again.

Yes. But she wouldn't admit it. Couldn't admit it. Refused to. How dare he. How dare he treat her this way. Like she was his property, something he could control and manipulate and terrorise. No. She wouldn't allow it, and she wouldn't let him do it to her child either.

She pushed off the wall, her fury filling her, and met his gaze. 'Stay the fuck away from me,' she hissed, her voice louder now, drawing the attention of the people around her. 'I mean it. Stay. Away.'

She spun on her heel, turning towards the door, intending on joining her sister and Emily, hiding within their circle, where he couldn't touch her. But his hands gripped her wrist, wrenching her backwards, and she yelped in surprise.

'Oi!' one of the men said, their laughter gone now. They glared at Jamie, and he dropped her wrist, putting his hands up as if in submission. 'Watch it, mate.' Another man stepped closer to Freya.

'You all right, maid?' He had a thick Cornish accent, and a gentle smile. But she didn't want him. She wanted Imogen. She wanted, needed, her sister.

Forcing herself to nod, Freya hurried past the men and back inside the club, eyes on her feet. She bumped into someone and gasped, an apology on her tongue, before realising who it was.

'Oh, Immy,' she said, throwing her arms around her sister's neck, who hesitated for a second, before wrapping her arms around her. 'Can we go?'

Imogen pulled away from her sister, looking deep into her eyes. Freya knew she could hear her thoughts, knew what she was feeling, even if she didn't understand it. After a beat, Imogen nodded, pulling Freya close again.

'Of course. We'll go get a pizza and watch a terrible movie.' She signalled to Emily, who grabbed their bags from the bar and hurried over. At the mention of her brother's name, Emily's eyes widened.

'Let's go,' she said, taking the lead, clearing a path through the writhing bodies to the exit. Imogen held Freya's hand as they left, their fingers linked. Freya smiled. Soon, they would be speeding away from this place, away from Jamie. Maybe forever.

42

IMOGEN

That evening, I eat a quiet meal with Mum, lost in our own thoughts. I wonder how Flo is going to tell everyone about her decision. I wonder how Emily will react. Does she need this job? Something tells me that she doesn't intend on staying for long, but there must be a reason she took the job in the first place.

I glance up at Mum, notice the way she's pushing her food around her plate, remember the way her face had dropped when I told her about Flo's decision.

'Oh, no. Poor Flo. And those poor people who are going to lose their jobs.' She wrapped her arms around me. 'I'm sure you did everything you could, Immy.'

But did I? I've been tormenting myself all day, thoughts going round and round in my head. Did I do everything I could? Did I try my hardest to give Flo another option? But her mind was already made up, her instincts telling her it was time to close the business. And with her sister so ill, and those kids needing their aunt, what other choice did she have? No, there was nothing more I could have done. But it doesn't stop the guilt from pulsing through me, my gut clenching every time I think about it. About the people who are going to suddenly find themselves out of a job. Everything will be turned upside down, and I can't help feeling partially responsible for it.

~

The bleeding starts at three in the morning, cramps waking me from a troubled sleep. Sweat prickles my forehead; blood seeping from between my legs, sticking my skin to the covers.

'No,' I cry, my voice breaking as realisation dawns. 'Oh, no. *No.*'

I struggle to sit up, try to tuck my T-shirt between my legs to catch the blood. There's so much of it; I turn back to find the bedsheets covered in murky red. A sob rises in my throat and I force it down, drag myself off the bed and stumble down the hall to the bathroom. I shut the door behind me, resting my back against it as another cramp runs through me, sending shockwaves of pain across my stomach. I slide down onto the rug, back against the door, my child's life draining out from between my legs. There's nothing I can do; it's too late. She is gone. Just like Freya. I am alone.

In that moment, I realise suddenly what happened to her. Freya. The memory rises up through my grief, the memory of the pain I felt all those years ago. But no, not mine. It wasn't my pain. I've never experienced this pain before. But the loss... I recognise this loss.

Images flash before my eyes. A balled-up sheet, a dingy room, dark wood panelling and yellowish walls. A figure in the doorway, face in shadow. And blood, so much blood. I wake sweating, tears streaming down my face, and it takes a moment for the bathroom to come into focus. *Immy.* My name whispered on the wind. *Freya.* A sob catches in my throat as I stare up at the ceiling, picturing my sister.

She told me not to step on the cracks. *It's bad luck*, she said, as she took my arm and we skipped over the cracks in the pavement. Sweet sixteen, making our way to our birthday party at our favourite restaurant. Our skirts floated around our thighs, our tanned legs dancing in the evening sunlight. Our innocence so bright, our futures clear. Always together.

Passing pubgoers on the street, men dangling over the railings outside the Wetherspoons, cigarettes between their fingers, their smouldering gazes lingering on our dancing forms. How oblivious we were to the dangers of the world. How little we knew of what awaited us.

Halfway through the night, we met in the toilets and swapped skirts, giggling. Taking our hair from our braids and fluffing it around our heads. Even Mum did a double take, before shaking her head. But Jamie knew. Jamie always knew. He sidled up and took Freya's arm, smiling down at her, and I think I knew then that this boy would be dangerous. That he would take my sister from me, one way or another.

I remember the last time I saw her. Biting words, cutting into our skin. Then she ran away, and I spiralled down. *I don't have time for this.* Her shadow moving across the grass. Gone. Calling her home, her name in my mouth, reverberating around my skull. Freya. Sister.

Mum finds me an hour later, slumped against the bath, face wet with tears. My legs feel numb, my throat raw from my silent screams. I barely react when she pushes the door open, freezing as her eyes adjust to the scene in front of her.

'Oh, Immy,' she breathes, reaching out and stroking my hair away from my face. 'Come on, sweetheart. Let's get you in the bath.'

I stand on shaking legs while my mother peels away my nightclothes, stained with blood. She helps me into the bath, the running water slowly covering my naked body. The citrus scent of the bubble bath fills the air, and suddenly I am transported back almost twenty-five years, to a time when Freya and I still bathed together. Dad filling the bath with rubber ducks and other bath toys, coating our hair in bubbles and crowning us as queens of whatever we were obsessed with at the time – Barbie dolls, cupcakes, bright pink socks with flowers on them.

I feel the tears slide down my face. Mum sighs heavily. 'Oh, love,' she whispers, perching on the toilet lid and reaching across to place a hand on my shoulder. 'I'm so sorry. I'm so, so sorry.' She sniffs and I can tell she's crying too. We cry together for the lost children, mine and hers, the ones we will never see again.

43

EMILY

'Good morning, early bird.' I jump at the voice, twisting to see Flo walking towards me, one hand shielding her eyes from the sun. I snap back to the present, the memories of Imogen and Freya disappearing as I drop the cigarette into the ashtray and smile back.

'Morning.'

Flo smiles. 'You're a grown woman, Emily. You don't need to hide your cigarettes from me.'

I laugh, remembering a time Flo caught me stealing a cigarette from Mum's handbag. I must've been about fourteen at the time, reckless and rebellious, desperately trying to find a way to deal with what was happening at home. Flo had put a finger to her lips, pulling out her own packet and handing it to me.

Her eyes twinkle now as if she's remembering the same thing. Then a cloud passes over her face, and my stomach clenches.

'Come into my office, Emily,' she says. 'I have something to tell you.'

~

I sit at my desk, still reeling from Flo's news. I've been sworn to secrecy for now – Flo said she'd be announcing it at the end of the week – and I could barely look anyone in the eye as I scuttled up the stairs to my desk. I stir sugar into my coffee absent-mindedly, the spoon clinking against the mug. Dave, who sits next to me, looks up in irritation.

'Are you making a speech?' he says, his words clipped.

I stare at him, my mind still on Flo's announcement. I wonder how he'll cope. He has three children under the age of nine – he's shown me enough photos, told me enough 'hilarious' anecdotes, that I even remember their names – and his wife doesn't work. 'So your daughter will be bringing herself up then?' he'd said when I'd told him about Ella being at nursery. I bristle now as I did then, softening my features as he glares at me, giving him an innocent look. He has no idea what's coming, and the thought cheers me slightly.

Aryan bursts through the doors, stomping over to his desk on the other side of Dave, who swivels round to face him. 'What's up, mate?' he asks in that jolly tone I now know is false. Everything about him is false. God, I'm not going to miss him.

'My mum's been denied residency,' Aryan says shortly, standing with his hands on his hips.

I frown as I take a sip of coffee. 'Wasn't she born here?'

Aryan shakes his head. 'She came over when she was a baby, barely two years old. But the government, in its infinite wisdom, has decided that she hasn't got sufficient evidence to prove residency.'

'Fucking Brexit,' Sally, on my other side, mutters, shaking her head. I nod, sharing her sentiments. I'm about to ask what will happen when Dave chimes in.

'Hang on,' he says, 'what's that got to do with Brexit? She's from India, ain't she?'

Aryan glares at him. 'Iran.'

Dave doesn't appear to notice the hostility in Aryan's tone. 'Well then,' he says, smirking, sitting back in his chair, his legs spread wide, chinos riding up to show coarse black hair and mismatched socks. 'You can't blame Brexit for this, mate.'

I take a deep breath as I watch Aryan wrestle with his anger. 'First of all,' he says, tone low, 'I'm not your fucking mate.' Dave looks visibly taken aback, sitting up in his seat and opening his mouth to retaliate, but Aryan continues. 'Second, I can blame the racists in this country, the same racists who voted to leave the EU.'

'That's a bit much,' Dave splutters. 'You can't call us all racists!'

'You misunderstand me.' Aryan moves closer, placing his hands on Dave's desk and leaning in. 'I didn't say everyone who voted to leave was racist. But I'd be willing to bet that all the racists voted to leave.'

With that, he turns on his heel and, grabbing his bag, pushes through the double doors and out of the office. I let out a breath. Dave turns to me, mouth open, arms up as if to say *what the hell?* I shrug, which he will probably interpret as support, but actually means that he deserved every angry word, before turning my attention to my computer, pretending to skim through emails while Dave mutters to himself. I remember the time he asked Aryan where he was from. 'You know, *originally.*' Aryan's eyes were like flint when he answered. 'Birmingham,' he said.

I shake my head, tuning Dave out. I might have spent most of my life in Plymouth, in a predominantly white area, but the university has always been a brilliantly diverse place, attracting people from all over the country and all over the world. My thoughts flit to Liana, the way her hand in mine made me feel, her large brown eyes pinning me to the spot. Her disappointment seeping through my phone as her text messages dwindled. I'd allowed my father's racism, his prejudice, to cloud my mind. I'd allowed him to control my life, even after he was gone. I feel my cheeks grow hot at the realisation. How strongly our childhoods influence us, the attitudes of our parents echoing down the passage of time.

My phone vibrates, startling me. Deb's name flashes up on the screen.

'Hello?' I answer cautiously. Deb hasn't called me in a long time.

'Emily,' she says, breathless. 'Sorry to call you at work. It's Imogen. Can you come?'

It's almost noon by the time I get to Imogen's house, the sun beating mercilessly down as I run up the front path. Deb throws open the door, one hand outstretched, and a memory flashes before my eyes. *Go, Emily. Run.*

'Thank you for coming, Emily,' she says now, taking me by the shoulder and guiding me into the house. The hallway is blessedly cool, the living room to my right cast in shadow, the curtains shut tight against the heat. 'I've spoken to her GP, she's going in later. But I... I didn't know who else to call.'

She wrings her hands, a tissue clutched between them. I lay a hand on her wrist. 'Where is she?' Deb nods towards the living room. I take a deep breath. 'Why don't you put the kettle on?' I say gently. 'Mine's two sugars.'

She gives me a watery smile. 'I remember.' I try to return it before turning to the living room door. My heart is hammering as my eyes adjust to the gloom. The TV flickers in the corner, sound muted, and the air feels heavy.

'Imogen?' I whisper, inching towards the sofa. She turns her face to me, and I can make out her tear-streaked cheeks, her curls scraped back into a messy bun on top of her head. 'Oh, Imogen.' I sit on the end of the sofa, by her feet, and try to arrange my features. Sometimes I forget how much she and Freya looked alike, how identical they were, and guilt floods me. I can never let myself forget Freya.

'Mum called you,' she croaks. It isn't a question. I nod, and she sighs. 'I'm all right. I mean, I'm not... It's passed.'

Her words hang in the air between us. *It's passed.* Her baby. Sadness engulfs me and I feel the sudden urge to hug her. I wrap my arms around myself instead. 'I'm so sorry,' I say, feeling the inadequacy of my words. Of my presence. I shouldn't be here. Not after Freya. Not after what we did.

44

FREYA

THEN

Freya stood before the mirror, top hitched up, the front of her leggings pulled down. She frowned as she turned sideways, cupping her stomach with her hands. She wished she could ask her mum whether this was normal, to have such a small bump. *Is my baby healthy?* She'd typed the question into Google the night before, scrolling through endless articles about bump size. She'd stumbled upon a forum full of worried mothers and strange acronyms. Reading through, she'd realised her pregnancy had been easy. Minimal nausea, a few stretch marks; her skin had even got better. She'd been craving strawberries and cream, and slightly overripe pears. And she had an almost invisible bump, hidden easily under stretchy leggings and flowing tops. Nothing to raise suspicions.

A part of her wished someone had found out. She'd almost told Imogen when she got back from the clinic, still reeling from the news. She was already eighteen weeks when she arrived at her appointment, the shock hitting her like a wave of cold water. The nurse had explained everything, her eyes kind and her tone gentle, and Freya had made her decision. She was keeping her child.

The door creaked open, Emily's face appearing in the gap as Freya tried to cover herself. Emily's eyes widened as she took in the sight of Freya's stomach.

'You – you're...'

Freya grabbed Emily by the arm and pulled her in, closing the door behind her. 'Shh!' she hissed, glaring at Emily, who stood in the middle of the room, frozen. 'You can't say anything.' Emily just stared at her, mouth open, eyes wide. Freya took a step closer to her. 'Please, Emily,' she whispered, taking her friend by the shoulders. 'I have a plan.'

'W-what plan?' Emily stammered, eyes flicking to Freya's stomach, concealed now beneath her clothes. 'How far... how long have you...?'

'Six months, almost.'

'Jesus...' Emily sat down on the bed, her shoulders sagging. Freya perched next to her. 'It's his, isn't it?' Emily said after a moment, staring down at the carpet in front of them, her socked toe rubbing at a hair-dye stain.

'Yes.' The word took the breath out of her, the admission of her carefully concealed secret. So close. She was so close. 'Listen.' Freya turned to Emily, taking her hand. 'I told you, I have a plan. We're leaving soon.'

'We can't still go!' Emily protested, eyes widening again. Freya shook her head, glancing at the closed door.

'Shh. Please, I don't want Imogen to know. Not yet.' Freya took another deep breath. 'We'll go to Scotland first, explore the Highlands. I'll have the baby there. And then...'

'And then?' Emily snapped, wrenching her hand from Freya's grasp. 'You have to tell Imogen. You have to.'

'No!' The word burst from her lips, surprising them both. 'You know what will happen, Em. She'll cancel everything. She'll tell Mum. She'll tell him.' Freya shook her head again. 'He can't find out. He can't be a father.'

Emily was silent for a moment. Freya knew she agreed, knew what he was really like. She wouldn't put her child in danger. She wouldn't let Freya's child grow up like Emily did.

'Okay,' Emily said eventually, and Freya let out the breath she was holding. 'But I'm going to help.'

Together, they found a cabin in the depths of Scotland, using Emily's card to book it for a month. Freya stared at the trees surrounding the little cabin, with its dark wood and huge windows. It looked... peaceful. Off the beaten track and hidden away behind large pine trees. Big enough for the three of them – no, the four of them – to have some privacy. Freya would take one bedroom, and Emily would share with Imogen.

'What about the birth?' Emily whispered, closing the laptop and setting it on the floor. 'You can't give birth by yourself.'

Freya leaned back so she was lying across the bed, her legs dangling off the end. 'Of course not. There's a hospital nearby. I'm not a complete idiot.' She pulled a face to lighten the mood. She didn't need Emily feeding her own fears. She didn't need someone else's anxiety pulling her under. 'Don't look so worried. I've got it all planned out.'

Emily sighed and laid down next to her. 'I can't believe this is happening. We're really going to do this.'

Freya reached out and took Emily's hand. 'We really are,' she said, smiling at her friend. 'All of us.'

'What do you mean, we're going to Scotland?' Imogen asked, raising an eyebrow at her sister's reflection in the mirror. She continued to scrunch curl cream into her wet hair, cupping the strands gently with her palms. 'I thought everything was sorted.'

Freya leaned against the doorway, watching her sister tip her head to the left and squirt some cream into her hand. She caught sight of her own reflection and quickly removed her hands from her stomach. It had become habit. She cleared her throat.

'I want to see the Highlands,' she said lamely, avoiding Imogen's gaze. 'Hadrian's Wall, you know.'

'You do realise Hadrian's Wall is in England?' Imogen said with a smirk.

Freya waved a hand impatiently. It felt as if, sometimes, her sister was trying to push her buttons. 'I've already spoken to Emily. She agrees.'

'Does she now?' Imogen put her hands on her hips and sighed. 'All right, if we have to.'

Freya forced herself to smile. Imogen had always been the easy-going one, preferring to let others make the decisions, pick the restaurant, choose the film. Always the voice of reason.

'Maybe we'll find the Loch Ness monster.' Freya grinned, reaching out to tug on a lock of Imogen's damp hair. 'We'll take the train up, stop off in the Cotswolds, Yorkshire, and the Lake District. Wherever!' She could feel excitement bubbling, their route mapped out in her head. 'We'll leave a month earlier than planned.'

Imogen had turned back to the mirror to begin applying her make-up. She paused, the mascara wand hovering in front of her eye. 'A month earlier?' she echoed. 'But that's only a month away. I can't, Frey. I have to give four weeks' notice.'

Freya lifted a shoulder. 'So give it tomorrow.' Her phone started buzzing in her back pocket; Jamie. She declined the call and shoved the phone back into her pocket with more force than was necessary. He just couldn't take a hint. The scene in the club flashed back into her mind, the feeling of his fingers tightening around her arm. She shook her head, focusing on Imogen. 'Flo won't mind. She knows we've been planning this for years.'

Imogen finished applying mascara before she spoke again. 'Is something going on, Frey?' She turned again, locking eyes with Freya. 'You seem... You haven't been yourself lately. Has something happened?'

Freya tried to keep her expression neutral, but her heart began to pound. *You would pick now to tune into the 'Twin Thing',* she thought, trying to smile at her sister. 'No, I'm fine. Why do you ask?'

Imogen sighed, leaning against her dressing table. 'Come on, Freya. You've changed. Ever since... Well, since Dad died, actually. I know it hit you pretty hard.'

Freya felt heat rush to her cheeks. 'It's been two years, Im.' Her voice was small, the pain rushing back with the memory of finding him on the bathroom floor, his eyes glazed over, his skin waxy with death.

'I know. But I know how close you were.' She raised an eyebrow again. 'We were never that close, were we?' Her words stunned Freya, but she knew they were true. She blew out a breath, trying to find the right words. Imogen smiled sadly. 'But maybe we can be. There's still time, right?'

The sadness in her sister's words hit Freya like a blow. She felt her eyes prickle with tears, the reality of how she had distanced herself from Imogen, shutting herself away, breaking the tie between them, finally dawned on her.

'Of course,' she said, holding Imogen's gaze. 'There's always time.'

But there wasn't.

45

IMOGEN

I spend the day on the sofa, drinking the endless cups of tea Mum brings me. I try to ignore the clenching in my stomach. The cramps have almost passed, the bleeding light, but I'm overcome with a sense of dread. A black cloud hangs over me, threatening to burst, overflow, flooding everything.

Après moi, le déluge. After me, comes the flood. Where was that from? It was something Freya had taped up on her bedroom wall, next to the mirror. How true it was, for her. After Freya, our lives were destroyed, flooded with grief.

My phone vibrates and I pick it up, squinting as the light hits my eyes in the darkness of the room. Max. I thought she'd given up, after all this time. After I'd packed up and left our little Melbourne flat, leaving only a letter on the kitchen table.

Gone home. Don't worry about me. Im x

But she's continued to worry. I scroll back through the messages she's sent since I left, dozens of them.

Immy, what's happened? Are u OK?

Have u landed yet? How long are u there 4?
When are u coming back?
Immy, pick up!

Then came the calls, the Facetime requests. All ignored. How could I answer? How could I tell her what had happened that night with her boyfriend?

I'd been alone in the flat when he'd let himself in, letting the door bang shut behind him. I poked my head out of the kitchen, expecting Max.

'Oh, hi Finn,' I said, wiping my hands on a tea towel. 'Where's Max?'

'She's at mine. I'm just popping back for her make-up bag.' He rolled his eyes. 'Can't live without it.'

I laughed. 'You know Max, she wouldn't be caught dead outside without her eyebrows on.' Finn hovered in the hall, not making a move towards Max's room. I hesitated. 'Do you want me to grab it?'

He grinned, showing even, pearly-white teeth. 'Nah, you're all right, Im.' I always liked the way my name sounded when he said it, how he stretched out the I. He disappeared into her bedroom for a moment, and I turned back to the pasta sauce I was cooking. The smell of garlic clung to my fingers and I moved over to the sink to scrub my hands again with washing-up liquid.

When I turned back to the hob, I caught sight of Finn in the doorway, make-up bag in hand, a look in his eye that I'd almost gotten used to from him; that glint as his hand lingered too long on my waist after a hug goodbye; as he brushed up against me at a party or in the hallway; as he sat too close on the sofa between me and Max, his thigh pressing into mine. The glint that should have warned me, warned Max, what kind of guy he was. The glint we ignored, telling ourselves that *it was just Finn*, just the way he was, over-friendly and touchy-feely, a good guy. He was one of the good guys. He had to be. We'd have known it if he wasn't, wouldn't we?

I still don't understand how it happened. I've gone over and over it in my head, trying desperately to work it out. Did I say something to make him stay, to make him believe I was interested? Was it because I was only wearing an oversized T-shirt with no bra? Was it because I engaged him in conversation, had made an effort in the months since Max first brought him back from the bar where they'd met, that I'd tried to get to know him?

Deep down, I know it was nothing I did or didn't do. It had nothing to do with what I was wearing, or what I said to him. I don't know if he planned to rape me when he let himself in that night, or whether he had truly popped back for Max's make-up bag. I suppose I'll never know.

I've tried so hard to block out that night, but the smell of garlic always takes me straight back, my face pressed against the kitchen table, my T-shirt bunched up around my waist. And after the test showed two blue lines, as my stomach swelled, as my back ached and my breasts felt sore, I pushed it further from my mind. I couldn't bear to think of my child as a result of that night. No, now I had a new *before* and *after*. Before I became pregnant, and after, and that night would play no part in any of it. I was going to raise my child alone – my daughter, the girl I pictured in my head from the moment I found out I was pregnant – never acknowledging her father, refusing to even think of him in that way. He didn't – doesn't – deserve to be a part of our lives. My daughter was going to be my missing piece, the piece Freya took with her when she disappeared.

But now she's gone too, and I'm alone again.

My phone buzzes and I switch it off, leaving Max's messages unread. I should tell her; I know I should. What if he hurts someone else, or hurts her? I'd never forgive myself. But I'm not ready yet. The pain is still too raw; the pain of losing my daughter rawer still.

I close my eyes, pretending not to notice Mum hovering in the doorway, her brow creased with worry, her eyes red from crying quietly in the kitchen, where she thought I couldn't hear her. I don't have space in my heart for her grief right now. It's too full of my own.

I hold Ella close that night, squeezing until she wriggles in protest, her little feet kicking against my stomach.

'Mumily! I can't breathe.'

'Sorry, darling,' I whisper, pulling away slightly. I kiss her forehead, brush her hair away from her face. That wild hair, those tight curls, prone to tangles and sticking up at odd angles in the mornings. I watch as her eyelids flutter, sleep trying to drag her down.

'Story, Mumily,' she murmurs, and I smile. I run a finger down her cheek, relishing the softness of her skin.

'Here's a story for you, my darling girl.' My words come automatically, without thought. They fill the space between us, drifting into the air, resting against the ceiling. 'There once was a girl who fell in love with a prince. But the prince was really a wolf, cleverly concealed beneath his fancy clothes.' Ella smiles and snuggles closer, tucking herself in against my side. I trail my fingers along her back, drawing invisible shapes, then words, imprinting the story into her skin. It's her story, after all. 'The girl didn't see the wolf until the day they were due to marry, but by then it was too late. The girl and the wolf were married, and soon, the girl gave birth to a child. But she was worried that her child would be part wolf, so she hid her in the woods, waiting close by to see if anyone would take her.'

Ella's breathing has deepened, her chest rising and falling. 'An old woman appeared, and, after a moment, she scooped up the child and took her home. The girl followed her to a cabin, and watched through the window as the woman put the child to bed, tucking her in with a pink blanket. The woman seemed kind, and the girl was happy that her child would be safe from her father, the wolf.' Ella murmurs in her sleep, flexing her fingers towards me like she did when she was a baby, her tiny fingers reaching out from the cot, searching for me. No, not for me. Not yet, anyway. 'When the wolf found out what the girl had done, he flew into a rage, killing her. But the girl died knowing that her child was safe, and would be raised in a house full of love, with no sign of the wolf to be found.'

A tear rolls down my cheek as I watch Ella sleep, a strand of hair fluttering as she exhales deeply. I took Ella from the wolf, stole her away in the middle of the night, hiding her to keep her safe. But I brought her back, and now I'm not sure I can protect her. If I can protect either of us.

I leave Ella sleeping, slipping silently out of the room, and join Mum downstairs. She's still lying on the sofa, her breathing ragged. The air is thick, the scent of her unwashed body filling the room.

'She's sleeping.' I jump at the sound of Jamie's voice, turn to find him sitting in the armchair. 'She was on the floor when I came in.' I can hear the accusation in his voice, and I feel my spine straighten in preparation for his anger, but he doesn't continue. I ignore him, focusing on Mum, watching her eyes flicker as she dreams. What does she dream of? Do past events still haunt her, still plague her sleep, like they do mine?

Jamie sleeps in the armchair, and I lay awake most of the night, running Ella's hair through my fingers, memories suffocating me. I remember the time *he* broke Mum's arm, the ambulance ride to Derriford, the way she'd thrown up in A&E after taking too many painkillers and drinking half a bottle of vodka, her hair plastered to her forehead, her eyes rolling back. I still remember the smell, that hospital scent of disinfectant and bodily fluids. I remember his face when I called 999, the first time I'd ever defied him like that. The only time.

Jamie helped me carry Mum downstairs, her body hanging limp between us. *He* followed behind, barking orders, but we ignored him. I had asked the police to come too; maybe, finally, we could be free of him. The paramedics arrived quickly, and as I jumped in the back of the ambulance, I saw him put a hand on Jamie's shoulder. I knew, then, that nobody would tell the truth. That we would continue to suffer in silence, wilting under his reign of terror. Until he finally disappeared, and we were free.

I think of Jamie, asleep downstairs, and wonder if he knows he's turning into the monster he used to hide from. If he knows he's let the darkness in.

47

FREYA

THEN

Emily started coming over every morning, saying she was there to give Imogen a lift to work. 'Save the planet,' she said, grinning, as Imogen yawned and wandered back upstairs to get ready. Emily would busy herself in the kitchen, making a cup of tea for herself and Freya, popping two slices of bread into the toaster.

'Will you stop fussing?' Freya said one morning, lifting an eyebrow to soften her words. 'You're like a mother hen, constantly clucking around me.'

'Shut up and eat your toast,' Emily retorted, placing the plate in front of Freya. 'Got to keep your strength up.'

Freya sighed dramatically. 'God give me the strength to deal with *you*.' Emily stuck out her tongue, watching as Freya dutifully ate her breakfast.

One Saturday morning, when Imogen was out with their mum and Emily wasn't due to come over, Freya realised just how much she looked forward to her visits. She felt better having someone to talk to, someone who knew her secret. She ran herself a bath, squirting too much bubble bath into the water, and lit a few candles on the windowsill. Maybe she would text Emily later, ask her to go out for lunch. They were leaving in less than two weeks. She had one week left at Starbucks, and she was looking forward to handing her uniform back. She doubted she would ever drink there again.

A noise from the hallway startled her. Turning her head, she saw Imogen walk past the half-open bathroom door. Freya sank beneath the water, hiding her bump. She was starting to show, but she wasn't ready to tell Imogen yet. Not until they were safely on the train to Scotland.

'Frey?' Imogen called, popping her head round the door.

'Christ! Can I have some bloody privacy, please?' Freya shouted, the water up to her chin.

Imogen laughed and turned her head pointedly in the opposite direction. 'All right, keep your hair on.'

'I thought you were out. Where's Mum?'

'I've just nipped back for my purse. We're going out for lunch. I was going to ask if you wanted to join us.'

'No thanks. I wanted some peace and quiet.' Freya knew she was snapping, knew that Imogen didn't deserve it, but her heart was racing. It was getting harder to conceal her pregnancy. *Just two more weeks.*

'All right, moody. See you later.'

'Later.'

Then the front door slammed, and she breathed out.

'You need to tell her,' Emily said later, sitting across from Freya in Goodbody's, a stack of pancakes in front of her. Freya sipped her milkshake.

'Not yet. I told you, she'll cancel our plans. I'll tell her when we leave.'

Emily sighed. 'I hate keeping secrets from her. I keep worrying I'll accidentally talk to her instead of you.'

Freya laughed. 'Can't you tell us apart, after all this time?' She shook her head. 'Jamie never had that problem.' The name made them both freeze, the atmosphere thickening. Emily reached out and laid a hand on Freya's wrist.

'We're doing the right thing, aren't we?' she asked, her brow creased.

'Of course we are,' Freya said, but her stomach clenched. Was she doing the right thing? Could she possibly make it work, taking a newborn baby travelling? On paper, it sounded like a ridiculous idea, something only an idiot would attempt to do. But she'd spent an evening the week before reading blogs and articles about women who had done exactly that, given birth and taken their child around the world. It *could* be done. But was it the right decision?

Freya shook herself. She had to stop going around in circles, driving herself mad with what ifs. It was her only option. She had to trust herself. She could trust Emily, could rely on her for help. Couldn't she?

Guilt blossomed as she thought of Imogen. She should have turned to her, she realised now. She should have let her in, told her everything. About Jamie, about how, at first, she'd loved being with him, the way he made her feel. How she'd seen a side of him she hadn't expected, and how much she'd enjoyed spending time with him. And then later, how he scared her, his moods changing like the tides, how unpredictable he became. But Freya had never been good at asking for help. She was too proud, her dad always said, preferring to suffer in silence than reach out. Now she felt alone, trapped inside her own head, building walls between herself and her sister.

I'll tell her soon, she promised herself, sipping her milkshake. *Once we're away from here. Once we're safe.*

48

IMOGEN

'What are you doing?' I stand in the doorway to Freya's room, staring at the clothes littering the floor, Mum kneeling in the middle of the chaos.

'Oh, Imogen, good. Do you want to go through these, see if you want anything?' Mum gestures to the pile on the bed. 'Christ, she had a lot of clothes. Most of it can go to charity, I don't think she wore half of this stuff. And boots! I'd almost forgotten how much she loved boots.'

I'm silent, too shocked to speak. She turns to me. 'I should've done this a long time ago,' she says. 'There's no point in it all gathering dust.'

'But what if she comes back?' I whisper.

Mum sighs. 'She's not coming back, Imogen.' She swipes at the sweat trickling down her forehead. 'It's been five years. If she's out there somewhere, she's not coming back.'

If. If she's out there. Her words fill the air between us. 'Emily came back,' I whisper. 'Freya could...'

'Do you truly believe she's coming back?' Mum snaps, her eyes blazing. 'You're her twin. You should know. Because I do. She's gone, Imogen.'

Tears fill my eyes. 'You don't know that. Nobody knows.'

'I do,' she says sadly. 'I really think I do.' Mum leaves the pile of clothes on the bed, bagging up the rest and putting them by the back door. I want to scream at her, to cry and smash my fists through the wall, but I don't. That was always Freya's way. But what is my way?

I drift into Freya's room later that night, pulled by an invisible thread. I lift the blue dress she only wore once and hold it to my nose, but all I can smell is washing powder. Mum's right. Freya is gone. I've been lying to myself for five years, convincing myself that my sister was still alive, that she is out there somewhere, just waiting to be found. But I know, I've always known, deep down, that she is gone.

A sob catches in my throat and I hug the dress to my chest, rocking back and forth. I've lost everything. My sister, my daughter. Even my job. What am I going to do with my days now? I should have been planning for my baby; I'd bookmarked so many websites, but I hadn't bought anything yet. A cot, a pram, clothes. Nothing. And now I would need nothing.

I drop to my knees, peering under Freya's bed. Dust fills my nose as I pull out shoebox after shoebox, full of yet more boots. I'm looking for a particular pair, black faux leather with a blocky heel. They were one of her favourites, ones I'd always coveted but she never let me borrow, and suddenly I want them, need them. I yank the lids off boxes, some empty, others with different shoes in, one full of nail polishes and files, before throwing them aside. The carpet is rough beneath my cheek as I reach in for another box, tucked up next to her bedside table, almost hidden from view. I tear open the lid and freeze, a hand fluttering to my mouth.

I lift out a Babygro, cream in colour with a baby elephant on the front. Next, a pair of booties and a blanket, pale pink, with embroidered edges. A few muslin cloths, a sleepsuit. A purple dummy, a cat toy with soft, ginger fur. A photo album, empty but for a scan photo. *A scan photo.* I rifle through my pockets, pulling out my own, the edges creased from where I've been clutching it to my chest, and place it next to the one in the album. I stare down at them, my mind racing. On the left, *Rivers, F.* On the right, *Rivers, I.*

I drop my head into my hands, unable to make sense of what I'm seeing. Rivers, F. Rivers, I. Freya and Imogen, Imogen and Freya. Pregnant.

I reach out for the Babygro, running my fingers across the soft material. I hold Freya's blue dress in the other, bringing the material up to my face. I can feel everything slipping through my fingers; Freya, my daughter, Emily. My grip on reality. I look up and catch my reflection in the mirror, YOU LOOK FINE stamped across my face. My eyes are bloodshot, my hair a mess, and, suddenly, I can see her. Freya. She's here, she's always been here. She isn't in her clothes or her boots or her forgotten passport, but in her absence. She has been inside me all along, and, finally, I'm ready to hear her.

A mother always knows. And so does a sister.

49

EMILY

Mum surprises us the next morning by getting up early, busying herself in the kitchen by making tea. 'How are you feeling?' I ask her, coming into the kitchen and sitting down at the table. She turns and smiles.

'Better. I feel like I've got a bit of a spring in my step. Haven't had one of they for a long time.' She winks, her Cornish accent stronger than usual. 'I think I'll nip to the shops this morning, get a breath of fresh air. It's another lovely day.'

I frown as she places a cup of tea in front of me. 'Are you sure, Mum? You don't want to push it.'

She leans against the counter, still smiling. 'My days are numbered, Emily,' she says softly. 'I'd rather enjoy them while I can.'

My heart flutters at her words, but I know she's right. I nod. 'I've got a doctor's appointment at twelve,' I say, and she smiles.

'I'll take Ella to the park then, give her a go on the round-about. I quite fancy a ride myself, come to think of it.'

I laugh despite myself, despite the knowledge that this is the end, these are the last days she will be able to enjoy, floating in the air between us. *Why not let her enjoy herself?* I think, sipping my tea. God knows, she deserves to.

Just after ten, Jamie stumbles out of the living room, stinking of stale alcohol. He rubs a hand over the stubble on his face, yawning.

'Where's Mum?' he asks, flicking the kettle on. I pretend to be absorbed in the newspaper in front of me, ignoring him. 'Hello?' he calls, waving a hand in front of my face. I look up at him. 'Where. Is. Mum?'

'Out,' I say unhelpfully, turning back to the paper. He slams a hand on the table beside me and I jump.

'You know something, dear sister of mine?' My heart begins to pound as I stare into his eyes, and I'm transported back almost ten years, to another time when a man used to terrify me in this house. 'You are starting to get on my fucking nerves. Isn't it time you pissed off?'

I glare at him, willing my heart to slow. *You don't scare me, Jamie.* But he does. I scare myself sometimes, too. I remember the wolf story and take a deep breath. *I am not my past. I control my present, and my future.*

Jamie shakes his head. 'You're all the same. You, Imogen, Freya.'

'Don't say her name,' I hiss, and he laughs again, before slamming both hands on the table between us. This time, I don't flinch.

'I'll say whatever the fuck I want.' His voice is a low growl. 'After you left Mum to sleep on the floor last night?' He looks me up and down. 'You're not fit to look after her.'

'I had to put Ella to bed,' I say, hearing and hating the whine in my voice.

'It's been too much for her. Looking after Ella, you being back. You shouldn't have taken that job.'

I suppress a sigh. 'I needed the money. What do you want

me to do, Jamie?' I feel my frustration building. 'She wanted me to come back.'

'No,' Jamie says, his voice low, 'she wanted Ella back.'

I recoil from his words as if slapped. Could it be true? Did she only want me to bring Ella?

'You know,' he continues, taking a pull from his e-cigarette and blowing a cloud of vapour into the air, 'I should've called the police back then, when you disappeared with my daughter.'

I feel my heart harden. 'You know full well why I did what I did,' I snap. 'I did the only thing I could.'

'Oh yes, that's right. Poor little Emily, never in the wrong.' He sneers at me. 'Always the victim.'

'You're sick,' I hiss. 'But you're right. I never should have come back. You don't deserve to be in Ella's life.' I go to leave the room, but in a flash he's behind me, grabbing my wrist and yanking me back. I let out a yelp.

'Who do you think you are?' His face is too close to mine, his shoulders squared, his fists now clenched at his sides. I feel my heart begin to pound. 'You should be in prison.'

'*You* should be in prison,' I growl back at him, planting my feet, clenching my own fists. 'How dare you? Who the fuck do *you* think *you* are?' I poke a finger into his chest, pushing him off balance. 'You know what you did. You know exactly what happened, why I had to take Ella. You gave me no choice.'

Jamie takes a step back, his eyes widening for a moment, before he smiles menacingly. 'You've changed,' he says, his eyes narrowing. 'I can see him in you now.'

The wolf. My heart gives a lurch and I feel my shoulders slump, the fight leaving me as quickly as it entered.

'He was always there,' I say sadly, almost to myself. 'I just try not to feed him.'

50

FREYA

THEN

The sun was going down, the sky rippled with red and indigo. She sat on a rock, legs dangling over the edge, head tipped back towards the sky. It was her favourite time of day, dusk. A flock of birds danced above her, whirling around in formation, and she watched them disappear over the horizon. Waves lapped below her; droplets of water cold against her bare feet. She'd ducked beneath the DO NOT ENTER sign, pushing her way through to this forbidden place.

She often came here with Imogen and Emily when they were younger. Fourteen, fifteen, bottles of vodka and packets of cigarettes tucked into their pockets. A blanket in her bag, a few packets of crisps. They'd always preferred their own company, just the three of them, laughing and talking. Emily was, Freya realised, like another sister, able to inspire both love and hatred in equal measure. Wasn't that what sisters did? Got under each other's skin, knew one another better than they knew themselves. Shared their secrets, kept them safe.

She thought of the box underneath her bed, the booties Emily had bought last week, and smiled. She was so different to her brother; though still haunted by the violence of her childhood, she hadn't let it consume her. Emily was nothing like Jamie, and nothing like Freya either. Emily would be a good influence in her child's life, with her strength and courage. Imogen would bring her level-headedness, her ability to see the bigger picture. *And what will I bring?* she wondered, her doubts plaguing her once more. Could she be a mother to this child? Could she manage? Yes. With Imogen and Emily by her side, she could. *The three of us, plus one more.*

She glanced down at the bruise blossoming on the side of her thigh and rubbed at it with her thumb. Her heart pounded as she remembered him ripping open the car door and grabbing her the night before, when she'd pulled up outside the house. She'd tumbled out, catching her leg on the steering wheel and almost falling onto the pavement. She'd quickly shielded her stomach as she fell, and Jamie had noticed, reaching down to yank her upright.

'Do you really think you can just run away?' he hissed in her ear. 'Do you really think I'm going to let you go now?' For a second, she thought he was going to hit her, before Emily came flying down the path, her fists clenched as she stood between them, her chin tilted towards her brother in defiance.

Freya took a deep breath, inhaling the crisp sea air, trying to push away the memories. She wasn't running away; she was escaping. She was protecting herself and her child from him, from the bad decision she made to ever get involved with him.

She leant back, tipping her head toward the sky. The day had been hot, but the evening was cooler, the rock damp beneath her. But she was content. They were leaving tomorrow. She could hardly believe the day had come, after years of planning and saving. Finally, they were ready to go. She put a hand to her stomach, rounded now, pressing against the waistband of her leggings. Tomorrow, she would tell Imogen the truth. She would let her sister back in as they sped away from this place, from him.

She rummaged in her pocket and pulled out the small black box. Nestled inside was a necklace, the silver glinting off the evening sun, colours rippling like the waves beneath her. Smiling, she ran a finger across the letters. It was perfect. She was ready.

51

IMOGEN

I stare up at the moon, fat and full, and watch as a wisp of cloud floats across it. Freya would know what type of moon it is; she always seemed to know. She read our horoscopes every day, did numerology readings for everyone, even strangers in the pub. Apparently, the night we were born, the moon was in Taurus, making us crave comfort and security.

'Taurus is an earth sign,' she said, reading an article from her phone. 'It means we don't like change, and we like to acquire things.' She glanced around my room, at my collection of candles, and raised an eyebrow. 'We also need a "running away fund".' She laughed. 'And we don't know how to let go.'

Oh, how right she was. No matter how different I thought we were, we were the same in so many ways. Freya could hold a grudge and would never be the one to concede in an argument. And when I get an idea into my head, I can never just let it go.

Like today. I didn't plan to do it. One moment I was leaving the shop, intending on walking to my car and going home, opening the bottle of wine I'd just bought and drowning my sorrows. The next moment I was taking Ella's hand and drawing her away.

Agnes was standing at the counter, leaning heavily on it, chatting to the woman who was bagging up her items. Milk, chocolate, gluten-free bread. She looked unwell, a hat covering her hair, pulled down almost to her eyebrows. She was bone-thin, her hands turning white as she held onto the counter.

Ella was looking at the postcards, twirling the stand around and around. It squeaked as it moved, but Ella kept spinning it. The photograph flashed into my mind again, of me and Freya when we were five or six, on a beach in Cornwall, her holding a bucket, me with the spade. Matching swimming costumes, identical plaits hanging over our left shoulders, tied off with a bright red bobble. My eyes are closed, screwed up in laughter, but Freya's are open, her lips turned up in a smile. That same smile I saw on Ella's face in that shop, spinning that display stand around and around.

So I took her.

She came happily enough. She must have recognised me as the woman next door. Or maybe she recognised something in me, saw something reflected in my features that made her feel safe enough to put her small hand in mine and follow me out of the shop.

Mum was out when we got back, visiting a friend in Bristol. She would be staying overnight, so we had the house to ourselves, Ella and me. I made her a snack, piling cheese on top of gluten-free crackers. As she ate, I realised just how familiar she is. How similar. She looks so much like me – like us, Freya – at that age. Bright, almost white curls, wide blue eyes. How could I have been so stupid?

'This looks like Nanny's kitchen,' Ella said, gazing around the room. I followed suit, taking in the layout as if for the first time.

'I suppose it does.' I'd always thought our houses were so different, but in truth, they are mirrored. And so are our lives.

We are so entangled, the Rivers and the Blighs, me and Emily, Freya and Jamie. So irrevocably tangled, like the vines on my arm. On our arms.

I put Ella in Freya's room, tucking her into the duvet that I spent so many nights sleeping beneath, curled around my sister, my twin. I watched her as she fell asleep, darkness falling outside, taking in her features, the truth hitting me like a bolt of lightning. Because it isn't just Freya she reminds me of. It's Jamie.

As I led my sister's child into our house, the house she should've grown up in, I realised that she is a poor substitute for Freya. For knowing what happened to her. But she is all I have left, now. And I intend to fight for her.

I pull out my phone, scrolling down to the photograph I took earlier. I find Emily's number and press send, and wait for it all to come crashing down.

I'm ready. Are you, Emily?

52

EMILY

Night has fallen, and Ella is still missing. It's been hours since Mum rang me, sobbing, her words distorted. 'E-Emily, I... It's...' She gasped for breath and I waited, my heart hammering in my chest as I gathered up my bag and left the pharmacy without my prescription.

'Where are you?' I could hear voices in the background, cars rushing past. 'Mum?'

'A-at the shop. I only turned my back for a moment. I... She's gone, Emily.'

She's gone. History was repeating itself, the past coming back to haunt me, as I always knew it would. I told Mum to go home, to wait for me there.

'Should I call the police?' she sobbed.

How could we call the police? They'd find out who she is, what I did all those years ago. But what if the person who took her wanted to hurt her? My chest tightened and I felt the edges of my vision darken. Then it hit me. Jamie. 'I'll ring you back,' I said to Mum, hanging up before she could respond and dialling Jamie's number.

'Have you got her?' I cried when he answered, my voice

cracking, my heart aching. I almost hoped he did, that it was Jamie who took her. At least then I would get her back. At least then she would be safe.

'Who?' he asked, and I knew. I knew he didn't have her. I sank to my knees on the pavement outside the pharmacy, clutching the phone to my ear as his voice rose in panic on the other end. 'Emily? What's going on? Emily? Emily!'

Jamie arrived at the house an hour later, red-faced and wild-eyed, before running back outside and jumping in his car. He drove all over the city, searching for her, ringing Mum every half an hour to ask for news. I paced the kitchen, fingers in my hair, nails digging into my scalp, while Mum sat at the table, head in her hands.

Almost five hours have passed. She could be anywhere, with anyone. We'll have to call the police soon; I know we will. Fear grips me as I imagine sitting in a police cell, ripped away from Ella forever, but it's a risk I have to take. I have to get her back. I have to keep her safe.

My phone pings now and I snatch it up, frowning when I see the name flash up. Imogen. I click on the message and a photo loads excruciatingly slowly. A gasp rips from my throat, my hands beginning to tremble as I take it in. Ella. She's asleep in a bed, hair falling in her face, her little body covered by a duvet. *She'll be hot*, I think stupidly, before scrutinising the rest of the photo. The room looks familiar. A small bedside table, a lamp with a purple shade. The duvet cover has bright red poppies on it, blooming from a field of white.

And then I see it. The map hanging on the wall. She's in Freya's room. Ella is next door.

I launch out of my seat, but Jamie grabs me, taking the phone from my hand.

'Fucking hell,' he murmurs, showing it to Mum while

holding me back with one hand. I struggle against him, but he's strong. He always has been.

'Oh, thank God,' Mum whispers, her voice thick with tears. 'At least she's safe. She's safe, thank God.'

I close my eyes as Jamie turns me to face him. He shakes me. 'Emily. She's next door, she's with Imogen. She must have found her, or–'

'Are you really that fucking stupid?' My eyes fly open and the words hiss from my mouth. Jamie's eyes widen in surprise. 'She took her. Imogen. She knows.'

Jamie releases me then and I stumble toward the front door, tearing it open and jumping over the low wall that runs between our houses. The wall Freya used to sit on, legs bare and tanned, waiting for Jamie that summer. The summer it all started to go wrong.

'Imogen!' Once again, I'm banging on this door with my fist, terrified. 'Imogen! Open the door. Please!' A sob escapes me and I screw my eyes tight to stop the tears from falling. 'Please. Give her back. Imogen!'

The letterbox opens and I fall to my knees, the pain barely registering as they connect with the paving slabs. We're level now; I'm finally looking into those eyes that have haunted my dreams. The eyes I've seen every day for almost five years. Imogen's are full of rage. 'How could you?' Her words batter me like fists. 'How could you do this to her?'

My mouth opens and closes, but I can't find the words. I always feared this day would come. I dreamt of it, always waking to Ella placing a cool little hand on my forehead, soothing me as if she were the mother and I the child. But I have never been her mother, and, desperate though I was to believe it, she was never my child.

Imogen's eyes are still blazing at me, the same eyes that

pinned me to the spot all those years ago. Freya's eyes. *Get her away.*

'I can explain.' Imogen raises an eyebrow at my words, but I press on. 'I can. I can explain everything. Just let me see her, please. Let me see she's all right.'

'I would never hurt a child,' Imogen hisses. 'I sent you the photo. She's asleep.'

I see it in my mind, the photo she sent. Her eyes, his mouth. The same nose as me and Mum; the same temperament as Deb. I've seen us all in Ella over the years, even *him*. But she is not just the sum of our parts. She is my sunshine child, the girl I swore to protect. To give my life for. And I would give it now, ten times over, just to keep her safe.

'Let me in. I'll explain. And then you can decide what to do.' My fate is in her hands. I can tell she knows that. I see her eyes close for a second, then fly open again at a noise behind me. Jamie.

'No, Jamie,' I say, getting clumsily to my feet, but he shoves me aside, and I realise that he is all *him*. All anger and self-righteousness. 'Don't!'

He crouches so his eyes are level with Imogen's. 'Give me back my fucking daughter.' His voice is a low growl, and I shudder.

'*Your* daughter?' Imogen sounds incredulous. Her eyes dart between me and Jamie. 'You don't deserve to have a daughter. Not after what you did.'

'And what did I do, Imogen? Hmm?' Jamie slams his hands on either side of the letterbox, and I see Imogen flinch. 'You've got no fucking idea. And you never will, if you don't give her back.'

Imogen hesitates, then I see her decide in an instant. 'Only her,' she says, looking at me. 'Back away from the door and I'll let her in.'

I rush at Jamie, pull him back by his T-shirt. He growls but I throw all my weight into him, shoving him backwards. 'You've done enough,' I hiss at him, shoving him again. Now I can feel *him* pulsing through my veins. The violence I've spent a lifetime running away from. I will embrace it if I need to.

Jamie seems to see it in my eyes and he takes a step back, then another, until he's halfway down the front steps. As I turn back to the door, I hear the letterbox clang shut, then the jingle of keys. She's opening the door. Oh, thank God, she's opening the door. My knees feel weak as I walk forward, my legs like jelly, but I force myself to move, inching through the gap before Imogen slams it shut, but not before I see the look on my brother's face. The hatred, the violence. I imagine it's the look Freya saw, the hints of his true nature beneath the mask, which made her try to flee.

53

IMOGEN

We stand facing each other, in the hallway of my childhood home. The home we were born in, Freya, the home where we learned to crawl and walk and talk. The home we played in, Emily snuggled beneath the duvet between us, her hair smelling of cigarette smoke. The home that was a refuge for them, the Bligh children, where my dad taught Jamie to play the guitar, and Mum baked cookies with us. The kitchen where Freya cut my hair and Dad had to fix it, before cutting Freya's too so we'd match, and then having to cut Emily's the same way. The bathroom where Dad collapsed, half-naked, dead from a heart attack before he hit the floor. The bedroom where Mum spent her days crying, empty wine bottles creating a minefield between her bed and the door, plates of uneaten toast congealing in the dark. The living room where we opened our GCSE results, then our A levels. The sofa with two bum prints, mine and Freya's, where we sat writing our dissertations for hours on end, cups of coffee cooling at our elbows, her Spotify playlist on repeat.

I lead Emily upstairs, to the room where we made our plans, the three of us, pointing at the map tacked to the wall. The room which contains our dreams, those foolish, happy dreams of the young. And in the bed Emily used to top and tail with Freya, is Ella.

Emily lets out a cry and rushes to her, pulling up at the last moment and laying a hand gently on the little girl's cheek. I watch Emily's back heave up and down as she sobs silently, her hair dangling in front of her. Ella doesn't stir, doesn't react to the grief of the woman she has believed is her mother. Her mummy. Her Mumily.

Sadness grips me and I turn away, tears pricking my eyes. Then I feel my heart harden. No. This isn't the time to be the voice of reason, the peacekeeper. The doormat.

'Tell me.' My voice is too loud in the quiet room, and Emily jumps visibly. She turns to me slowly, eyes wide. I watch her, see the expressions flickering across her face, the thoughts racing behind her eyes. She's wondering if she has time to snatch up Ella and push past me. If she's strong enough. I see her weighing up her options, then I see her deflate, as if the past five years have hit her all at once. Her shoulders sag, and I know it's finally over.

'Better yet,' I say, 'show me.'

I make Emily walk ahead, Ella slung over her shoulder, her light blonde curls tangling with Emily's in the wind. The night sky is heavy with clouds; for the first time in months, I think we're going to have rain. I can smell it in the air.

I close the back door behind me and follow three paces behind Emily as she walks down the garden to the alley beyond, and my waiting car. I picture Jamie with his face pressed to the letterbox, shouting through to an empty house, and smile.

I secure Emily in the front seat, Ella on her lap, and jog around to the driver's side. As I start the car and pull away, I hear

Freya's voice on the wind. *You've lost it, Immy.* And maybe I have. Maybe I lost it all those years ago, when Freya was ripped away from me. When I lost my other half, my reflection. Maybe I've only been clinging onto reality for the past five years. Maybe this was inevitable.

I follow Emily's mumbled directions, but I don't need them. I know where we're going. There's an old house on top of Trevaunance Cove which used to belong to Emily's uncle. And as we cross the Tamar into Cornwall, I curse myself for not thinking of it sooner. For not realising where my sister lost her life, and where she gave Ella hers.

54

EMILY

Terror grips me as we fly across the bridge, the water below reflecting an ever-darkening sky. Ella still hasn't stirred; I wonder if Imogen gave her something to make her sleep. It's not the Imogen I know, but, by the wild look in her eyes, I wouldn't put it past her.

I stop giving directions as soon as she gets on the A30. She knows where to go. Maybe she's always known, deep down. I've always believed she and Freya were linked, that 'Twin Thing' going far beyond their quirky similarities; the way they wore their hair, how they bought the same outfit without consulting one another. No, this ran deeper. And so I've been waiting for this day to come, for Imogen to finally realise what happened. What we did.

I should never have come back. I cry silently into Ella's hair, whispering apologies into her ear. I did this. I put her in danger by coming back here. I might deserve whatever's coming tonight, but she doesn't. *Please. Please let Ella go.*

Imogen rifles in the centre console and pulls out a packet of cigarettes. 'Want one?' she asks. I stare at her, unable to speak. She shrugs and uses the car cigarette lighter, unaware of the box of matches that must have slipped into the dark crevice under her seat, just inches away from me. 'Like old times.' Her grin is manic, her hair flying around her head as she rolls down the window to let the smoke out.

I try to speak but my throat is too dry. She must hear me because she glances over and grins again. 'I have nothing left to lose,' she says, and I go cold.

As Imogen pulls off the A30 towards St Agnes, I notice a drop of rain hit the windscreen. I think of Mum, of how she joked that her parents were so unimaginative, they named her after the town where she was born, and I think of the house we're speeding towards now, its ghosts waiting for us.

Imogen doesn't slow as we reach the village, taking the corner onto Town Hill too fast. A young couple, probably holidaymakers, sit on the wall outside the church, cans of beer and an empty pizza box beside them. As more drops of rain fall, they hold up their hands, as if receiving a gift from the heavens. The road bends sharply and they are gone, and we're speeding down the hill towards the roundabout. Imogen turns, again too fast, and I feel my seat belt straining across my chest. I hold Ella close, one arm supporting her head like when she was a baby.

Imogen slows as the road narrows, the sea shimmering in the moonlight below us. She turns off, heading up the narrow road towards the cottage. She flicks her cigarette butt out of the window and turns to me as if to say, *are you ready?*

No. I'm not ready. I'll never be ready. But it's time. It's time for the truth to come out, for Freya to finally be laid to rest.

55

FREYA

THEN

Shadows in the corner of the room. Whispered voices. Pain tore through her and her vision blurred, the low ceiling spiralling until she felt nausea rising. *I can't breathe. I can't breathe.*

Another shadow darted across her vision and she tried to raise her head, but hands pushed her down. 'Come on. You can do this. You have to.'

She shook her head, squeezing her eyes shut tight. *No. No. I want to go home. Imogen. Where is she?* Another wave of pain gripped her as she thought of her twin. She remembered the last time she'd seen her, her face pressed against the window of her bedroom, hair swept up in a bun on top of her head, watching as Freya disappeared into the night.

Freya hadn't wanted to go. She'd tried to fight, but her eyes were so heavy, her limbs refusing to move. The memory hit Freya as she felt a gush between her legs. A needle slipping into her arm, the world spinning as she fell to the ground. Hands reaching for her – whose? She'd tried to scream, but nothing came out, and she couldn't fight the darkness that dragged her down.

Now hands were pressing her into the bed, fingers gripping her shoulders. 'Come on,' the voice said again, and she shook her head. She wouldn't forget to scream this time.

'No!' The word tore through the room, leaving a trail of fire blazing down her throat. 'Get off! Let me go!' She tried to move her arms, but they were tied to the headboard, the rope burning her wrists. She kicked out and screamed as another wave of pain hit her.

'Mum.' The voice was quiet, and Freya wondered if she'd imagined it. Was it Imogen, come to save her? Her vision blurred, making it difficult to see the face to her right, the features hidden in shadow. 'Mum, stop it. We need to get help.'

The hands gripping her suddenly let go and she felt the presence to her left move away. She heard a sigh. 'I can't. It's too late, Emily. It's gone too far.'

Emily. Freya turned her head sharply and finally found her friend's face in the darkness.

'Em,' she croaked, tears welling up. 'Emily, help me. Please.'

Emily laid a cool palm on Freya's cheek. 'I'm trying,' she whispered. 'I–' The door burst open and there he was, silhouetted in the doorway. Freya struggled to sit up, to catch his eye, but they slid away from her, guilty.

'Jamie.' Emily moved towards him, blocking the light and throwing him into darkness. 'What have you done?'

'Emily.' The voice was sharp, right next to Freya's ear. Who was it? Why was the room so dark? She panted through the pain, her wrists straining against the ropes binding them. 'Enough.'

Freya watched Emily turn away from Jamie, revealing his face full of anguish. Did he do this to her? She tried to cast her mind back to the night she was taken, but the memory was too confused. Emily strode across the room, grabbing the shadow and shoving her into the light. Agnes staggered, catching herself on the wall before she fell.

'Em. Don't,' Jamie said, stepping forward to support his mother. 'It's not her fault.'

'No!' Emily screamed. 'It's both of you! It's always been both of you! Look at what you've done.' Quick as lightning, Emily's arm shot out, her fist connecting with her brother's nose. He staggered, blood dripping down his face as Agnes pulled Emily away.

A wave of pain coursed through Freya. Looking down, she saw the sheet beneath her had turned red.

'H-help,' she stammered, her voice struggling to rise above the others shouting. 'Help!' she tried again, and Emily's head snapped towards her.

'Mum!'

They all rushed towards her, Agnes pushing her knees apart, only the top of her head visible. 'It's time,' she said, her head rising and her eyes meeting Freya's. Understanding passed between them, and despite Freya's terror, she knew what she had to do.

She pushed.

56

IMOGEN

I stare down at the bed in front of me, the wooden bed frame empty and rotten. The evidence of Freya's ordeal disposed of, hiding what they did to her.

I remember the pain I felt that night, how I knew it was Freya, trying to communicate with me. But I couldn't reach her. I remember curling up in a ball on top of her duvet, my face in her pillow, her pain flowing through me. I didn't know where she was, what was happening to her. But I didn't get help. I lost myself in my own grief, taking the pain as penance. And I pushed the knowledge away, deciding instead to flee across the globe, searching for a ghost. I grimace at my cowardice, at the cost of it. I think of all the years I lost, trying to find my sister's footprints in the sand. And all the time, she had been here. She hadn't left me. She'd been taken. I felt her leave this world, but I didn't let myself believe it. Instead, I wasted five years searching for her, scouring the fjords of Norway and the plains of Australia, searching my own eyes in the mirror for the answers. But I'd known all along.

I can't stop the sobs from taking over. I bury my face in my hands, a wail of anguish tearing through my throat. *Freya.* I imagine how she suffered, how terrified she must have been. How she'd tried to reach me from across the Tamar, desperate for her sister. But I'd closed myself off from her.

'I'm so sorry.' Emily's voice startles me. I turn to see her holding Ella, one hand cradled against her head. My sister's daughter. 'I couldn't help her. I couldn't do anything.'

'You could have called the police, an ambulance,' I say, but the words are empty. I don't have the energy to fight her anymore.

'I know,' she whispers. 'I was scared. Jamie... He reminded me so much of our... our *father*.' She spits the word out. 'I wasn't brave enough.'

I turn to look at her, see the slump of her shoulders, the grief in her eyes. The fight has gone out of her, too. She reaches into her pocket and brings out a necklace, shining in the dim light. ELSA.

'It was what she wanted to call her,' Emily says, holding the necklace up to the light. 'Elsa. But I thought... I changed it at the last minute. I'm not really sure why. I suppose it seemed like such a... *Freya* name.' She swallows before holding it out to me. I take it, feel the cool metal against my palm. 'Her birth certificate says Elsa. I did what Freya wanted. She asked me to take her, to get her away.'

'Why?' I whisper. 'Why couldn't she go with you?'

'She... It was so sudden. Mum said... Mum said she haemorrhaged. She said she tried to save her, but she couldn't.' Emily starts to sob. 'It was too late. I was too late. I couldn't save her.' She buries her face in Ella's hair. 'So I took her. Ella. Like she asked me to.'

I stare at Emily. 'You left her here.' She flinches at the accusation in my voice.

'I had to. She was already... It was already too late. Jamie had gone out for supplies.' Her voice breaks on the word and I close my eyes. *Supplies.* To dispose of my sister's body. 'It was the only chance I was going to get.'

I imagine Emily wrapping my sister's child in a blanket, tiptoeing past Agnes, and fleeing into the night. I imagine my sister lying on the bed, the life draining out of her, her whispered plea. *Get her out.* And I know that I do not doubt Emily's words. I know she is not to blame, that she tried her best. But her best wasn't enough to save Freya's life.

Complications. Would things have been different if my sister had given birth in hospital? If paramedics had been called? I will never know what exactly led to her death, but I do know that she never had a chance here, chained up in this room like an animal. They never gave her the chance to live, to see her daughter grow.

Emily takes a deep breath. I watch the tears slipping down her face, and I hear Freya's voice when she speaks. 'Please. Take care of her. She... Don't let him take her. Like he took Freya.'

'He...? It was Jamie?' Emily is nodding, her face wet with tears. I knew it, had known it all along. Jamie. Jamie killed my sister.

'No.' The voice makes us both turn in unison. Agnes stands in the doorway, one hand gripping the frame. Mum waits behind her, her face contorted with anxiety, her eyes flitting between Emily and me. 'It wasn't him,' Agnes says, her gaze locking me in place. 'It was me.'

57

EMILY

I reel backwards, feel my shins bang into the bed frame. Ella stirs in my arms, her eyelids fluttering. I hold her tighter and stare at my mother. Deb takes a step back, her eyes locked onto the back of Mum's head, and I feel my chest constrict.

'No.' Imogen shakes her head. 'No. It can't be.'

'Agnes?' Deb croaks, and Mum closes her eyes. 'What's going on? Why have you brought me here?'

Mum shuffles further into the room, sitting painfully on the hard-backed chair in the corner. 'It was me. I took Freya that night.' She looks up, her eyes fixed on Deb's face. 'She was trying to leave. She was going to take my grandchild away from me. I couldn't let her go.'

Nausea rises and I struggle to take a breath. I feel Imogen step up behind me, rage pouring off her. But it is Deb who speaks.

'How could you?' Her voice shakes, but her eyes blaze with fury. 'How could you do that to her? To my daughter?' The words echo around the room and I am cast back to that night. *Take her. Please. My daughter. Get her out.* I bury my face in Ella's hair and let the tears fall. Once again, I am too scared to move, too afraid to do anything but watch. *I am a coward*, I think bitterly.

Mum doesn't move as Deb looms over her, her shrunken body made smaller by the size of Deb's fury. I watch her arm fall in slow motion, hear the crack as her palm connects with Mum's cheek. But she doesn't flinch. She stares up at Deb, her eyes hard as flint.

'I've taken worse in my time, Deb. You know that.' Deb's chest is heaving as Mum speaks. 'But what you didn't know is that I gave as good as I got. In the end, anyway.'

Memories play behind my eyes, my ears full of white noise. *His* boots on the stairs, stomping hard enough to make the perfume bottle on my desk rattle. I switched the light off, hiding under my duvet, the small computer chair pushed ineffectually up against the bedroom door. I watched his shadow pass my room without stopping, his boot connecting with his door, kicking it so hard it smashed through the plaster. Mum's screams as he dragged her out of bed; the heavy thud as she fell to the floor. His breathless anger as he hit her, breaking her arm, his foul words muffled by the duvet pulled tight around my ears. Her sobbing, begging. The soundtrack to my childhood.

I remember again the day Jamie held him up against the wall, the belt tightening around his throat. The hatred in Jamie's eyes, the anguish in Mum's voice as darkness took me under.

'You killed him,' I whisper, my eyes flying open.

Mum shakes her head. 'We all get what we deserve,' she says with a watery smile. 'But I didn't kill him, though I wanted to. Oh, how much I wanted to.' She looks up at the doorway, and I feel the world tilt sideways as my gaze follows hers. Jamie.

Imogen grabs me as I sway backwards, one hand going to Ella's head, the other to my shoulder, holding me upright. She takes Ella from my arms, murmuring softly to the still sleeping child. Jamie's confession rings in my ears as I stare at him, the memories threatening to swallow me whole.

'He was going to kill her,' he says, his eyes locked on mine. 'He was going to kill *you*, that day. I had no choice.'

I shake my head to clear it, but he must think I disagree, because he takes a step forward.

'Em, you know it's true.' He's right. He would've killed her, might have killed all of us one day. I stare at my brother, see his features morph into the teenager he was, the *child* who killed his own father.

'But why take Freya?' Imogen cries, looking between Mum and Jamie, her eyes wide with grief.

'I told you,' Mum sighs, 'she was trying to take my grandchild away. She was going to ruin Jamie's life. I couldn't let her, not after what he did for me.'

'You killed her!' Deb screams, her face so close to Mum's, their noses are almost touching. Mum just stares straight ahead, unflinching in the face of Deb's fury. Jamie moves towards Deb, taking her by the shoulders and trying to move her away. She fights against him, elbowing him in the chest, and I watch anger flicker across his face. But I can't move to help her, I can barely breathe. My brother, the murderer. My mother, the abductor. How many lives have been ruined by this family? How much more pain can we take?

'And yet,' Mum says, her face still impassive, 'you finished the job. Didn't you, Deb?' Her eyes meet mine, and I realise that she knows. She's always known. 'You helped Emily escape. With Ella.'

I hear Imogen gasp behind me, and Deb's eyes close for a second, the room silent as she speaks. 'Yes, I did. I had to get her – them – away. I'd always known what went on in your house, Agnes. We heard it, all too often. When Emily turned up on my doorstep that night, I...' Her voice breaks and I want to step forward, to take her weight as she crumples to the floor, her mouth open in a sob. But I am frozen, caught in the memory of that night. The wild drive from this house to Plymouth, desperately racing ahead of Jamie, Ella wrapped up in a blanket laid precariously on the passenger seat. I kept one hand on her stomach the whole way, trying to keep her still, praying, begging her to be okay. For us to be okay.

'I thought she was yours,' Deb wails, staring up at me through her tears. 'I thought... I thought he'd hurt you.' She points at Jamie. 'Or maybe Sam had come back. I didn't know. I didn't...' She breaks down again and my heart lurches. I crouch down beside her and wrap my arms around her shoulders.

I'd pulled up outside our house, intending to run in and grab the rucksack I'd packed for our trip. We were travelling light, taking only the essentials, but Freya had hidden the things for the baby in my bag in case Imogen went through hers. It was ready, sitting beside my bed upstairs, my passport and some money tucked into the front pocket. I only had to run in and grab it. But Deb had appeared on the front path, cigarette dangling between her lips, and her eyes took in my wild hair, the blood on my clothes, the baby in my arms. She'd misunderstood, and I'd let her.

'I'm so sorry,' I whisper, grasping her as she leans into me, pouring out her grief. 'You couldn't have known. It's my fault. It's all my fault.' I look up at Imogen, who stands in the opposite corner of the room, Ella on her hip. How alike they look, I realise with a jolt. Like twins.

As Deb and I cry together, I notice Jamie slinking around the edge of the room, his eyes trained on Imogen. I rise, bringing Deb with me, and guide her towards the door. Jamie is watching me now; I have to act fast.

Suddenly, the roles are reversed. With my eyes, I beg Imogen to take Freya's daughter away from here, from us. From the poison that has infected us all. She knows what to do. What we have to do.

As Imogen runs past, Ella cradled in her arms, Jamie lets out a roar. I stand in the doorway, blocking him from following them. I plant my feet, fumbling in my pocket for the box of matches I'd taken from Imogen's car as Jamie comes for me. I am finally facing my family, the mother I trusted, the brother I ran from. The match sparks and flares, illuminating his features. I'm not running anymore.

58

IMOGEN

I urge Mum down the hallway, one arm around her shoulders, the other holding Ella close. I breathe in her scent and find Freya, and my heart twists with pain. I hear Jamie bellow behind us and we run faster, bursting through the front door. I can almost feel Freya's hand in mine, fingers gripping tight as I stumble through the rain.

Mum trips and I reach out for her, pulling her towards the car. 'Come on,' I say over the rain, 'we need to leave, now.'

Mum sniffs, tears still flowing down her face, mingling with the water pouring out of the sky. 'Immy. Oh, Immy. What have I done?'

'You didn't do anything,' I hiss, fumbling with the car keys in the darkness. 'You didn't know.'

'But I should have,' she cries, burying her face in her hands. 'Why didn't I know?'

'I didn't either.' I lay Ella on the back seat, brushing her wet hair from her face. She mumbles and rolls over, and guilt washes over me. I should never have taken her from Emily. If I'd known what she'd done to protect her...

I get into the car and start the ignition with shaking fingers.

Mum clicks her seat belt in, and I take a deep breath before putting the car in reverse. It's tight, and the front of the car scrapes against the wall, but I manage to turn the car around. The sea crashes beneath us, the sound echoing in the cove, and I shudder. Images flash before my eyes, of Jamie carrying Freya's body to the top of the cliff, the bedsheets set alight on the beach, the evidence burning under the midnight moon.

I'm putting the car in gear when Mum grabs my arm. 'Im, look!' She points through the windscreen, and I squint, following her finger to the top of the cliff. My stomach lurches as I take in the scene before us.

The house is on fire. Flames crackle up the side of the building, smoke billowing out of the windows. I press a hand to my mouth, watching the fire take the curtains in the living room window, blossoming like a flower in the darkness. A crack of lightning splits the sky open, and the rain begins to pour. But it isn't enough to put out the flames. The house continues to burn, and, for a split second, I think I see Freya's face in the window, her eyes fixed on mine, her mouth open in a shout. *Go!* she screams. *Immy, now!* Ella groans in the back seat, and I turn to look at her. When I turn back to the window, Freya is gone.

I slam my foot on the accelerator, the headlights on full, the windscreen wipers flashing furiously across the glass. As we round the corner and the road opens up, a figure is caught in the headlight, blocking our escape. Jamie. And he has Emily.

I stop and rip open the door, jumping out into the pouring rain. I hear Mum scream my name, but I keep running, thunder booming above our heads, drowning out her cries. Jamie has Emily's hair in his fist, his eyes blazing as I approach.

'Let her go,' I shout above the rain. The sea rages beside us, the waves smashing against the rocks to my left. 'It's over, Jamie. Let her go.'

Lightning splits the sky open as his lips curl into a sneer. 'I'll let her go, when you give me my daughter.'

'She's not your daughter,' Emily cries.

Jamie silences her by tugging on her hair. 'Give her to me,' he growls, 'and you'll never see us again.'

I glance over my shoulder, take in Mum's terrified face. Ella is sitting up now, just visible between the front seats as she stares at us. What have I done, Freya? I took your daughter, brought her here to this awful place. And for what? You're still dead, and Jamie is still haunting us. Jamie is still controlling our lives.

I turn back, meeting Emily's gaze. She tries to shake her head, her lips moving silently. *Don't. Please.* But before I can speak, a shape appears from the darkness and slams into Jamie, knocking him sideways. Agnes. She must throw all her strength into it, because his grip on Emily loosens. She stumbles, feet slipping in the mud as she tries to grab hold of a rock, her eyes wide with fear. But Jamie still has hold of her, his fingers curled tightly in her hair, and before I can move, all three of them disappear over the edge.

'No!' I scramble across the mud and slide down the rocks, my fingers gripping the slippery heather. The fire rages behind me; a window bursts and I hear glass shatter as I let myself drop to the ledge beneath. Something glints in the darkness. I inch towards it and pick it up, holding it in the air. I swipe at the rain pouring into my eyes. It's the necklace. ELSA.

I call Emily's name, trying to pick her out in the darkness. A flash of lightning and, there! I catch a glimpse of her, the top of her head. She's gripping onto the side of the cliff, her fingers caked in mud. 'Emily!' I yell, pocketing the necklace and searching desperately for a way down. I have to help her. I can't lose her again.

I turn and begin to climb down, my foot seeking the next ledge below. A hand grabs me by the ankle and I scream, trying to scrabble backwards, my fingers desperately grasping the muddy earth beneath me. I kick my leg, trying to dislodge the hand, but it clings on, fingers tightening around my ankle.

'Pull me up!' a voice growls, and I freeze. Jamie. I can see him now, his eyes blazing, his hair plastered to his head.

'Imogen!' Emily cries, her fingers slipping on the rocks.

Fear floods through me as I slide down another inch. I kick again with both legs, and my other foot connects with his jaw. He bellows but his grip around me loosens a fraction. I look around for something to use, something to throw at him, to get him off me, and my fingers close around a rock. I lift it and reach as far as I dare. The sea roars beneath us, the rain lashing down, and I feel myself start to slip again.

'No!'

For a moment, I think the word has burst from my lips, but, suddenly, Jamie's hand is no longer gripping me. He has disappeared. Rolling onto my front, I peer over the edge to see Agnes and Jamie beneath, her arms wrapped around him as if in an embrace. He struggles against her, knocking them both off balance, and I see Agnes close her eyes as they drop off the ledge and into the sea below.

EPILOGUE

Ella

20 years later

We come here every year, to the house on top of the cove. The house we rebuilt, where my mother gave me life, and then lost hers.

I don't remember my mother, though Immy says they looked the same. She gave me a photo album full of pictures of them both, their identical smiles and their twinkling eyes. I stare down at the woman, my aunt, who lost her sister the night I was born. My mother. She must sense my gaze because she looks up, shielding her eyes with a hand, a bemused smile on her face.

'What are you doing up here?'

I turn at the sound of her voice, my heart leaping. She steps up behind me and throws an arm around my shoulders. Mumily. I smile at the childish name I gave the woman who raised me. Who fed and clothed and loved me. Who took me away from here, from the terror that happened here, and tried to keep me safe. Who almost died to protect me.

I will forever be grateful to Immy for going back for her that night. For jumping out of the car, running down to the cliff, slipping on the wet heather. She risked her life for Emily, to bring her back to me.

I breathe in her scent, the smell that reminds me of a place far away, a cabin hidden amongst the trees, a river trickling past the window. Her hair is still the colour of autumn leaves, her eyes bright and full of life. I stare out across the water, one arm around her waist, listening to the waves crash against the rocks below, the gulls shrieking above me. Immy and Nanny Deb are in the house, unpacking the small suitcases we brought. We only come once a year, spending one night in the small bungalow. It's a kind of ritual, I suppose, a way to remember the past. To ensure we don't repeat it.

The fire was ruled as an accident. The storm put out the flames long before any emergency services were called, and the blackened cottage was discovered by an early morning dog walker. It's always a dog walker, isn't it? They'd reported it as arson, what they'd thought were kids messing about, but we knew what it really was. It was her way of distracting them, the old wooden bed frame bursting into flames, buying Immy a few moments to get me out. But it wasn't enough. They've told me all about that night, the three of us huddled around the kitchen table, Emily and Immy clutching my hands as the tears fell from their eyes and the room filled with their words. They told me about my mother, Freya, and how fierce she was, and I could almost feel her in the room with us, the brush of her lips against my cheek.

Emily tucks a strand of hair behind my ear, bringing me out of the dark past. It's the first time she's come with us, and I turn to see tears sparkling in her eyes. I hug her tighter, feeling the pain radiate from her. But I'm glad she's here. Every year I've imagined her rattling around in that house, the house she grew up in which is now ours. Which is now full of our memories, our laughter, our lives. I always imagined her sitting alone in the growing dark, waiting for us to come home. This time, we're together. This time, she can lean on me, as I have always leaned on her. I can see the ghosts dancing behind her eyes, the way the past wraps her up when she thinks I'm not looking, threatening to drag her down. But I won't let it. She's my mum, after all.

Immy's daughter is here too. The twin who hadn't made herself known until she was ready to be born, after her sister was lost. *The hidden girl*, Immy calls her. *The lost girl*, she calls me.

Emily pats my cheek before turning and picking her way down the cliff, down towards the sea. I close my eyes and breathe deeply, letting the scent of the ocean fill my lungs. I've always loved being by the sea, listening to the waves crashing against the sand. It's where I go to forget, and to remember. To hold onto the past, and to let it go.

'Found you.' I don't turn at the sound of her voice. Aoife steps up beside me and I smile as she links her arm with mine. We're off to travel the world next year, once Aoife has finished her degree. We're going to follow the route our mothers planned, the same map that's now pinned on my bedroom wall, yellowing with age. We've rearranged some of the pins, after Emily reminded me of a lake we used to visit in Scotland, and Immy told us how she always wanted to visit Canada. She's going to meet us there, Emily too, after we've travelled around Europe. I picture the cabin she wants to book, surrounded by trees and snow, and smile. Aoife bumps my shoulder and I can tell she's thinking the same thing.

We've become inseparable over the years; cousins, best friends, sisters. Together we look out over the water, Imogen's daughter and Freya's daughter. The hidden girl and the lost girl, found.

THE END

ACKNOWLEDGMENTS

Girl, Lost was one of those stories which planted a seed inside my head and, although I tried to avoid watering it, it continued to bloom. But for many reasons, this book was a hard one to write, and I wouldn't have managed it if I didn't have the support and friendship of so many wonderful authors. To Sarah A. Denzil, Alex Kane, Valerie Keogh, Rona Halsall, Ruth Heald, and Lesley Sanderson, thank you all for listening to me whinge and for sending encouraging messages. And an extra thank you to Anna Mansell for her daily Instagram stories, for making me laugh and keeping me on track.

Shout out to the Savvy Writers' Snug and Psychological Suspense Authors' Association for keeping us all sane, and to everyone in the Retweeting Psychological Suspense Group for your continuous support and cheerleading. A huge thanks to the Fiction Cafe Book Club and Skye's Mum and Books for all you do for authors.

Thank you to everyone in Coeliacs & Gluten Free UK and GUTs Group for your help with symptoms of coeliac disease in children. I was diagnosed in 2018, and I realised that the only mention of a gluten-free diet I'd ever seen in fiction was as a 'weird' quirk or a lifestyle choice. Coeliac disease is neither, and so I wanted to introduce characters who live with it, just as 1 in 100 people do in the UK. I hope I've done it justice.

A big thanks to PC Ricky Carter for his help on all things policing, for the measly price of a hot chocolate. All errors are my own. Thanks also to Georgina Carter for organising, and for confirming to her boyfriend that I am indeed a 'real author'. Special mention to Courtney (@teabooksandreviews) for naming Finn, and to my wee pal Kayleigh Meldrum for helping me get the Scottish Liv right, even if it did take three months for her to remember.

I've always believed that writing a book is a collaborative effort, and I'm lucky to be working with such an amazing team at Bloodhound Books. In particular, thanks to Tara Lyons for her enviable organisational skills and never-ending support; to Ian Skewis for his excellent editorial work and ability to spot repetition a mile away; and to Shirley Khan for her brilliant proofreading. Thank you all for shaping this book into something better. I'm also grateful to my fellow Bloodhound authors for being so welcoming and supportive.

Thanks to Danielle Henley for her flexibility and support, and for allowing me to kill her once in a short story. I hope she'll forgive me for this one too. They say 'write what you know', and unfortunately I could draw on a lot of real life for Imogen's job, but, unlike Flo, we continue to push on. Thanks as always to my friends and family, who continue to support me and provide invaluable feedback on my early, often terrible drafts. To Amy Fergus, whose excitement is only really good for boosting my ego (but it is nonetheless a necessary service), and to Christian Lyne for naming my first car Percy when I wanted to call it Mufasa. A decade later and I still haven't forgiven you. And finally to my partner, the moon to my sea. My true partner if not in crime, then in lazing around on the sofa with the cats while nibbling on Quality Street (which are indeed gluten-free, but not suitable for cats).

Lightning Source UK Ltd.
Milton Keynes UK
UKHW040809150520
363228UK00004B/338